ROGERS MEMORIAL
LIBRARY

D1503610

The Peaceful Season

The Peaceful Season

a novel

✳ ✳ ✳

by Melanie Lageschulte

The Peaceful Season: a novel
© 2018
by Melanie Lageschulte
Fremont Creek Press

All rights reserved.

Kindle: 978-0-9997752-0-2
Paperback: 978-0-9988638-8-7
Hardcover: 978-0-9988638-9-4

This is a work of fiction. Names, characters, businesses, places, events
and incidents are either the products of the author's imagination or
used in a fictitious manner. Any resemblance to actual persons, living or
dead, or actual events is purely coincidental.

Cover photo: 3523studio/Shutterstock.com
Cover design: Melanie Lageschulte

Web: fremontcreekpress.com
Twitter: @FremontCreekPR

Also by Melanie Lageschulte

Novels:
Growing Season (2017)
Harvest Season (2017)
Waiting Season (2018)

Short fiction:
A Tin Train Christmas (2017)

❋ 1 ❋

The paper caught fire so fast, and burned so quick, that she had no choice but to add it to the pyramid of dead leaves. Soon the flames were rising, the heat pushing against her face and the tang of smoke filling the air. Melinda Foster took a quick step back, the damp chill of the early November morning enveloping her as soon as she moved out of the fire's circle of warmth.

"At last," she whispered, a content smile slowly spreading across her face as the paper was consumed by black soot and orange flames. "All that wondering, all that worrying about what I should do next in life. This is it. This is where I'm supposed to be."

The lease extension for her Minneapolis apartment had waited, unsigned, on the farmhouse's kitchen counter for weeks, a tangible reminder of the life she left behind at the start of the summer. She hadn't meant to walk away, hadn't planned to stay in rural Iowa when she returned home to help Aunt Miriam run Prosper Hardware, her family's longtime business in a tiny town of barely two-hundred residents.

But even as Uncle Frank recovered from his heart attack and a job offer in the city finally arrived, Melinda realized it was too late to turn back. This acreage had found its way into her heart. The cozy farmhouse was now her home, the dear animals that lived here were now part of her family.

And then Horace said he wasn't turning back, either. He would remain at the Elm Springs care facility with his brother, give up the farm that was his lifelong home, and leave the reins in Melinda's hands. Horace's faith in her came with a promise that changed everything: He'd sell her the acreage in the spring if she wanted it. But the winter sheep chores might be too much for her, Horace decided, and made plans to sell his twelve ewes at auction last week.

When it was time to load the sheep, Melinda hadn't been able to get the gate's latch open and started to cry, first tears of despair and then joy. The sheep stayed, and she knew then that she would do the same.

After she decided she would not return to Minneapolis, she'd been so eager to get rid of the renewal form for her apartment lease. Tearing it up hadn't seemed final enough. Instead she tucked it away, waiting for the day she could use it to light this bonfire of fallen leaves. And as Melinda learned quickly when she decided to rent this acreage, life has a way of taking its own time.

First, the oak and maple trees had to let go of the last of their leaves. Then her neighbors, Nathan and Angie Hensley, had to finish harvesting their crops so Nathan could make his final passes across Melinda's yard with Horace's lawnmower. Then it rained. Then came days brilliant with sunshine, but so windy that lighting a leaf pile was too dangerous.

Today, at last, was dry and calm. The bonfire popped and sizzled. Shreds of charred paper, a few carrying a pinprick of orange heat, rose toward the heavy gray skies and vanished. As she kept watch over the flames, Melinda felt a weight lift off her shoulders that she hadn't realized was there.

"Bet that feels good. Burn that lease to a crisp!" Nathan suddenly appeared beside her and gave her shoulder a friendly pat. He was in his late twenties, only a dozen years younger than Melinda, but Nathan fussed over her as if she might be his mother. It was a kindness that she found both touching and cringe-worthy. She had so much to learn about country life, but she wasn't an old lady quite yet.

"I put the lawnmower back in the machine shed," Nathan added. "And I covered it with that blue tarp Horace always uses. It'll be good until spring." His words were followed by the same contented sigh that Melinda found herself using lately. It was the one that said yet another task was complete, and her farm was one step closer to being ready for winter.

"As soon as it warms up in the spring, I'll come over and get the mower tuned up and ready to go. If you want me to keep doing the lawn next year, just let me know," Nathan said hopefully. "I've been doing it for Horace for over five years now. We're so glad you're going to stay on."

"Thanks, Nathan. So am I." She didn't know what else to say, how to express everything she was feeling: excitement, a twinge of fear, gratitude, hope. Melinda had to laugh at herself. She'd spent more than fifteen years writing dynamic copy for some of the Twin Cities' best advertising agencies, and now she was at a loss for words.

The pile of leaves was fully engulfed now, but it still felt good to pull her heavy gloves back on, her fingers already turning stiff from the cold. She pushed her brown, wavy hair further back under the hood of her chore coat, and gave its drawstring the quick pull that was already becoming second nature as the days shortened and the temperatures dropped.

There was a whimper and a mournful bark from beyond the pasture fence, and Melinda turned to see Hobo push his brown nose through the wire panel, the white tip of his fluffy tail beating out his frustration in the tall, dry weeds that lined the pasture's boundary. One white paw came up on the fence, then another, and there was more whimpering.

"I'm sorry, Hobo," she called over her shoulder. The poor dog had been heartbroken when Horace left, but his bond with Melinda was growing stronger every day, every month. "You love to help all the time, I know. But a bonfire is no place for you, or the sheep, either."

Melinda had tiptoed behind the ewes at breakfast and locked their access to the pasture, causing Annie, the most indignant of the bunch, to give her a nasty look. And Nathan's arrival, so soon after last week's near-transport to the auction barn over in Eagle River, only increased the sheep's suspicions. But come late afternoon, when Melinda would splash the leaf pile with a few buckets of water, ownership of the pasture would go back to the sheep.

Hobo's disappointment turned to excitement when Nathan passed through the pasture gate, as he took a moment to crouch down and rub Hobo's ears. Melinda spotted her two barn cats, Sunny and Stormy, ambling across the yard as if they couldn't care less about attention from Nathan. But they noticed Hobo getting his share, and she knew the cats would want their turn.

As she walked toward the gate, she pondered the once-shy cats' progress. They were strays, coming from who-knows-where and arriving at the farm only weeks before Horace's departure and Melinda's arrival. It took time, patience and special treats to win their trust.

Sunny, the more social of the two, now dipped his fluffy orange head to the side as Nathan scratched his neck. Melinda could see the caution in Stormy's green eyes as he hung back, his tail curled around his gray-and-white fur, waiting for Nathan's gentle greeting. Both cats' noses were twitching and curious, the smoke in the air and the pyre of flames on the other side of the fence an unusual sight.

Melinda picked up Stormy and turned so he couldn't see the fire burning merrily over her shoulder. She glanced to the northwest, where a line of low-lying clouds hung heavy above the now-barren fields. More rain? She might not have to worry about smoldering embers in the leaf pile after all.

The weather was a constant presence here, one that affected every aspect of rural life. When Melinda started working at Prosper Hardware, she tried not to roll her eyes when the store's coffee group discussed how hot it would be tomorrow, or when the next front would come through or when the first frost would arrive. But she soon found herself watching the skies and listening to the forecast, seeking clues about the future.

Nathan noticed Melinda studying the horizon. "I'd better get home and get our garden tilled under before it rains," he shook his head. "And I'll be back to turn your plot over some day next week."

She could only nod gratefully as they started for where Nathan's truck was parked by the house, Hobo trotting proudly at her side. She knew better than to offer Nathan payment for his morning's work. He always waved her money away, insisting everything was covered by what Horace paid him to mow the lawn all summer.

Angie and Nathan raised a wide range of livestock and crops, and had two little girls to run after, but never seemed to run out of steam. Melinda was constantly amazed as what her friends accomplished. She found the never-ending work around her own acreage to be both gratifying and exhausting. The coming months would be a test of both her skills and her resolve, and Melinda hoped she could pass.

"I've got so much to do before winter gets here," she told Nathan as she gently deposited Stormy on the picnic table by the back porch. "I have to get that snow fence up, winterize the house, clean out the sheep straw in the barn ... my list just gets longer and longer."

She glanced around the yard, as if scanning for what she might have missed. Or what might have cropped up while she wasn't looking. "Cassie and Susan are coming down next weekend, and I plan to put them to work. And being retired, my parents are willing to help, too, especially my dad, who's a former farm boy. I just hope I can hold things together out here this winter."

"It can get rough, no doubt," Nathan fished in his coat pocket for his truck keys. "But it sounds like you've got a plan. We farmers always have to have one of those. More like three." Nathan's easy grin lifted Melinda's spirits. "Your city friends seem capable enough. And I'm sure you'll have everything ready before the snow comes. Besides, there's been years that we've had snow on the ground by Halloween. We've been lucky this year."

Melinda's eyes widened. Nathan only laughed and adjusted the brim on his flame-orange canvas cap.

"You'll do just fine," he assured her. "It's not pioneer times, just remember that. We've all got electricity, and propane heat, and cell phones and internet service. You've even got a basement full of canned produce, which is more than Angie and I can say this fall."

A severe storm churned through the area in late July and spawned a tornado that destroyed Angie and Nathan's barn and uprooted their entire garden. Melinda's place had received only a glancing blow and her plants bounced back, stronger and more productive than before.

"As I've said all along," she reminded Nathan, "you two are more than welcome to whatever I've got down in the cellar. I wouldn't have been able to preserve all that produce without Angie's help."

"Appreciate it," Nathan gave Hobo one last pat on the head and climbed into his truck, the rusty old one he used to bump around in the fields. He cranked the ignition and the truck growled in protest. "If winter gets really bad, I guess I could wade through the drifts to load up a plastic tote with tomatoes and green beans and ... oh, what's that nasty-sounding stuff Horace loves so much?"

"Corn relish," Melinda grimaced. "I've got more than two dozen jars of it in the basement. I told Horace I'd bring him some in the next month or so, before the weather turns nasty. And guess what I plan to give away this Christmas?"

"Santa would never be that cruel!" Nathan shouted over the roar of the truck's engine. "Just watch that leaf pile. There's plenty of humidity in the air today, that'll help. You know, it almost feels like ..."

"I don't want to hear it. Don't you say it feels like snow!" Melinda called back, jokingly covering her ears with the palms of her padded chore gloves. Nathan only laughed and put the truck in gear, his dented tailgate soon disappearing in a fog of gravel dust.

✳ 2 ✳

Hobo dashed down the lane after Nathan's truck, a bad habit Melinda had given up trying to break. As long as her dear dog ran behind vehicles instead of in front of them, she decided, she would let him have his fun.

The farm settled into a reflective quiet as the hum of Nathan's truck died away. The chickens scuttled about in their run, seemingly oblivious to the chill. Although the coop was on the far side of the yard, between the garden and the windbreak, Melinda could just make out all eight hens behind the fence. They might as well enjoy the fresh air and scratch for what bugs remained after the frost, as they soon would spend most of their time inside.

Thanks to the crew of volunteers who helped her clean up after the tornado, the chickens' run was once again straight and sturdy. And Horace's nephew, Kevin Arndt, made good on his promise to have the missing-shingle gaps in the barn's and machine shed's roofs patched before winter arrived. His cousin, Dave, arrived one morning last week just as Melinda was leaving for work, and she returned home to find both buildings repaired.

"There's advantages to renting, that's for sure." Melinda turned for the back porch, pausing for a moment to take in the farmhouse's unassuming charm. While she admired the two-story home's faded white clapboards and the gray-green shingles that hugged its steep roof and cottage-like dormers, she knew not to look too closely. The house was solid, but it had been decades since it received much love beyond the most-needed repairs.

"I've got big dreams for this place," she told Hobo, who was back from his run down the lane. "Someday, I'll be able to do it all. But it's going to take a chunk of cash to turn this house back into the showplace it surely used to be."

Melinda really didn't care if the paint crackled a bit on the gray window trim, or if there was a slight sag to the floor of the screened-in front porch. She'd fallen in love with the charming farmhouse the first time she saw it, that day in early June when she set off in search of what was behind the "for rent" sign she spotted on the county blacktop.

The farm was lush and green during the height of summer, then lit up with blazing oranges, reds and yellows when fall arrived. Now it was cloaked in shades of tan and brown, and she could already imagine the stark, snowy beauty that would blanket her acreage once winter arrived.

A squirrel chattered in the oak tree between the house and garage, flipping its bushy tail at Hobo, and she decided the peaceful stillness of the harvested fields was deceiving. Animals all over the township were gathering food for winter, reinforcing their nests and dens. The human residents were doing the same. She'd better get to work.

The pegs on the farmhouse's enclosed back porch were already weighed down with an assortment of coats and sweatshirts. Melinda planned her chore-time attire based on the temperature, and many days she sported an evening ensemble far different from what she'd modeled for the sheep and chickens that morning.

"I put as much thought into my clothes now as I ever did in the city," she said to herself as she pulled off her heavy coat, which was one of Horace's left-behinds, and the thick stocking cap borrowed from the top shelf of the porch closet. "Except now it's all about staying warm, not following the latest fashion trends."

Next came the zip-up sweatshirt and her new chore boots, which Melinda purchased with her employee discount from the shelves at Prosper Hardware. And rather than an of-the-moment handbag or a pair of sleek new heels, her biggest fall shopping splurge had been the insulated coveralls that hung in the closet.

The heartening aroma of simmering chicken and herbs greeted her as she came through the wooden door that separated the back porch from the kitchen. Melinda never had much use for a slow cooker when she lived in Minneapolis, preferring to prepare simple, fresh meals or roast meat in the oven. But now she wondered how she survived so many years without one.

Horace's crockpot bubbled away on the laminate counter, held level by a wood block. Sometime during its years of service, one of the slow cooker's three plastic legs must have snapped off. The plywood chunk was on the shelf, collecting dust next to the crockpot, and she put it to good use.

She washed her hands in the deep porcelain sink and anxiously checked the spread of noodle dough drying on the counter. This was her first attempt at recreating her Grandma Foster's recipe. "I don't know if these are rolled thin enough," Melinda worried as she used two metal spatulas to turn over the delicate sheet of dough, then scattered another generous handful of flour over both surfaces. "Mom said they can't be too thin. But chicken and noodles will be perfect for supper, especially if it does rain and ..."

She jumped as a sharp *snap!* echoed around the kitchen. The sound, one she had become all-too-familiar with the last few weeks, came from under the kitchen sink.

"Another one." She rolled her eyes, then dropped the spatulas and reached for the jar of cheap peanut butter kept in the cabinet above Horace's wall-mounted phone. "Where do they all come from? And why my house? It's a good thing I can use my Prosper Hardware discount on mouse traps."

Melinda had carefully considered her choice of weapons once she decided to stay at the farm through the winter.

There were hair-trigger snap-traps and slow-death glue traps, and those little plastic poison houses that lured the mice inside to die. There were even electrical devices that emitted shrieks at a frequency only the mice could hear. Overwhelmed by her morbid options, she consulted someone with decades of experience fighting off rodents of varying species and sizes: August Kleinsbach, owner and proprietor of Prosper Feed Co., the local co-op.

"Don't waste your time and money on those newfangled things," Auggie warned her one morning around the coffeepot at Prosper Hardware. "The old-school kind are cheap and deadly. If they're lucky, the mice go like that." Auggie had snapped his fingers and raised his bushy eyebrows behind his black-framed glasses. "Just keep your hands out of the way."

Melinda had reluctantly followed Auggie to the back corner of the store, where mousetraps had been for sale since he worked at Prosper Hardware during his high school days forty years ago. Using a metal screw as a decoy, Auggie had her set and reset a wooden mouse trap until she got it right.

She was glad for Auggie's help, as her other option, which was giving Sunny and Stormy the run of the house, had been met with glares and yowls of disapproval.

Seeking an end to her infestation and imaging herself sprawled out on the sofa with two cats purring in her lap, Melinda tried to lure Stormy and Sunny into the back porch with a tasty treat of tuna and chicken. Despite the wonderful aroma and her cooing pleas, neither cat would inch closer than the second porch step. She'd picked Sunny up and snuggled him close, hoping to overcome his suspicions, but he'd howled and clawed a fresh rip in her chore coat when she tried to carry him inside.

"At least those kitties will eat the dearly departed," Melinda muttered now as she opened the cabinet under the sink and used one of Horace's left-behind grabber sticks to lift out the trap. She shrugged into a coat, slipped on her boots and headed for the barn, holding the still-loaded wood scrap far ahead of her with timid fingers.

Stormy and Sunny were nowhere to be found. Melinda closed her eyes, unhinged the trap and left the corpse next to the cats' food dishes in the grain room, a peace offering for the upheaval caused by the roaring bonfire. Satisfied that the flames now burned low and the wind remained calm, she returned to the house for a cup of coffee, a pumpkin-walnut scone and another spin through her winter-preparation checklist. Cassie and Susan would be eager to help, but Melinda knew she'd have to tackle the rest of it on her own.

"Let's see ... the storm windows need to be put on the front porch. If I have time, I'd love to get that cold frame going in the garden. But the cats' house has to come first."

Since Stormy and Sunny refused to move indoors, Melinda decided to bring warmth and light their way. She'd spent a few lunch hours sketching designs that used plywood to wall in the cats' space under the haymow stairs, then added a hook for a heat lamp to the underside of the steps. Bill Larsen, Prosper Hardware's only other full-time employee, cut the plywood to her dimensions and helped her load the sections into the hatchback of her car. The panels were now stacked in the barn, waiting to be installed.

Melinda wandered into the dining room, admiring the farmhouse's built-ins, original wood floors, and substantial oak window trim. She hated to wrap those lovely windows in plastic, but she had to be practical.

She pulled a tape measure from her jeans pocket and worked her way around the downstairs, including the back bedroom where Horace used to sleep and that Hobo still favored, curling up each night on the faded crazy quilt draped over the iron bedstead.

Upstairs, her bedroom, the little office and the bathroom were a priority. The tiny bedroom that once belonged to Wilbur, Horace's older brother, and the spacious front room now used for storage would have to fend for themselves.

"I need at least four boxes of window plastic," she calculated and made notes on her list. "Good thing I know where Horace keeps the stepladder. I'll have to move all that stuff out of the way in the garage to get at it, though. We'll need it to change out the screens on the front porch, too."

Melinda thought it was comical how both Horace and Wilbur so closely fit the stereotype of the thrifty bachelor farmer. They had kept the house just-clean-enough since their mother passed away thirty years ago, never updated the interior, and apparently saved just about everything. A cleaning crew organized by neighbors Mabel and Ed Bauer swept through the farmhouse before her arrival to cart out the stacks of newspapers, wash the curtains and scrub the walls and floors.

Horace, thankfully, was happy to share his decades of farm knowledge. She called him frequently to tap his expertise. Wilbur, who had dementia, often chimed in on the conversations even though he lived inside his memories more every day. Last night, when she called Horace to get his opinion on what needed to be done at the farm before winter, Wilbur eagerly offered suggestions.

"Tell her to make sure those sleigh runners aren't rusty," Wilbur had told Horace. "Pa wants us to keep them smooth and sharp, it makes it easier for the team to pull it through the snow."

Melinda heard Horace's patient response. "You're right, Wilbur, I'll remind her about that."

Then he turned back to the phone, using a louder voice than usual to be sure Wilbur could hear. "Melinda, make sure you get that done."

She laughed now as she ticked off the items on her list. "Thank goodness I don't have to worry about a sleigh this winter, or horses either, for that matter. I've got my hands full with the chickens and sheep. And the holidays will be here before I know it."

Thanksgiving and Christmas would be perfect opportunities to make new memories, to embrace her new life. Melinda was eager to become more involved in the rural community that was now her home. And she could just imagine how beautiful the farmhouse would look once it was decorated for the holidays. She had already announced her intentions to host her family's Christmas celebration. Maybe she needed to start another list ...

"One thing at a time. And you know, I can take all this up tomorrow," she decided, then tossed the notepad on the kitchen table. "It's barely November. It's a sleepy day. I think this will be the perfect afternoon to kick my feet up and read."

Thanks to the farmhouse's still-drafty windows, her restful afternoon was interrupted by the hum of another pickup truck barreling up the lane. She looked out to see neighbor John Olson's truck arrive in the yard, gravel dust billowing behind the small metal trailer hitched to the back.

Melinda glanced at the clock above the kitchen sink. It was nearly evening chore time, the hour when everyone in the township would tend to their animals, make their final rounds outside before sundown. Why was John here now? She frowned, but started for the enclosed back porch to pull on her boots and Horace's old coat.

"I didn't think he was bringing that load of hay and straw until the weekend." She hurried back into the kitchen and rummaged in her elegant tote, the city-girl purse she couldn't quite give up, and reached for the folded twenties tucked in her wallet.

"Good thing I've been to the bank and got out the money. It's a cash society out here."

Little Prosper didn't have a convenience store, much less a bank or an automatic cash machine. With the bank in Swanton nearly eight miles from the farm and about fifteen from Prosper, she learned the hard way early on to keep cash on hand. The same went for groceries and other necessities. If she couldn't get something at Prosper Hardware, she had to drive over to Swanton or go without.

"No wonder Horace always planted such a huge garden, canned all that food every year, and kept chickens." She remembered something. Horace insisted she keep the proceeds from his few regular egg buyers, and the money jar was her last-resort stash. She hadn't checked it lately.

She opened a cabinet and reached in for the large glass jar stuffed with coins and small bills, her fingers making a quick count. "Good. At least thirty in there, just in case."

It seemed odd when John pulled his rig up between the garage and the house, rather than park by the main barn door. And Melinda's curiosity grew when Dylan and Tyler, John's teenaged sons, hopped out of the back of the trailer.

Hobo, however, didn't mind at all. He was too busy getting head scratches from John, one of his favorite people. Hobo ran away during the tornado, and his fear and confusion took him to the Olsons' farm, two miles to the east. John's family had cared for Hobo until he could be reunited with Melinda.

"Hey, John," Melinda waved as she came down the back steps, still pulling on her chore coat. "Surprised to see you today. But I've got your money for the straw and the hay."

"Made a last-minute decision to head over this afternoon," he replied as he adjusted his fleece-lined cap, which sported a thick flap that covered his ears and the back of his neck. Melinda had nearly died from holding in her laughter the first time she saw one of the local men wearing an Elmer Fudd hat, but now she hardly noticed.

"The boys don't have sports practice this afternoon, so I brought them along to help," John said as he dropped the trailer's metal ramp. "And we've got a little something extra for you, Melinda. Maybe I should've called you, but Horace's is paying for it, so I guess ..."

"Sure, that's ... fine with me."

Just when she thought she had a handle on things out here, something else always seemed to come up. She might as well roll with it, whatever it was. "But, John, why are you pulled up here by the house?"

John motioned her to join him behind the trailer. "Horace probably didn't tell you, but every fall, he stacks straw along the west and north walls of the house's foundation. Helps break that terrible wind that'll be driving in from the north any day now."

Tyler and Dylan ducked inside the trailer and reappeared, each carrying a golden bale of straw. Melinda didn't know the boys well, only that Tyler was the older of the two. They grinned at her and started past the picnic table to the back corner of her house as if they knew just where to go. It was obvious Dylan and Tyler had been doing this for years. She couldn't stand there and let the guys do all the work.

"Let me help, at least." She adjusted her thick gloves and climbed into the trailer with John. It was nearly full, the faded green of the hay bales barely visible behind the stacks of straw. "How ... how many bales does this take?"

John grinned, pleased by her offer to assist, and slid a straw bale her way. "I count out forty for the foundation. We stack them two rows tall. Start there behind the back porch, then bend around and do the whole north side."

Melinda confidently reached for the twine strings on the bale and tried to drag it out of the trailer. It was heavier than she expected. Were these bales bigger than the ones John usually brought her? She struggled down the loading step, hurrying to get out of John's way.

"Grab the strings right in the middle," Tyler nodded at Melinda as he returned for another bale, which he picked up as if it were an empty laundry basket.

"Will do," She called after him, trying not to be annoyed. What did it matter how she carried the darn thing, as long as she got it where it was going? She'd carried some bales in her time at the farm, brought them down from the haymow when the stacks by the sheep's area got low and Kevin hadn't made it down from Mason City to give her a hand.

Of course, she used a little wheeled cart in the barn, and she had been known to kick and slide bales down the haymow stairs, which Stormy and Sunny found amusing from a distance, but still ...

She barely made it past the picnic table before her wrists started to hurt. Dylan had already put his first bale snug against the concrete blocks of the house's foundation. All she had to do was set hers next to it. Melinda counted twenty more steps, and only got as far as the far corner of the enclosed porch. The charming yard had never seemed so big.

At last, she got the straw bale to the side of the house and dropped it with a sigh of relief.

"We'll need to pack them closer together," Tyler said gently as he came back with another bale. Melinda reached for hers again, her arms already stiff, and shoved the bale against its neighbor. John was waiting behind her. "That's good," he nodded. "Nice and tight. That'll keep the cold out. Now, we've only got about thirty-five to go."

Hobo enjoyed all the commotion. He tried to run back and forth with each trip from the trailer to the house, then decided to do his sniffing inspections as the bales were set against the foundation. Stormy and Sunny suddenly appeared but refused to help and instead crouched, alert and suspicious, on the picnic table. Stormy's green eyes were wide and watchful, and Melinda noticed an annoyed flip in Sunny's fluffy orange tail.

"Quite the surprise, isn't it?" she whispered to them as she stopped to pat their heads, a good chance to catch her breath. Her wrists hurt, her shoulders ached. Itchy bits of straw were climbing under her stocking cap and wriggling inside the cuffs of her coat, but she reached for another bale. The guys were outpacing her two-to-one, and she wasn't going to quit.

John at last took pity on her, and she was grateful. "How about you stay here by the house, stack the bales as we bring them over? That'll save us some time."

This part was actually fun, Melinda decided once she got the hang of it. She lined the bales up, making sure they were snug to each other and the house, then started the top row in a staggered pattern. It was like setting up bricks, building a wall without mortar. Except each of these bricks weighed over forty pounds.

While she finished stacking the bales in place, John pulled the truck and trailer around to the barn and he and the boys unloaded the rest of the straw and hay. They graciously turned down her offer of cookies and coffee, saying they had to get started on chores. Melinda, who was trying to act as if she didn't ache all over, was rather relieved when the truck and empty trailer bumped away down the lane.

Stiff and sore, she could barely make it up the back steps. She should have shaken out her cap and coat before she came in, she realized too late, as bits of straw chaff flew all over her freshly swept porch floor. She had her own chores to do, but surely she could rest for a minute ... or ten.

"No wonder Horace decided to stay at the nursing home," she sighed as she gingerly lowered herself to one of the kitchen table's chairs. "I'll want to get myself a room, too, if this is what lies in my future."

* 3 *

Melinda tried to distract herself by shuffling the stack of documents in her lap, then shifting her elegant leather tote from one side to the other and finally to the floor. Her wrists still hurt from wrangling all those straw bales just a few days ago, but she was almost sure she had removed the last of the straw from her hair, which no longer showed any stray grays and was styled into a chic, low ponytail. She glanced nervously at the sleepy clock above the bank's water fountain, squeezed her fists and tried to relax.

Like a Cinderella racing to return to her humble beginnings, she had to be back in her usual jeans and sweater and behind the counter at Prosper Hardware by noon. Her meeting with the mortgage officer should have started ten minutes ago. Where was this guy?

The bank was as quiet as a vault, the silence broken only by the sigh of shuffling papers. First Federated of Swanton had updated its decorating scheme from blue to beige, but little else had changed since Melinda first visited years ago, a little girl clinging to her mother's hand as she opened a savings account with her birthday money.

Last week's visit to transfer her accounts from her bank in Minneapolis had been easy, casual. Today's meeting, however, had so much more at stake. She loved to shop online, even more so since returning to such a rural area, but

Melinda had no intention of getting a mortgage through some internet bank. First Federated, which had stood on Swanton's town square for more than a century, was her best bet for the financing she needed.

There was a container of lollipops on the counter, but she refrained from pawing through them to find cherry, her favorite. She tried to relax and not watch the clock.

Her net worth certainly had changed over the years, from babysitting dollars through part-time college work and, at last, a soaring marketing career in the Twin Cities. Aunt Miriam and Uncle Frank were surprisingly generous with her salary at Prosper Hardware, given it was a retail job, and Melinda was grateful they treated their few employees so well. However, she cringed to think of how her income had fallen since she was laid off from the copywriting department at WP&S. As for buying a house sooner, things just hadn't fallen into place. She'd discovered her vintage Minneapolis apartment years ago, hadn't wanted to leave. Of course, she was going to give it up and buy that bungalow with Craig, right after they got engaged, but then ...

Melinda squared her shoulders and tried to stay positive. Craig had been a mistake, but she'd seen that in time to call off both the wedding and the bungalow. And so what if her income had dropped? She still had her investments. She was spending less, too.

No more fancy coffees, no more self-induced pressure to keep up with the latest arrivals at her favorite boutique in downtown Minneapolis. She rarely went out to eat, packing her lunch to Prosper Hardware and enjoying quiet dinners with her parents or her few new friends here.

She and Horace had discussed a price for the acreage, and it sounded manageable. It fit her new financial situation, which she had carefully mapped out on a spreadsheet just for this pre-approval meeting. Melinda was so thankful for Horace's patience. If he'd demanded a quick answer, she surely would have bolted back to Minneapolis, too afraid to give the idea, and herself, a real chance.

She gazed out the bank's wall of windows and saw a scene that matched her mood. Restless splats of cold rain hit the glass and gathered under the bare trees along the sidewalk. It was a dreary day, that time in November when the brilliant hues of fall were already carried away by the brisk winds, but the fresh snow hadn't yet arrived with the promise of the holidays to come.

She adjusted the neckline of her silky blouse, smoothed the creases in her dress pants. Melinda hadn't worn these clothes in months and was elated that they not only fit, but were just a bit loose. All those hours of hard work at the farm were paying off in more ways than one. But her stylish clothes, she noticed as she looked around, outshined the business-casual attire of many of the bank's employees. Maybe she had overdressed for the occasion. Maybe rolling into the bank in jeans and a sweatshirt would have looked more, well, serious farmer-like.

The thought of the farm made her relax. It was the reason she was here, after all. She imagined Hobo napping in his doghouse while the light rain tapped on its roof. The chickens would have gone inside, too, enjoying the clean coop that Melinda prepped for winter only a few weeks ago. And the sheep were probably inside the barn, lounging in some of the fresh straw she spread out for them last night. She wouldn't be surprised if Annie was in the doorway, glaring at the rain, willing the dark clouds to drift away so she and her friends could run back out to the pasture.

Sunny and Stormy were likely sleeping in the haymow, curled up together on the new stack of straw bales in the southeast corner. How many bales were there now? Melinda closed her eyes for a moment and tried for a quick count. Was there enough straw to get by until Christmas? Or even through the winter? And then the hay bales ...

"Miss Foster."

She looked up with a start. A dour-faced elderly man was, at last, waiting for her in the doorway to the loan department. His three-piece suit told Melinda she was right to wear her silk blouse and heels. He adjusted his tie with an impatient flip of his wrist. "Why don't you come on back?"

The man studied Melinda over the top of his wire-rimmed glasses, not smiling, not frowning, as she gathered her things and started in his direction. She suspected he was of the traditional, no-nonsense type, but he was so contained she couldn't read him well. The man's unflappable personality was no doubt a great asset to someone in his position, a job where he could approve or deny people's dreams with a few scratches from the expensive pen that Melinda was sure waited on his desk.

Tony Bevins, the chief of Prosper's volunteer rescue squad, gave her a cheerful wave from his desk in the investments department. She returned Tony's smile, wishing she could meet with him instead. But maybe his acknowledgement would put a few points in her favor.

The dour loan officer gestured to a padded chair across from his desk. "Perfect day for a nap, isn't it?"

Melinda sank into the chair and slid her ankles back. "Yes, it sure is dreary out there," she replied, then suspected he was mocking her. She set her jaw and felt her irritation rise. First, he made her wait. She was sure of it, as she had seen no one exiting this office. Now, he was talking to her as if she were a child, not a grown woman with investments and a job and common sense.

She had seen this before. She'd dealt with difficult people many times in her career, whether it was a high-maintenance co-worker or a corporate client eager to control every step of the creative process. Maybe she now spent her days behind the counter at Prosper Hardware, but Melinda could still hold her own in a business meeting. The man hadn't introduced himself, but "Donald Hawkins" was lettered across the nameplate on his desk.

"Well, Don, I'm glad you could meet with me today," she kept her voice level and gave Don a cool smile. "Here are my recent pay statements, my last two years of tax returns and the investment documents you requested."

Don looked momentarily impressed, and Melinda chalked up a point for herself. She waited calmly, quietly, as Don slowly paged through the stack, nodding as he went. Then he paused, and frowned.

"If you're missing something or need more information, just let me know," Melinda relaxed back in her chair. She would not hover over Don, nervously chattering on about why he should approve her request. She suspected that's what he wanted her to do.

"So ..." Don's brow furrowed deeper. "These are your last two pay statements for your current position, correct?"

"Yes. Yes, they are," she replied. "I know that my salary has decreased in the past few months. But so have my expenses, as you can see by the spreadsheets I provided."

She reached over the table and searched through the pile, pulling out another document and sliding it Don's way. "I also have some contract work coming from one of the best public relation firms in the Twin Cities. An estimate of that income is here, on this next page."

Don only grunted. "Miss Foster, contract work is fine and all, but it's not steady income. And it looks like you haven't completed any projects yet. How do you know for sure that these estimates will bear out?"

"You are correct," Melinda nodded. "That's why I haven't included them in my new monthly budget. Those amounts will vary, as you said."

As Don studied the income tax forms, the documents that reflected dollars Melinda was no longer earning, he hesitated again.

"Miss Foster," Don said at last. "I understand you're looking to purchase an acreage between here and Prosper. That's some of the finest farm land in the county. It has some of the richest soil in these parts of Iowa."

"I'm sure that's true." Melinda hadn't known that, but fought to keep her voice confident as she described the acreage. "The parcel is small, just under two acres. What's not part of the yard and outbuildings is in pasture, with a stand of trees along the north and west sides of the lot. None of this land is being cultivated for crops."

Don nodded, possibly impressed. Melinda felt her shoulders relax. "That may be the case," he said slowly, "but the quality of the land still raises the per-acre value of the property. Add in the house and barn, and the outbuildings, and you've still got a substantial piece of real estate."

"The house is in solid condition," she countered, "but it is old, and it needs updating. Two bachelor brothers, now very elderly, lived there all their lives until the last year or so. While they kept the place going, it's nothing fancy."

"Exactly." Don tapped his expensive pen on his desk. "Have you considered what it might cost to upgrade the property?" He raised an eyebrow, but didn't pause for Melinda's answer and leaned forward.

"Even with insurance, there's so many things that will come out of your pocket if they break down or need repairs. This isn't like a house in town, Miss Foster, or even a condominium where HOA fees cover exterior improvements." Don paged through more forms. "I see you've filled out paperwork for our first-time homebuyer's program. I dare say, you're looking to take on quite a bit of risk."

So that's what this was really about. Don wasn't just concerned about her ability to repay a mortgage. He didn't believe she was capable of running the farm, and maybe even assumed she was one bad day away from running back to the city. Melinda now wondered if Don would have taken her more seriously if she'd shown up in her grubby chore clothes, her ratty orange knit hat plastered over her forehead and mud stuck to the bottom of her shoes.

All Don knew about her was what was right in front of him: her elegant clothes, the wide-ranging dollars on her documents. Melinda saw she would have to get personal to convince Don to take her seriously.

"Don," she tried again, "you are correct that this will be my first mortgage. I had a wonderful apartment in Minneapolis, a vintage building in a trendy neighborhood. It just happened to be a rental, not a resident-owned property. But I'm not afraid to get my hands dirty. I wasn't afraid to fix a leaky faucet on my own, and I only called building services if there was an absolute emergency."

Of course, there was the time she crafted a flaming cherry dessert for a dinner party, and a neighbor called the fire department, but Don didn't need to hear that story. The memory hit Melinda square in the heart. In just a few weeks, she and her parents were going to Minneapolis to clear out her apartment and turn in the keys. One of her final connections to her old life would soon disappear.

Don was listening intently now. She gathered her emotions and continued. "You would also be prudent to question my intent to stay around Prosper. It's true, I've lived in the Twin Cities since I left home for college, and I loved it. But I grew up here in Swanton, and it's good to be back."

Melinda explained how she was downsized from her public relations career, then came back for the summer to help Aunt Miriam run Prosper Hardware while Uncle Frank recovered from his heart attack. Don's eyes lit up with interest when she described how she discovered Horace's farm was for rent, and her eagerness to take over the acreage.

She told how she'd kept Horace's large garden thriving, cared for the sheep and chickens, won over Hobo and the cats, and helped Horace's family clean up the property after the tornado. She saw the surprise and respect on Don's face when she admitted she recently turned down a promising job in Minneapolis to remain in Iowa.

"So, you see," Melinda finished, "I'm not going back. I want this farm to be my home, and Horace wants me to have it. Now, what do I need to do to make that happen?"

"It sounds like you've had quite the time of it, Miss Foster." She noticed a change in Don's tone, and silently cheered at this small victory. "I admire your determination. But this is a legal matter, not simply an emotional decision."

He glanced again at the documents and turned to his computer, his fingers tapping the keys while she waited.

Whatever was he doing now? A few clicks, and Don let out a low whistle. "Just as I suspected." His mouth set in a firm line. "Do you know what this property is assessed for?"

"Well, no," Melinda was taken aback. "Horace told me what the taxes and insurance premiums amount to, and they didn't seem outrageously high." She had all but laughed at how small those fees were compared to the ones tied to the Minneapolis bungalow she and Craig almost purchased.

"The taxes are indeed low, given that Hartland County is predominantly rural," Don conceded.

"But I'm looking at the listing on the assessor's website and ... well, all I can say is, this figure Mr. Schermann provided to you is quite the bargain." Don was giving her the strangest look.

Melinda felt her palms start to sweat. "Horace said the acreage has never been mortgaged and it's been in the family for more than a hundred years, so he's not concerned about making a profit, he's just ..."

"Miss Foster," Don broke in, "based on its assessed value alone, this piece of property is worth double what you've been quoted. If not more."

Melinda blinked. She didn't know what to say. *Double?* She hadn't realized ...

Don seemed to consider something, then finally spoke.

"I know we are only here to consider a pre-approval application, but I'm guessing you don't have this offer in writing?" Don peered at his computer screen. "And I see this land is currently held in trust. Mr. Schermann ... does he have family? What do they say about this idea?"

Melinda felt herself sinking into her chair. Of course, Don was right. Horace was all but giving away the farm at that price. She had been so busy trying to decide what to do with her life, and so excited and overwhelmed by Horace's offer, that she hadn't stopped to think how odd it might seem to anyone not involved.

"Horace has a sister and nephew in Mason City. I've gotten to know both Ada and Kevin very well in the past several months, and they also want me to buy the acreage," she assured Don. "You see, Horace and Wilbur inherited this parcel when their mother passed, and their siblings divided up the proceeds from the sale of the rest of the acres. Wilbur now has dementia, but Horace has the authority to make financial decisions on his behalf."

Don nodded gravely, and chose his words carefully. "Well, I'm guessing Mr. Schermann ... the one that's still mentally fit, I mean ... must have a lawyer to advise him on these matters." He waited, a hopeful look on his face, seeking her assurance the offer would stand.

Melinda hadn't asked Horace if he had a lawyer. But she'd gotten to know Horace well enough to believe his word was good. Horace was quiet, but he was direct. He meant exactly what he said, and nothing more.

"Look," she leaned forward. "Horace is adamant that I buy the acreage if I want it. No one else in the extended family is interested in it. We're waiting until spring to finalize the sale so I can have a few more months to be sure this is what I want to do. Horace insisted on it. He says no one else will want to buy the acreage this time of year, anyway."

"That's for sure," Don chuckled, taking her by surprise. "I grew up on a farm myself. Winter is hard. You'll find out soon enough if you're really cut out for country life."

Melinda wasn't sure if that was meant as a reassurance or a challenge.

"I want to stay," she said firmly. "That place is home now. I can't imagine being anywhere else."

Don considered for a moment, then shuffled the documents back into a neat pile. "I guess if the family doesn't object to the proposal and the property carries no debt ... Tell you what. If Mr. Schermann holds true on his price, I would expect this application to be approved."

Melinda smiled and nodded, but Don raised a warning finger. "You won't get approved for much more than that, I'd say. Your income is greatly reduced. However, Prosper Hardware is a landmark business in this area and doesn't look like it will go under any time soon. You have excellent credit, and a decent amount of savings in your name as well. If you change your mind about the farm, you'll have just enough for a small house, either in Prosper or Swanton."

Don took another look at the documents before he added them to the new file folder he pulled from a desk drawer. "You mentioned livestock on this farm. Any possibility of additional income there? From the sale of any animals you raise, perhaps?"

"Well, Don, there might be." Melinda hadn't thought about that. "I suspect a few of the sheep are pregnant."

"Just a few?" Don looked confused. "You must have a ram, then, running with your ewes and ..."

"Well," she sighed as she gathered up her wool coat and tote. "Not actually. Actually, it all was an accident. A sort of *neighborly* accident."

Don chuckled and shook his head. "It's a good thing you've been saving carefully all these years, Miss Foster. It's been decades since I've mended any field fences, but I can tell you they are very expensive to replace."

✳ 4 ✳

Stormy and Sunny were hungry, scared and furious. The yowling started as soon as the car rolled into motion, a hair-raising duet that had Melinda grateful it was only six miles into Prosper.

"Six. Long. Miles. And a half," she corrected herself, barely able to hear her own voice over the racket echoing from the two cat carriers in the backseat. "I know, I know," she said soothingly. "I'm sorry I had to trick you like that last night, bringing out that yummy raw hamburger-and-tuna mixture and feeding you inside those portable prisons. But don't worry, we'll be to town soon."

Melinda grasped for anything positive she could offer her anxious kitties. The unfamiliar rattle of the gravel under the car didn't ease Sunny and Stormy's nerves, nor did the harsh gust of wind that slapped the vehicle as soon as it was out on the open road. "And guess what? You'll get to see Karen. You love her, I know."

Sunny, who was to the left side of the backseat, let out some sort of questioning gurgle.

"Yes, Sunny, Karen will be there," she replied in a soothing voice.

"She's Doc's assistant and my friend. Karen's the nice lady that brings her dog, Pumpkin, out to our farm to play with Hobo. Both of you let Karen pet you last time, remember?"

There was silence for a moment and she felt her hopes rise. Then Stormy, who was to the right, let out a vicious growl that may have been directed at Melinda. That brought Sunny out of his silent sulk, and the cats' wails rose in both volume and pitch. She clicked the radio on at a soft volume, found an easy-listening station she otherwise would have rolled right past, and tried to tune out the cats' howls.

It was a raw, windy day even though the sun was shining bright at this early hour, the ditches' dry grasses and weeds doubled over as they were pummeled by the stiff northwest wind. Swirls of dead leaves scuttled across the gravel road as they approached the bridge over the creek, the trees along the waterway already bare-branched and the willows showing their stalks.

Melinda knew she was doing the right thing, something she should have done as soon as she won the cats' trust. She suspected neither cat had ever been evaluated by a veterinarian. They needed to be neutered, then get their vaccinations and anything else Doc and Karen recommended.

But for so long, she hadn't been sure she would stay, or if Horace would come home, or what might happen to Stormy and Sunny if he didn't. Now that she knew they were her kitties to keep, it was time to step up their care.

Her cat carrier, the one she used for years to escort her dear Oreo to the vet clinic in Minneapolis, was still in her apartment. She'd left it behind, the stylish top-load tote a painful reminder of that final trip to the emergency pet hospital in March. Oreo's bowls and toys were donated to a shelter the following week, but she hadn't been able to let go of the carrier.

How often Melinda wished she had in those weeks after Oreo passed away, the tears welling up every time she spotted the carrier in the back of the spare bedroom's closet. She held out hope she would need it again someday, that the pain would ease enough so she could adopt another cat.

Oreo had claimed her the night she found him, a cold and hungry kitten, under the Dumpster behind her apartment building. And once again, she didn't seem to have much say in the matter. Unbeknownst to everyone but Horace, Stormy and Sunny were waiting for her here at the farm, two travelers who chose their true home on their own.

The hard-sided carriers she borrowed from vet clinic were bulky and scuffed, appropriate transport for two barely tame cats like Sunny and Stormy. Melinda had tried to scrub away the lingering scent of the vet office, then wired the cages' doors open and set them out in the barn days ago, tossing innocent treats inside whenever she passed by. Last night, when she bribed the cats to enter the carriers one more time, Sunny and Stormy hadn't noticed the doors were locked behind them until it was too late.

"The worst is over," she reminded herself as she reached the intersection with the state highway. One more mile east, and she'd be to town. The impressively tall storage tower for Prosper's co-op was already visible on the horizon.

"We're almost there," she called back to the cats, who had at last settled into a resigned silence. "You'll be knocked out soon, and will be as sleepy as little kittens when I pick you up this afternoon."

With this mission nearly complete, Melinda could turn her thoughts to her visit to the bank. Her conversation with Don was both exciting and unnerving. On the one hand, it was a big step toward her dream of buying the acreage. The pre-approval letter wouldn't arrive until next week, but Don had all but said it was a lock. And she'd quickly learned that Don, just like Horace, didn't say things he didn't mean.

But the more she thought about her arrangement with Horace, the worse it all sounded. Was she crazy to want to buy the acreage? Melinda decided she might be, especially when she thought about the extra bales of straw John Olson brought over to set around the house's foundation.

She knew her neighbor didn't have a high markup on his straw and hay, according to what Auggie's farmer sources told him about such things, but those dozens of extra straw bales added up to a significant amount of money. The fact that

Horace was paying the bill didn't ease her concerns. The whole incident was just one more thing she hadn't expected, one more expense not built into her budget.

There would be more such surprises. Don was right; owning a farm was a financial gamble at best. But Melinda couldn't imagine leaving, and she had to smile at the scene before her as she eased her car into a spot right in front of the vet clinic's door. The last of the faded autumn leaves drifted across the brown lawn, and the building's forest-green siding and crisp white trim radiated comfort and reassurance. Just what Melinda needed right now.

"Well, we're here," she sang out to the cats as she turned off the engine and reached for her purse. "Too late to turn back now."

Flustered but triumphant, Melinda marched through the front door of Prosper Veterinary Services with a wailing Sunny in tow. "You look like you've had quite the morning," Karen Porter said as she looked up from some paperwork. "I hope you've got one more out there."

"Yes, I do." Melinda reached over the counter and accepted Karen's high-five. "And I have all my fingers, too."

Stormy was huddled in the back of his crate, his eyes wide and dark as Melinda reached into the car and brought him into the sunlight. The terror on his gray-and-white face deepened as he peered out at the unknown buildings and cars parked along Main Street, his senses assaulted by so many strange sights and smells. The medicinal odor of the vet office hit Stormy's nose the minute Karen opened the door for them. Stormy began to wail and Sunny, who was still in his crate behind the counter, responded with his own yowls.

"Oh, Stormy," Karen cooed. "Don't you remember me? Today's a big day. You boys are on the list for spa time. You'll get a nice nap while I perform a small procedure, then we've got a few shots, fecal and urine samples, some blood tests ..."

"You're a brave one, Karen," Melinda said as she began to fill out the admission forms Karen placed on the counter. She knew Sunny and Stormy were males, and that was about it.

She guessed them to be two or three years old, then wrote in question marks on most of the other lines. "I don't know how you and Doc plan to handle these two. They aren't exactly lap cats."

"Well, I think the anesthetic will help with that," Karen whispered and offered her friend a knowing grin. Melinda imagined it was the same smile Karen gave to the startled farmers who wrongly assumed a petite blond woman couldn't handle large, angry livestock. "Doc's got a string of farm calls today, so I'll be going it alone. Once Stormy and Sunny are out cold, I'll get them neutered and work in the rest of the stuff before they start to come around."

Melinda agreed to pick up the cats right after four, when she got off work, and promised Karen she would lock Sunny and Stormy in her barn's grain room that night so they would be forced to rest after their surgeries.

A man with a gentle golden retriever on a leash was coming up the walk as she left the clinic, and two more cars were pulling up near the entrance. John "Doc" Ogden had served as Prosper's veterinarian for over twenty years, and his practice was certainly thriving. Karen's arrival in August had brought more than a few raised eyebrows from many of the farmers in the area, especially when she answered their calls to come wrestle a disgruntled bull or help a horse give birth. But Karen had proven herself many times over, and now was mostly accepted as Doc's business partner and, someday, his likely successor.

Judging by the muffled laughter and animated conversation Melinda heard when she came in Prosper Hardware's back door, most of the coffee group's regulars were already gathered around the sideboard up front. The store was about the only place residents could meet at this hour as the Watering Hole, the town's only bar and restaurant, didn't open until late morning.

Auggie had his own key to the store, and Melinda knew she could count on him to set out the chairs, plug in the coffeepot, and steer the conversation in the direction of whatever was on his mind that day. Now that harvest was over, Auggie was no longer in a rush to get down to the co-op. Dan, his longtime assistant, would watch the shop until Auggie arrived.

The men often discussed the weather in great detail, and didn't need Auggie to encourage such conversation. However, Auggie's fascination with the weather went beyond his role as owner of a farming-related business.

Prosper Feed Co. had been an official weather recording station for decades and, like everything else he was involved in, Auggie took his role seriously. He was fascinated with temperature swings, severe storms and high winds, anything he could add to his logs.

Today, however, the coffee group's first topic was the local high schools' basketball teams.

"I tell you, the boys are going to state this year," Auggie's voice boomed out as Melinda shouldered through the squeaky-hinged door that opened into the main part of the building. There were groans and sighs, but Auggie pressed on, leaning out of his chair and shaking a finger for emphasis.

"They can make it, I know they can. We've got three starters coming back, you know. And our bench will be deep, thanks to those sophomores. They went undefeated back in seventh grade, remember?"

Jerry Simmons, a retired school principal and Prosper's mayor, just shook his head as he topped off his coffee mug. "They're good, but I don't know if they're *that* good. A few of the boys have some injuries to deal with, Auggie. Playing football's supposed to get them in shape before basketball starts, but sometimes that plan backfires."

It didn't matter that Prosper's secondary-level students now attended school in Swanton, leaving only elementary classes at the brick building just two blocks away. Activities were still followed with a fervor Melinda recalled from her own days at Swanton High School. She noticed that despite Jerry's lukewarm review of the basketball team, he was once again wearing his purple team-spirit sweatshirt. He'd be there in the stands all season, Melinda knew, supporting the local athletes no matter what the scoreboard said.

Uncle Frank was part of the circle that morning, the coffee group about the only part of his old routine that his cardiologist and Aunt Miriam let him keep. No more lifting merchandise, no more long hours on his feet behind the counter, no more cutting lumber in the workshop. But he had a new role to fill in the community. Frank Lange would soon be the newest member of the Prosper City Council, handily winning the vacant seat on the board in a special election held just days ago.

"He was so touched that thirty-five residents actually wrote his name on the ballot," Miriam told Melinda. "Of course he won. No one else filed papers to formally run for the seat, and the only other vote cast was for Pepper, Jerry's black lab. And I suspect Auggie was behind that one."

Frank was still adjusting to his sudden retirement, but he seemed in good spirits today. Even so, he shared Jerry's caution about the boys' basketball team's prospects.

"It's too bad that Hinton boy broke his leg on that tough tackle at the last football game," Frank was saying, "but if the kids didn't go out for more than one sport, I don't know if we'd have much of a chance at anything. Even after the merger, it takes most of the kids playing multiple sports so we've got enough numbers to take the field."

Melinda spied some sort of forbidden treat in Uncle Frank's hand, possibly a chocolate muffin. No wonder he was grinning like a fool. One of the guys must have brought snacks, and Aunt Miriam wasn't around. She was about to reprimand Frank, but decided to let it go. She stepped around the stack of ice-melt bags Bill had set by the counter just yesterday, went behind the oak showcase, and added her purse to one of the shelves on its back side.

"Melinda, what do you think?" Auggie turned in his chair. "Are we going to state this year, or not?"

"I don't have any predictions for basketball season," she answered carefully. She knew better than to wade into that debate. It could go on half the morning, and she had to get the store ready to open at eight. "Sorry I'm running late, Uncle Frank. I had to drop Sunny and Stormy at the vet."

George Freitag, the group's eldest member at eighty-two, carefully rose from his chair and topped off his coffee mug. "Oh, that's right! How was the rodeo?"

"The best kind. Short ... and done. Both cats were taken into custody last night without incident. They've been turned over to the authorities."

"Bet Karen and Doc won't have an easy time with those two, if they're as skittish as you say," George chuckled, adjusting his overall straps and reaching for another muffin. "I've wrangled many an irate animal in my time. You never know what they're going to do next."

Melinda could just about transition her seasonal wardrobe based on what George was wearing. Only a few weeks ago, he'd swapped his plaid long-sleeve shirts for a selection of thick flannels. George loved to tell a good story, and she sometimes wondered what was true and what came straight from George's active imagination. But George was also one of her best resources as she tried to navigate the seasons at her acreage. He and his wife, Mary, sold their farm and moved into Prosper just a few years ago, and Melinda was grateful for George's sage advice.

She added her coat to the hall tree next to the sideboard and reached for an empty coffee cup. She was already behind on her workday, but those muffins looked fantastic and smelled even better. Mary probably sent them along, unless Jerry's wife was in a baking mood. Melinda promised herself she'd bring treats someday soon. She loved to bake, but time had gotten away from her in the last week.

"Doc's out on farm calls all day," she told George as she settled into the last empty chair. "So Karen's on her own with Sunny and Stormy. But they're probably asleep by now and getting prepped for surgery."

"Doc will have an interesting day today, driving out on the gravel with all this wind," Auggie glanced out to where a few stray leaves skidded down Main Street. "Could have gusts up to thirty-five this afternoon."

The men's conversation veered off in the expected direction, and Melinda settled back in her chair with a contented sigh. The coffee was strong, just the way Auggie liked it, and she didn't mind. She'd not slept well last night, worrying about Sunny and Stormy locked in their crates in the barn, and it would take more than one cup to get her going for the day.

She glanced around the store, taking in the simple white lights that glowed in the towering artificial Christmas tree now holding court by one of the front windows, and had to smile. Prosper Hardware's high, pressed-tin ceilings and shining oak floors hadn't changed since Melinda's Shrader great-grandparents opened the store in 1894, and the original interior set the tone for Aunt Miriam's old-fashioned Christmas decorations and displays.

Faux evergreen garlands twisted with more clear lights swooped over the two plate-glass windows, and a small-but-carefully chosen selection of toys filled the deep display shelf near the Christmas tree. But the store's second picture window was packed with shovels, battery-powered lanterns and snow boots, practical items that Miriam promised Melinda would be in demand long after Santa came and went.

More lighted garland was draped over the railing to the upstairs office and storeroom, and a small display of holiday-themed towels and household accessories beckoned to shoppers from the end cap of one of the store's four aisles.

The holiday season was an important source of revenue for Prosper Hardware, just like any other retail business, but Frank and Miriam insisted no Christmas decorations appear until Halloween passed. And while the store was now decked out in its Christmas finery, a basket of autumn gourds still greeted customers at the checkout counter.

"Everything arrives in its own time," Miriam told Melinda back in October, when the stores over in Swanton were already trotting out their Santa inflatables, reindeer and glitter. "I don't care what anyone says. Thanksgiving needs to be honored, too."

Aunt Miriam wasn't the most fashionable woman, with her close-cropped brown-gray curls, and she rarely wore makeup or changed out of her usual uniform of a sweatshirt and jeans. But as Melinda studied the simple holiday decorations, she had to admit Miriam had impeccable taste.

The most beautiful item was draped along the front of the antique oak-and-glass showcase that served as Prosper Hardware's main counter. The faux evergreen swag was lush and bright, despite its age, and dotted with clusters of red plastic berries. The day Miriam reverently lifted the garland out of its wooden crate, Melinda knew she was seeing a special piece of family history.

"Melinda, check right under that top molding and you'll find a tiny nail," Miriam had said. "This evergreen has hung on the front of this counter every year since 1949, when your Grandpa Shrader purchased it at what used to be the five-and-dime store over in Charles City. You should have seen the horror on your grandma's face when he brought out the hammer and drove all these nails right into the front of this antique showcase."

Miriam had shuddered, then laughed. "I thought our mother might faint. Needless to say, supper was a quiet one that night. But Mom came around at last, and had to admit the garland was beautiful. But she put her foot down: No more defacing of this cabinet, and we all agreed to abide by her wishes."

Melinda snapped out of her reverie and pushed herself out of her chair. It was nearly eight, and Bill was coming in through the back to grab his own cup of coffee before the store opened.

Bill Larsen was a little younger than Melinda, but his life had followed a similar path. He moved away for college and later to Des Moines, but he and his wife returned to Prosper to raise their young family. Bill was an experienced carpenter, and was in high demand with customers needing wood pieces cut to size for projects. That included Melinda, when she got inspired to do something at the farm that exceeded her limited skills.

"Hey, Frank," Bill said as he reached for the last chocolate muffin. "Weren't we going over to City Hall today to get a look at the town's Christmas lights? I'm slammed with orders, unfortunately. It seems like everyone turned the calendar over and decided that if they're going to build any handmade Christmas gifts, they'd better get on it."

"Don't worry about it, Bill," Frank replied. "I can go by myself. We just need to get some notes on which fixtures need new bulbs, if there's any loose wires, that sort of thing. I bet Nancy could help me." Nancy Delaney, the little town's only full-time employee, kept the wheels turning as both city clerk and library director.

Melinda was tired, but found she wanted to go, too. She loved history and old buildings, and was curious about the little town that had been so important to generations of her mom's family.

She couldn't pass up a chance to snoop around. And besides, Aunt Miriam would want someone to go along to make sure Frank didn't overdo it, lift things he shouldn't.

"I can go, Uncle Frank," she said, trying to sound casual, as Frank would bristle at any hint of assistance. "Miriam's coming in later, she can watch the register." Frank shrugged his approval and Melinda was suddenly energized.

Jerry reluctantly rose to his feet, and set his coffee cup on the battered metal tray on the sideboard.

"Well, I'd better get across the street. Let me know what's needed to get those Christmas lights in shape. No one has time to hang them until next week. Two of the guys who usually help us are out of town this weekend."

Jerry turned suddenly as he pulled on his parka. "Oh, and Melinda, I think I need your help with something."

She hesitated. "Jerry, I don't care for heights, so you won't get me up on a ladder to hang the holiday lights. If it's anything else, I might be able to do it."

"Oh, we just pull up under the poles with the fire truck, get them that way," Jerry chuckled. "But that's not it. I need another volunteer for the committee that's planning the holiday festival. This is just one evening, it's not a big event like the Fourth of July celebration. We could really use your marketing expertise again."

She could tell Jerry was trying not to beg, or to guilt her into saying yes. But she'd learned quickly once she arrived in Prosper that while many residents wanted to pitch in for the greater good, it was difficult to find people willing to make decisions and guide outcomes. Melinda had been in town only a few weeks when she'd found herself in charge of publicity for the Fourth of July festival.

She already had plenty on her plate. But everyone was looking at her, hoping, waiting. And hadn't she decided she wanted to get more involved? How could she say no?

"Put me down, Jerry," Melinda heard herself saying. "Let me know when the next meeting is."

* 5 *

Uncle Frank pulled the collar of his parka up against the chill as another gust of wind rushed down Main Street.

"Feel that cold, Melinda! Tells you winter's on the way. But you know what? I'll take it." Frank reached up to yank his knit cap farther down over his thinning white hair. "You don't miss the simple joys of life until they're out of reach. All those weeks in the hospital, all I could think about was getting out of that bed, coming home, and firing up the lawnmower or picking tomatoes out in the garden."

"And getting back to Prosper Hardware." Melinda laid a cautionary hand on her uncle's arm as a truck suddenly appeared just past the post office, from where Third Street met Main.

"That's right." Frank waved to the truck's driver, who tooted his horn in return. Frank Lange apparently knew everyone living or working within ten miles of Prosper Hardware's front door. "People probably think I'm crazy, but oh, I love this quiet, in-between time of year. The harvest is over, the garden's cleared off. It's a nice time to catch your breath before the holiday rush comes along."

If Prosper's Main Street was any indicator of what people were up to, Frank was right. There was only one car parked in front of City Hall, and Melinda knew it was Nancy's. Three vehicles were clustered by the Watering Hole's entrance in the next block. The rest of Main Street, which stretched only four blocks from the co-op on its northwest end to just past the vet clinic, was vacant and sleepy.

It didn't help that several of the buildings in the little town's business district were empty, a fact that pained Melinda. The farm crisis of the 1980s had not been kind to Prosper, or many other rural communities in the Midwest. This middle block of Main was Prosper's busiest, with City Hall and the adjacent library on one side and Prosper Hardware and the post office on the other.

The city buildings were surprisingly elegant, their tan-brick structures bolstered by limestone corner blocks. City Hall and the library had a common wall and shared an interior cased opening that made Nancy's jack-of-all-trades job possible. Through the library's picture window, Melinda could see Nancy straightening up the library's antique circulation desk and sorting a pile of books that probably came in through the night drop box.

While the library was only one story in height, City Hall was much grander in scale. Its second-floor windows were topped with arches and a heavy portico protected the building's double front doors. The historic property dated from the 1880s and had once been some sort of mercantile, a business that was already booming when Prosper incorporated in 1890.

For whatever reason, that venture died away while Prosper Hardware thrived across the street. The imposing building was vacant for years before city leaders, short on office space and not wanting one of the town's most impressive structures to crumble, snapped up the current City Hall and library for mere dollars several decades ago.

Melinda could see why residents wanted to preserve the ornate building, but had to admit she preferred the cozy elegance of Prosper Hardware. Two stories high and stacked with warm red bricks, her family's store had a dark green canopy that welcomed customers and sheltered the wrought iron benches in front of the generous first-floor windows. An ornate metal sign, a reproduction of the one ordered by her great-grandparents more than a hundred years ago, greeted passerby from above the awning.

Melinda squinted against the sharp sunlight and gazed up at the shade-covered windows on City Hall's second floor. "I can't wait to get upstairs," she told Frank. "I've only been inside a few times, and I only saw the front lobby."

"Well, I'm sure Nancy will be happy to give you the grand tour." Frank battled against the whistling wind to pry open City Hall's front door. "Me, I've got to give those Christmas lights a good once-over. Who knows how many bulbs might be out?"

It heartened Melinda to see her uncle so excited about a project. But she remembered Aunt Miriam's honest-yet-loving assessment of her husband's sputtering electrical skills. Bill would handle any needed wiring updates. And Frank wasn't supposed to lift anything heavy ...

"How about we settle for just taking inventory today?" she suggested. "I can slide the light frames out of their hiding places while you take notes."

Nancy came through from the library, eager to greet Melinda and Frank. Nancy was always in motion, and Melinda admired her intellect and drive. In addition to keeping the city of Prosper running smoothly, she was raising two teenagers as a single mom. Doc, who was also a member of the City Council, joked that the roof of City Hall would likely collapse the day Nancy retired. Thankfully, that was still at least a decade away.

"Come in, come in!" Nancy pushed back her reading glasses and rubbed her hands together, momentarily chilled by the breeze that blew in with Melinda and Frank. The generous collar of Nancy's burgundy cowl-neck sweater nearly reached the bottom of her razor-cut dark bob.

"Melinda, I'm so glad you can help us with the holiday celebration. Jerry told me all about it this morning. Frank, I trust you're preparing yourself for the heavy lifting that comes with serving on our City Council?"

Frank only chuckled. Melinda knew Nancy was just giving Frank a hard time. The council only met for an hour or so once a month, and socializing seemed to be the biggest item on every agenda.

"Well, I promised Miriam I'd head home for a rest after this," Frank replied. "Bill's too busy to come over today, but we've got to start on these lights. It's already November."

"We're only getting a list together for Bill," Melinda gently cut in, reaching for a pad of paper on the front counter and giving Nancy a knowing look.

"We won't be hauling anything out of storage today. Bill will come over with new wiring and bulbs yet this week and bring the lights downstairs."

"Sounds good." Nancy grabbed another sheet of blank paper and wrote out a hasty sign, "*upstairs, just yell*," and taped it to the edge of the counter. Then she stepped behind the desk and pulled a ring of keys out of a top drawer. "Well, let's go take a look."

The front room of City Hall, whose walls were a random shade of municipal pale green, was mostly taken up by the counter to one side and a modest desk and set of file cabinets on the other. The desk, Jerry's mayoral command post, was still cluttered with stacks of paper despite his stop at City Hall earlier that morning. A few barren chairs rested by the front window, where Nancy was determined to keep a stand full of plants alive.

A battered wooden door tucked in a wall of paneling, obviously added during some long-ago renovation, opened into another work space. The original ceiling moldings were still intact in this area, where two more metal desks lounged in the dim sunlight from a window that faced the gap between City Hall and the vacant building next door.

One table, stacked with emergency manuals, belonged to Tony Bevins. The other desk was dusty and empty. Prosper hadn't had a police force for decades, instead relying on a county sheriff's deputy to cruise through once a day. County crews also handled snow removal for the little community.

Through another half-open door, Melinda could make out the long desk and few rows of chairs that passed for a City Council chambers. Beyond that was the entrance to a modest kitchen. Instead of continuing into the council area, Nancy made a quick turn down a short, awkward hallway and paused before an insulated steel door. Melinda was all but holding her breath as the key clicked in the lock and a set of steep wooden stairs appeared.

Nancy flipped a light switch and a series of bulbs flickered to life far above, barely piercing the gloom. Melinda was reminded of Horace's haymow, with its towering roof and deep shadows. The upstairs of City Hall wasn't much warmer than a barn, and she was glad she hadn't removed her coat.

Nancy reached for a dented metal handrail bolted into the stairwell. "These steep steps wouldn't be to code these days, they're an accident waiting to happen. Be careful, Frank. Melinda, maybe you should take up the rear."

Frank protested but Melinda fell in line behind him, their footsteps echoing through the lonely space as they reached the top of the stairs. Discarded desks were everywhere, and a row of tired file cabinets slouched against the water-stained plaster of the far wall. There were stacks of lumber, mounds of cardboard boxes and pyramids of wooden crates. A henpecked manual typewriter, missing three of its keys, inexplicably slept on a pile of dirty traffic cones.

"All the holiday decorations should be over there," Nancy pointed to the left as she turned around stacks of stuff to reach the four front windows. One plastic shade snapped up with a screech of protest, and then another. Now that Melinda could see more than a few feet in front of her face, the cavernous space looked even more lost and neglected.

The once-rich stain on the wide-plank hardwood floors was scuffed away in many places. A row of shorter windows, their dingy shades still drawn, stared out over the roof of the single-story library next door.

The back wall of the space was the most interesting. A wide cased opening still held a set of rusting and empty curtain rods. The floor behind it was raised by about three feet, and a short run of steps met what must have been the front of a stage. Melinda could imagine long-ago children putting on a play for their proud parents, or a band tuning up for a community dance. She zigzagged around boxes and piles, trying to get a closer look while keeping the worst of the dust off her coat.

"I remember when I was a kid," Uncle Frank called over his shoulder as he stepped around boxes to reach the Christmas decorations, "there was something going on up here nearly every Friday night. Concerts, community plays, dances and such. It was the place to be. The Watering Hole was just a tavern then, but there was a little diner in the next block, there by the old bank. And a soda fountain at the drug store, two doors down from here. They were always packed."

Melinda could hardly picture how Prosper used to be. She made her way to the front windows and looked out over the little town, its streets barely sheltered by the bare limbs of the empty trees. The village ended only three blocks behind Prosper Hardware, the empty fields reaching right up to the backyards on the edge of town. Melinda knew it was the same scene in the opposite direction.

And just as the co-op was the west edge of town, the water tower marked the other end of Main Street. From there, the county blacktop bent to the south, passed a cluster of houses, and crossed the river bridge.

"It's been many years since any gatherings have been held up here, that's for sure," Nancy said wistfully. "Jerry says once times got hard, the city started using this whole upstairs for storage. The city used to rent out one of the other storefronts for that, but even at rock-bottom rates, they couldn't afford to keep that space. Oh, Frank, let us help you with that."

Melinda pivoted to see Uncle Frank was about to shove some wooden crates out of his path. She was closer than Nancy, and reached Frank just in time to discretely move one box so he could get through.

"What's in those other file cabinets, Nancy?" Melinda pointed to a row along the far wall.

"Oh, only most of the town's historic records," she sighed. "Things from the past twenty years are computerized, of course. And there's a small vault in the back of the library, from when that was a store years ago. But most of the rest is up here, in stacks of dusty old paper, just waiting for ..."

"Don't say it, Nancy! You'll jinx it," Frank pleaded. "These records are too valuable to be left up here like this. Prosper needs to join the modern age. Even at the hardware store, we converted our ledgers and records to digital ten years ago. Took me months up in the office, but we got it done."

Nancy's face lit up about the same time Melinda got an idea. Frank needed something to do, he was driving Miriam crazy because he was stuck at home ...

"Frank, in addition to joining the City Council, you may have just found yourself a part-time job!" Nancy exclaimed. "More like an unpaid internship, unfortunately. But we've got a scanner down in the library, and I wouldn't mind the company. Except for story time on Wednesday afternoons, it's pretty quiet around here."

Frank considered for a moment, then his smile spread from ear to ear. "I accept! If you keep me in coffee, Nancy, I think that's all the payment I'll require. Talk to Jerry about it, and we can get a motion on the agenda for the council meeting next month. I'll abstain from the vote, of course."

Then Frank pointed at a tumble of dusty metal frames leaning against the wall, his enthusiasm quickly evaporating. "Well, when it comes to holiday decorations, here's what we have to work with."

"Wow, they're ... needing a little work," was all Melinda could say.

She wasn't really sure what she expected, but her vague idea of colorful decorations glowing on all the lamp posts along Main Street didn't match what she saw. There were only twelve in all, five trees and seven snowflakes, meaning at least a few frames had long ago landed on a scrap heap.

The shapes were only about four feet tall and gray and dull, the wiring that peeked out from the inner channels a hot-mess mix of dirty old lines and new sections that Bill must have patched together.

"It's not much," Frank sighed. "But it's all we've got. So much for a winter wonderland."

"Jerry says the city's had these since the sixties," Nancy skirted around Frank and lifted a tree frame off a snowflake. A dirty, loose bulb dropped from a top branch of the tree and shattered on the wood floor. Nancy shook her head. "That was the last time they had the cash to spend on anything like this. I think at one time they had sixteen, or eight of each."

"Good thing Main Street's not very long," Melinda offered, searching for something positive to say. "These might be enough for, what, two blocks?"

"Not quite, but close," Frank rubbed his chin. "We alternate light posts, to start with. We try to catch this block, of course, then put a few down in the next block to get them in front of the Watering Hole and a few other storefronts. There's a few left to go back the other way, at least to the Methodist church."

He noticed Melinda's expression and shook his head. "Yep, that means the Catholic church doesn't get a city decoration out front. Good thing they have that beautiful lighted nativity display."

"So, none by the vet clinic, then, either. Or the co-op." Melinda paused. "What's Auggie have to say about that?"

Frank rolled his eyes. "Auggie's a bit of a Grinch, Melinda. Well, at least when it comes to decorations. He always reminds us that his front shop is newer and not so fancy as the buildings in this part of Main Street, as if that matters. And how he's just got that one plain front window, not much room for festive displays, anyway."

Frank paused long enough to make a few notes.

"But way back when, the co-op's previous owner always set out a lighted star at the top of the main storage tower. Auggie continued the tradition for many years, but now says he can't find the star, and that it's too much work to install it. We don't push him on it. You know how Auggie can get."

"He's got one too many excuses, I'd say," Nancy said with a raised eyebrow. Her tone told Melinda that Nancy had more than one story she could tell about Auggie, but was too discreet to do so. "He either has the star, or he doesn't. Well, I guess it's his call. Melinda, let's pull these out in the middle of the room and see what we've got to work with."

As she and Nancy lifted a snowflake away from the pile, Melinda heard the skittering of little claws back along the wall. "I know that sound all too well," she said. "Those mice are coming in everywhere out at the farm. The seasons are changing, and they know it."

"I need to set some traps up here," Nancy shuddered and reached for one of the tree forms. "With a soon-to-be-member of the City Council present, I hate to disclose how many mice I've caught in the library just this week. Melinda, it'd make your skin crawl. You know, what we need in this building is a cat."

Melinda's eyes widened. "Nancy! That's a wonderful idea! You should get one, it could be an ambassador for the library, have its own Facebook page ..."

"Don't get too excited," Frank shook his pen at Nancy and Melinda. "I know for a fact that Jerry's allergic to cats. And I don't know about Tony. Would be a problem if your emergency services director couldn't stand to come inside City Hall."

Nancy waved away Frank's concerns. "Jerry's only in here maybe ten hours a week, and Tony less than that. And he mostly hangs out in the garage out back." Nancy was about to wipe her dusty hands on her black pants, then thought better of it. "It's everyone else I'd be most concerned about. Prosper may be tiny, but it's a sure bet some of the residents have allergies. We want both City Hall and the library to be as welcoming as possible."

Melinda felt a pang of sadness. How she still missed Oreo. Too many nights she settled into Horace's leather recliner and wished for a furry friend to sit in her lap. Sunny and Stormy refused to come in the house. Hobo was too big to fit in the chair with Melinda and besides, he had quickly claimed her stylish chenille sofa as his own. After all, it was a great improvement from Horace's old couch, a sagging, orange-velour thing still wedged into the downstairs bedroom.

"Let's check all these light sockets," Melinda suggested, eager to change the subject. "Where can I plug these in?"

Nancy rummaged in a nearby cardboard box and came up with an extension cord. Only about half of the snowflake's bulbs would light.

"Oh, dear," Nancy sighed. "Frank, do you carry this size of bulb at the store? If the rest of the decorations are as bad as this one, we'll need all you've got, and then some."

Frank counted the burned-out lights he could see and motioned for Nancy to turn the frame so the other side was visible. "We can certainly order more," he said as he made notes on the pad. "Could get them in by next week."

Melinda reached for one of the Christmas-tree frames and tried to brush the dust away.

"These are so drab, with this plain gray metal. And they're scuffed, too. I could see the snowflakes painted white, and the trees a nice dark green. They'd look especially good during the day, when they aren't lit."

"Well, if you want to take that on," Frank shrugged, then stopped. "You know, we've got plenty of spray paint over at the store and can always get more. Either way, Bill's got to haul these over to our building with his truck to check the wires and change the burned-out bulbs."

Frank paused at the looks of relief on Melinda's and Nancy's faces. "Yes, you heard right," he said quietly. "No more heavy lifting for me. It's time to pass this all on to Bill."

"Maybe you could help me paint," Melinda suggested, touched by the wistfulness in her uncle's voice. "We can open some cardboard boxes in the back room of the store so we don't make a mess, tape off the decorations' sockets. These will look amazing."

A muffled voice echoed up the stairwell. "Hey, Nancy, you still up there?"

"On my way!" Nancy called out, then turned to Melinda and Frank before heading toward the stairs.

"Can you pull those window shades back down when you're done? I'll keep an eye out for Bill to stop by tomorrow to pick up the light frames."

Melinda dragged out another snowflake and moved to plug it in, but Frank waved her off. "You know, I'm really starting to get into the holiday spirit. I think this is a good year to replace all the bulbs on every frame. We'll have to take all the lights off, anyway, to paint them."

"Won't that get expensive?"

Frank just grinned. "Nah, not when I write all of it off as a tax-deductible donation to the city. The spray paint, too. Maybe I can't wrestle these lights around anymore, but I sure can make them look like new. That green and white's going to look sharp."

✳ 6 ✳

There was a knock at the back door, then Cassie burst into the porch before Melinda could run out to greet her.

"We're here!" Cassie sang, dropping her designer luggage on the painted-wood porch floor and giving Melinda a hug. Melinda glanced out the windows to see Hobo greeting Susan by Cassie's cherry-red Escalade, which now carried a distinctive underbelly of gravel dust.

"I was trying to watch for you," she said, pleased that Cassie seemed so relaxed and happy. Cassie's divorce was proceeding at a snail's pace, thanks to Jim Blake's significant investments, but it was clear she made the right choice. "I was making sure the bathrooms are stocked with clean towels. I've got a list of dirty jobs for this weekend, you know."

The three women had known each other since their early twenties and worked together at several marketing firms in the Twin Cities over the years. Cassie Blake and Susan Vinter were Melinda's closest friends. Although her life was changing and new people had appeared in it, she was so grateful that Susan and Cassie were still beside her, cheering every step she took.

And better yet, they weren't afraid of a little hard work. During their July visit, her friends helped her paint the living room and kitchen, transforming the spaces in just two days. Now, with winter coming, she needed their help outside.

"I can't believe that wind out there!" Susan's strawberry-blonde bob was askew and her fair cheeks flushed from the sudden heat of the kitchen. "You told us it was blowing hard today, and you were right. It all but pushed us down here from the Cities."

"We don't exactly have skyscrapers out here to slow it down." Melinda reached for Susan's nylon bag and set it around the corner on the dining room floor. "It's supposed to calm down tonight and clear off for tomorrow, which is good, because we may be outside most of the day."

"I'm just glad it worked out for us to come visit," Cassie said as she rolled her black waves into a casual bun. "It's so hard to get our schedules to match up. And this will probably be our last chance until spring. Are you sure you don't need extra hands when you clear out your apartment next weekend? Will your parents be enough?"

The manager of Melinda's building had a new tenant lined up for her apartment. The young woman had just been promoted and wanted nothing more than to move into the gentrifying neighborhood. But she needed access Thanksgiving weekend, not December first, and Melinda promised to have the place cleared out as soon as possible.

"Mom and Dad and I can get it," she assured her friends as she set out chips and dip on the kitchen table. "You know, it'll be sad in a way to give up my place, but it's time."

Susan gave Melinda's shoulder a squeeze. "And just look what you'll be coming home to. I think our painting efforts this summer really paid off. This place looks amazing."

"Well, wait until you see my to-do list. You might want to get back in the car and head north."

"Not in this wind," Cassie shuddered. "We'd fight it all the way. What's on the agenda this time?"

Melinda reached for the notepad and joined her friends at the table. Just as Susan began to pour out the red wine Cassie brought along, a "*snap!*" echoed from behind the stove. Cassie flinched and lifted her sock-covered feet up to the rungs of her chair.

"That," Melinda said soothingly, "is something I will handle on my own. Let's just say, this charming B&B has been rather busy lately. If you get up overnight, always turn on a light. And put on your shoes."

"Oh, my gosh," Cassie grimaced. "I'm sleeping in the car. How cold is it supposed to get tonight?"

"Into the thirties. If the wind dies down sooner rather than later, it could get down to freezing."

Melinda started to laugh. "Listen to me, I sound like Auggie giving his weather report! Anyway, I think you'll be more comfortable in the house, Cassie. And Hobo will be on guard. He sleeps on Horace's bed, you know, if you want to use that room again."

"I would love to bunk with Hobo," Cassie took a sip of her wine. "So, back to this list."

"OK," Melinda read down the page. "We need to swap out the screens on the front porch for the storm windows in the basement. There's snow fence to tie to the wire panels there behind the garden. Out in the barn, there's plywood for Stormy and Sunny's house under the haymow stairs. If we have time, you can help me shrink-wrap every window in this house." She sighed. "I doubt we'll get that far. And I don't want us to work the whole time. There's a craft bazaar and lunch down at the church tomorrow, so we'll go to that, too."

Susan reached for the chips and dip. "What's with all those straw bales around the back side of the house? Seems those weren't there the last time we visited."

"One of my neighbors brought those over last week, said Horace has him do it every year. It's supposed to keep drafts away from the foundation." Melinda shook her head. "I got into a little bale-hauling competition with the guy's teenaged sons. Guess who lost?"

Cassie smiled. "I love it how everyone helps everyone out here. You must feel so blessed." Cassie was about to reach for more chips, then stopped. "Speaking of staying warm ..." She rose from her chair and started for the living room. Melinda and Susan followed.

"Melinda, what's your fireplace like?" Cassie was suddenly all business, pushing aside the hearth's screen and crouching before the flue. Despite her manicured nails and hefty bank account, Cassie was full of handy information from spending her college summers working on a Twin Cities home restoration crew.

"I'm not sure," Melinda faltered, handing Cassie the extra flashlight she kept in the fireplace's left-side bookcase.

"I haven't had the nerve to start a fire in it yet. There's a bit of dry wood out in the machine shed, and I have a number for a guy over by Swanton who delivers. But I almost hate to ask what you're seeing in there, Cassie."

"Well, I think you've got a lovely family of spiders up in this chimney," Cassie's voice echoed out from the fireplace. "And the opening seems to be clear. The good news is, I don't see any bats."

"*Bats?*" Melinda shuddered. "Oh, no, I hadn't even thought about that. This house is a hundred years old. I'm sure they could find their way in. There's not an attic, really, but there's crawlspaces behind the half-walls upstairs, and in the tops of the ceilings ..."

"What a great image you just put in my head," Susan wrinkled her nose. "I was already imagining the mice camping out in Wilbur's old room, the one I'll be sleeping in. Now at bedtime, I'll be wondering what's flying around above my head, too."

Cassie carefully backed out of the hearth and wiped a sooty hand across her cheek, then brushed her dirty palms on her designer jeans. She glanced out picture window behind the sofa and got to her feet.

"It's almost dark out. Girls, get your coats. We're going bat-hunting."

"I don't think that was on the list ..." Susan cringed.

"We just need to sit in the yard," Cassie gave Susan a reassuring pat on the arm, "and watch that chimney. This is the time of night they'll be getting active. Melinda, can dinner wait a bit?"

"I just have some lasagna in the slow cooker, the salad is in the fridge. The garlic bread won't take long." She looked at Susan, then shrugged. "Well, let's get out there."

There were a few ragged lawn chairs in the garage. Cassie gathered them in front of the evergreens on the north side of the house, where the brick chimney was in full view.

"I hope we don't see anything," Susan whispered as she wrapped a blanket around her parka and settled into the dusty webbed chair. The wind was diminishing, but it was turning colder. The stars were still only faint pinpricks in the darkening sky.

"Me, too," Melinda admitted. "I've met many interesting people since I moved here, but I don't know any chimney sweeps." Hobo settled in the dead grass at her feet, listening, and she gave him a pat on the head. She scanned the yard, searching for Sunny and Stormy, but the cats apparently had better things to do during the twilight hour.

Hobo suddenly jumped up from the lawn, his ears alert. Susan and Melinda froze in their chairs.

Cassie tugged on the brown knit hat she borrowed from the porch closet and slid down in her seat. "He's watching the windbreak," she whispered. "Oh, I feel like I should turn around, but I can't ..."

"It gets dark out here so fast," Melinda said quietly, then craned her neck to study the roofline of the house, where the gables' peaks were being erased as shadows fell across the farm. There was no movement above, no fluttering around the chimney.

Hobo let out a whimper, and Melinda reached for his collar with one hand and soothed him with the other.

"He senses something," Cassie gripped her chair's arms tighter. "Oh, this was a bad idea. I'm sorry, girls. Forget the bats. What if there's something else out here?"

"Melinda," Susan's voice wavered, "didn't Horace tell you something about, well, larger wildlife roaming around?"

"That was a few years ago," Melinda tried to shrug off her own unease. "He had this story about something he shot at behind the chicken house, a bobcat, I think. But Kevin said Horace likes to stretch things a bit."

"Means nothing," Cassie tried to dismiss their fears with a flick of her wrist. "We're supposed to be watching for bats. Just little, innocent, endangered critters that eat bugs." The three friends trained their eyes on the silent chimney cap.

"So far, so good," Melinda tried to lighten the mood. "Maybe we're alone out here, after all."

But then ... was that a snapped twig in the windbreak? Hobo gave a low growl.

Cassie shifted in her chair, the metal frame letting out a squeak that made the other women jump. "What is that thing, up in that tree?" She pointed into the windbreak.

Melinda felt her blood run cold. She didn't want to admit it, but this wasn't the first time she'd been afraid out here. Sunset came earlier every night, and she found herself gripping the steering wheel tight as her car rolled over the creek bridge, half afraid of what might jump out of the shadows and into her headlight's beams.

But enough. If she was going to live here, she couldn't be scared of every strange noise. Melinda forced herself to turn and stare into the bare-limbed trees of the windbreak.

"Oh, girls, look," she whispered in awe. "It's an owl. A big one, too. Isn't he majestic? He's only out hunting for his supper. Maybe he'll serenade us later. I hear one, sometimes, out north of the house just about the time I'm off to bed most nights. This might be him."

Cassie pulled her throw blanket over her head. "My grandma always said if you hear an owl hoot in the middle of the night, it's a bad omen."

"I'm so tired that I'm always in bed by ten," Melinda assured Cassie. "Living in the country will do that to you."

"Cassie, pull it together," Susan snapped, but Melinda heard the relief in her voice. "Do you really think that cute owl over there is telling fortunes instead of hunting for a mouse? It's a good thing Stormy and Sunny don't have black fur. Cassie would be nervous about them, too."

"Well, I know you were scared, too, Susan Vinter," Cassie huffed. "Huddled over there in your chair. Good thing you have Hobo to protect you." Hobo made a snuffing noise and leaned against Susan's leg, as if to reassure her.

Melinda stifled a laugh. Hanging out with Susan and Cassie was never dull. How she missed her old friends. Phone calls, emails and texts just weren't the same. And spring was so far away. Melinda thought she could gather enough courage to clear out her old apartment and turn in her keys, but she never wanted to give up the special bond she had with Susan and Cassie.

The women waited in silence for a few more minutes. Then, as if someone had flipped a switch, the yard settled into a thick darkness.

Cassie studied the farmhouse's roof again, then at last gave a satisfied nod.

"No sign of bats." Cassie rose to her feet and motioned for Melinda and Susan to do the same. "I think you're in the clear. You might as well call that firewood guy and tell him to bring you a load. I still can't get over the fact that you can't get a pizza delivered out here, but people will just show up in your yard with stacks of wood and straw bales."

"I say we get inside and dig into that lasagna," Susan stretched her arms above her head, then folded her lawn chair with one smooth motion, her unflappable nature already restored. "I could use another glass of wine after all this excitement. And we better get to bed early. We've got a busy day planned for tomorrow."

✳ 7 ✳

A fine layer of frost covered the back sidewalk when Melinda went out for chores Saturday morning. The sky was calm and clear, a welcome change from the heavy clouds and driving winds of the day before. But while the farmyard was quiet, something was definitely happening out in the chicken coop.

Even with the new sunrise glowing in the chicken house's small windowpanes, she could tell the lights were on inside. Susan was still asleep in Wilbur's old room upstairs, but Cassie was nowhere to be found. And while her stylish brown topper remained on its hook by the back door, one of Horace's old coats was missing.

"Whatever is she up to?" she asked Hobo as they cautiously approached the coop. "I don't hear any shrieking or squawking, at least."

"Good morning!" Cassie crowed as Melinda slid the door latch and slipped into the chicken house, Hobo waiting on the grass outside. Melinda couldn't remember when she had ever seen Cassie looking so frumpy, nor so happy. She had to laugh at the ragged yellow-yarn chore gloves Cassie had found on the back porch. Horace's old coat was two sizes too big, and patched at the elbows.

"What do you have there?" she teased Cassie, gesturing at the red plastic bucket whose handle Cassie carefully balanced on one wrist. "I didn't know you wanted to help with chores.

Hobo will escort you to the hydrant by the garden. Just fill the bucket, then dump out the pans in here and in the chicken run, and give them a refill."

Cassie looked a bit defeated. "Oh, I thought this cute red bucket was for gathering eggs, so I did." Some of the hens scuttled nervously around Cassie's too-clean boots and edged toward Melinda, as if relieved to see a familiar face. Pansy, the queen bee of the bunch, glared at Cassie from her favorite perch on the far wall.

Unlike Pansy, Melinda was impressed with Cassie's efforts. "You rooted around the roosts in this dusty chicken house? Did anyone peck you?"

"I was pretty fast," Cassie raised her chin and straightened the coat's hood, which was decorated with random flakes of straw. "A few of us exchanged some harsh language," her brown eyes slid in Pansy's direction, "but I got it done. I found six eggs. Does that sound right?"

"I'd say so. There's eight hens, but their egg production slows as the weather gets colder. At least, that's two eggs apiece for our breakfast."

The hydrant handle was stiff from the cold. Melinda had to give Cassie an assist to wrench it open. As always, Hobo took a generous slurp from the tap before the bucket was hooked in place.

"Isn't that water terribly cold?" Cassie wondered as Hobo lapped at the stream gushing from the faucet, his muzzle quickly soaked. "How can he stand it?"

"I don't know," Melinda shrugged. "But it's his favorite part of doing chores. I hope this hydrant doesn't freeze up come winter. If it does, I'll have to haul water from the barn or the house."

"You have so much to do out here," Cassie sighed as they started for the barn, Hobo leading the way.

"I know," Melinda groaned.

"No, I mean, I wish I was this busy." Cassie looked down at her vinyl boots, which were a sophisticated shade of tan and surely expensive. "I always thought I had such a crazy life, running from one charity meeting to the next, taking the kids here and there and, well, shopping." She rolled her eyes.

Cassie had put her marketing career on hold when her first child arrived. With her soon-to-be-ex a successful lawyer and a member of a wealthy family, money hadn't been a concern. Until now.

"Since Jim moved out, I've been so restless." She shoved her fists into the pockets of Horace's old coat. "All of that, it's not enough anymore. I still have the kids, but I need to get out of the house, get a job again. Find a new purpose."

"Well, I'm not sure I'd recommend you go the way I did," Melinda answered dryly. "My new career came with a sharp pay cut, and I'm on my feet all day. I'll need to freelance for Susan's company if I want to save some real cash every month. I live in a charming-yet-drafty house, and winter's coming on. I'm flying by the seat of my pants out here."

"But you love it," Cassie countered.

"You're right," Melinda gently pushed an eager Hobo aside so she could reach the iron latch on the barn door. "But sometimes, I can't believe I actually did it. That I decided not to go back to Minneapolis. You know, Susan's firm is still hiring, if you want to get back into marketing." That brought a knowing smile from Cassie, as the position Melinda turned down just weeks ago had yet to be filled.

Hobo rushed inside the barn, where Stormy and Sunny were perched on top of the grain barrels. Cassie reached for the open door and got it latched on her second attempt.

"You know, I wasn't all that surprised you decided to stay here. When Susan and I came to visit, back in July? I could see how overwhelmed you were. But I could tell, even then, that this place was special, and that you loved it already."

"Maybe I did, but it took me some time to figure that out." Melinda raised her voice over the chorus of bleats coming from the sheep, who crowded to their feed bunks and demanded their breakfast.

"Yes, girls, you're stuck with me," she told the ewes, their "baaas" growing louder as they watched her remove the bricks from the lid of the left grain barrel. Next came some random lengths of lumber, and then a scattering of metal-post scraps.

"What's with all the junk?" Cassie's eyes widened in surprise. "It's like some kind of low-tech security system. Do you keep your secret stash of money in that barrel, too?"

"I might as well," Melinda gave the metal lid an expert tug that lifted it loose, "seeing what the price of shelled corn is these days. Don't run back to the house, Cassie, but I'm sure there's raccoons hiding out in this barn since the weather changed. Maybe rats, too."

Cassie turned from petting Sunny, who was strutting along the ridge of the half wall between the aisle and the sheep's quarters. She quickly took a step back, then deliberately stepped forward again. "Fine. I'm fine with that," she said in a trembling voice. "Sunny, shouldn't you and Stormy be keeping the rodent population under control?"

Melinda reached for the grain scoop, and the ewes at last fell silent as they focused on their feed.

"The cats spend more time lounging than hunting, I think. Cassie, if you're expanding your horizons this morning, I could use your help. How about I feed Stormy and Sunny while you give the sheep their hay?"

Cassie shifted on her feet, hesitating. On her first visit to the farm, she had climbed over the pasture fence with a bowl of vegetable peelings and ended up in the dirt, surrounded by a circle of spoiled-but-friendly sheep. Only her pride and her designer sandals were injured, but Cassie swore she'd never again get up-close with Melinda's flock.

"Are ... are you sure?" she faltered. "How about I feed the cats? Or I hand you the hay and ..."

Melinda raised an eyebrow and pointed at the gate. "Go. This time, you're dressed for it, at least."

Cassie stepped over to the fence. "You're right. I can do this." She fiddled with the gate's latch. "Oh, it's stuck."

Melinda reached around and jerked the clasp free. As if on cue, the ewes turned from their bunks and swarmed toward the entrance. She gave her friend a gentle push. "Start walking, and just keep moving. The sheep will get out of your way. If you go down to the other end, you can reach over the fence for the hay."

"Which one is Annie?" Cassie's gaze searched nervously among the nearly identical sheep. "She's so bossy, if she tries to trip me ..."

Annie was too busy glaring at Melinda to attempt to run Cassie down. Melinda returned Annie's eye roll and raised her voice over the din. "Don't worry about Annie. She's way down here, on the end. Just get the hay and shake it into the feed bunks. Three-quarters of a bale is about right."

Melinda left Cassie alone long enough to set out the cats' food and refresh their water bowl. By the time she returned, Cassie had finished with the hay and was back in the aisle. "I'm done," she announced proudly. "Nothing to it, just like you said. No one attacked me. Maybe it helped that I'm wearing Horace's old coat?"

"Maybe," Melinda admitted. "But even in your chore gear, I'm not sure anyone would mistake you for a ninety-year-old man. Speaking of Horace, let's get inside and see if Susan's got his old coffeemaker on."

She did, and was setting the table when Cassie and Melinda returned from the barn. Hobo let himself in through his set of new doggie doors, his tail wagging with delight.

Once Hobo showed Melinda he intended to spend most of his hours inside during the colder months, she'd worried about what to do. Horace had rarely left the farm for more than an hour or two, and obviously served as Hobo's doorman. With Kevin's approval, Melinda's dad helped her install dog entrances in the back porch's wall by the top step, and then within the wooden door that went into the kitchen. It took some coaxing and several rounds of treats, but Hobo soon learned the small openings were just for his use.

The cinnamon rolls Melinda popped in the oven earlier were nearly ready, the sweet smell of baking bread mingling with the comforting aroma of brewing coffee. Cassie chopped ham, green pepper and onions for omelets, the vegetables some of the last from Melinda's garden, while Susan whipped the eggs and heated the pan. Melinda frosted the rolls, and soon the friends gathered around the kitchen table for a hearty breakfast.

"I'm famished," Cassie sighed as she reached for another roll. "Must be all that fresh air and hard work."

Susan laughed so hard she almost choked on a bite of her omelet. "Seriously, you walked a few yards and lifted a little hay over a fence. Don't forget that I grew up in a small town, Cassie. I'm at least a little bit familiar with this sort of thing."

"Eat up," Melinda waved her fork at her friends. "I'll put you both to work soon enough. Those storm windows for the front porch won't drag themselves up from the basement."

They lingered over another cup of coffee, then Melinda led the way down to the dark, dusty corner where several tall windows leaned against the cinder-block wall.

"Sorry I didn't get them cleaned up yet," she sighed. "Maybe it would be best to hang them on the front porch first, then wash them?"

"I think so," Cassie nodded, pulling on the chore gloves she wore earlier that morning. "As long as we don't take any of their neighbors along with us." She pointed to the corner's thick nest of cobwebs, then took a deep breath. "I'm going in."

Melinda retrieved a ladder out of the garage while Susan and Cassie brought the storm windows outside. Susan scaled the ladder and reached for the metal clasps on the screen closest to the front porch's door. She tugged and twisted, but the latches wouldn't budge.

Melinda rubbed her face. "Let me guess, they're stuck."

"More like painted over," Susan threw up her arms. "We'll need a flat-head screwdriver and some WD-40 if we ever hope to get these things down."

They also needed a second ladder. Cassie leaned the storm windows against the front yard's maple tree and washed their panes, trying to save time, while Melinda and Susan jabbed and dabbed at the screens' hinges.

Hobo sprawled out by the front steps, watching the women work, while Stormy took up a spot on the brown lawn just out of Cassie's reach and supervised her cleaning. Sunny was a nuisance, climbing Melinda's ladder and leaping through whichever opening was new, sniffing the front porch and trying to solve its mysteries.

"I hope they don't run out of chili down at the church before we get there," Susan said from around the corner, where she was trying to loosen the last few latches.

Melinda picked up one of the freshly washed frames and marched over to the house. "All we have to do is hook them in, and we'll be done. Except for that little one by the front door, they're all the same size." She pushed and shoved, but the window wouldn't slip into the opening.

"It's a tiny bit too big. How can that be?" She turned on the ladder to look at the other storm windows now stacked against the side of the house. "Aren't they all the same?"

Susan lifted one storm window and held it close to its neighbor, then shook her head.

"Let me guess," Melinda's shoulders slumped as she studied the porch's framing. "These openings aren't perfectly square, or exactly the same size. This house is only a hundred years old. We just need some tape measures, a marker and, oh, another hour of work."

Susan measured the openings and called figures out to Melinda, who checked the width of the windows and handed her best guesses to Cassie, who served as the go-between. Once the puzzle was complete, Melinda opened the porch door and dodged just in time as a puffy-haired Sunny, yowling furiously, flew past her and dashed for the barn.

"I forgot he was in there," she gasped, doubling over with laughter. "Oh, Sunny, I'm so sorry!"

Starting on the north wall, she wrote tiny numbers in the lower-right corner of each storm window.

"Never again!" Melinda recapped her marker with a snap of triumph as she came back outside, giving Hobo a happy pat on the head. "Girls, I'd love for you to come back in the spring and help me swap these out again. I promise it will go much faster, but I still could use ...

A crack of rifle shot echoed across the empty fields. Cassie let out a shriek, and she and Susan ducked down in the grass. Melinda reached for Hobo's collar.

"*What. Is. That?*" Cassie whispered, glancing nervously around. "Who's shooting out here? I can't believe ..."

There was another shot, then two more. Melinda motioned for Susan to take ahold of Hobo, then hurried toward the north side of the yard and the windbreak.

"Melinda, get back here!" Cassie called after her. "You'll get yourself killed!"

Melinda stopped when she reached the trees. Through the bare branches, she could just make out the blaze orange of the hunters' vests and sweatshirts as they moved along the creek. A dusty pickup was parked on the gravel's shoulder near the bridge, and two dogs, also wearing orange vests, rustled through the tall grasses along the waterway.

"All clear," she told Susan and Cassie when she got back to the house. "It's just some hunters down by the creek."

Hobo barked and tried to get out of Susan's grasp. "It's OK, Hobo," Melinda soothed him. "But we'll have to tie you to your post by the garage when we go for lunch. You need to stay in the yard, OK?"

Cassie cautiously got to her feet, wiping the damp earth from her sweatshirt. "Well, I guess if you're sure they're only shooting at deer or turkeys or whatever. Don't they have to get permission to do that, though?"

"Yes, but they're way down by the creek and that's someone else's land. I guess I've gotten used to it the last few weeks," Melinda said. "I've got a blaze-orange sweatshirt that I wear when I walk Hobo, and he's got his own matching vest, thanks to Kevin."

More hunters' trucks were parked in front of the small Lutheran church, and the men sat side-by-side with the ladies enjoying the craft bazaar's luncheon. Angie, who was in the serving line, assured Melinda it was all part of the plan.

"There's a reason the bazaar is always this weekend," Angie said with a knowing grin. "These hunters may not buy of our crafts, but they can pack away the chili. And the pie."

The afternoon passed quickly, the friends moving from one project to another. The snow fence was stationed on the north side of the garden, its narrow wooden slats fastened to the year-round fence with lengths of sturdy wire. Melinda pulled out Horace's stash of old tools and, with Susan's help, walled in the cats' hideout under the barn stairs with the pre-cut plywood. They hung the new heat lamp from a hook drilled into the underside of the stairs, and piled more straw in the thick bed below. Cassie was eager to take the lead on chores while Melinda put away her supplies and Susan started the from-scratch pizza that would be their dinner.

"I can't believe I'm saying this, but it feels good to just kick up my feet," Cassie yawned as they gathered in the living room. "Where did we get all that energy we used to have? I can remember when Saturday night was the time to see and be seen."

"We rarely went downtown until ten," Susan sighed as she flopped onto Melinda's couch. "Now, Ray and I have the kids in bed by nine and we're sound asleep by eleven, at least."

"Well, we should rest well tonight," Melinda said as she brought in a bottle of wine and a plate of brownies. "I couldn't have done it without you, girls. With your help, I just might be ready to take on winter."

Susan reached for a brownie. "The porch windows are changed out, you've got straw bales around the foundation, the snow fence is up. I don't know what else you could need."

Melinda pointed into the downstairs bedroom, a proud smile spreading across her face. "Actually, quite a bit of stuff. Let me show you something."

Susan and Cassie followed. Melinda opened the paneled closet door with a flourish. "Oh, my," Cassie gasped. "Are you expecting a blizzard? Maybe tomorrow?"

Six flashlights, recently cleaned and their batteries replaced, stood at attention on one shelf. A red metal lantern waited nearby. There was a new box of matches, some candles and two antique kerosene lamps. Another shelf held a hand-operated can opener and several jugs of water.

"Are those old lamps safe?" Susan eyed them dubiously.

"They are now," Melinda answered. "I took them to the store one day last week and had George look them over. He's in his early eighties, you know, and had to clean those things when he was a little boy. George showed me how to fill them and trim the wicks. We don't carry kerosene at Prosper Hardware, but Auggie has a small stash down at the co-op and he sold me a container."

Melinda pointed above their heads. "There's extra blankets upstairs. I've got plenty of canned food in the cellar, of course, and I stocked up on soup, toilet paper and some other items the other day at the grocery store. There's bags of ice melt on the back porch, along with extra sacks of dog and cat food. And I've got more bags of oats, corn and chicken feed weighed down in spare barrels in the barn."

"Are they covered with bricks?" Cassie gave Melinda a knowing look.

"Yes."

"Oh, how I remember you as a city girl," Susan laughed and raised her wine glass in salute. "Walking down to the neighborhood grocery every few days for whatever inspired your next dinner. Taking transit as much as possible in the winter so you didn't have to clear the snow off your car. I remember that girl well; I used to live that way, too. Now I'm out in the suburbs, but I've got it easy; I'm only eight blocks from a grocery store."

"Tell you what," Cassie rubbed her hands together. "I may not be an expert shepherd, but I'm pretty good at building a fire. Melinda, how about we get a blaze going? You show me what you know, and I'll teach you how to keep from burning this lovely farmhouse down around your ears."

The firewood was already piled behind the grate. Melinda reached for her box of matches and the friends gathered on the hearth. Cassie lifted some twigs from the kindling bin by the bookcase and handed them to Melinda. "Now that you've got your stack, just light it under there ..."

At first there was just a thin golden flame winking from below the kindling, but then a soft glow spread through the twigs and branches.

There was the slap of a doggie door and Hobo, who had refused to come in when chores were done, now hustled in from the kitchen and gave a contented sigh as he sprawled out just in front of the fireplace grate.

"I think that's his spot," Susan smiled at Melinda. "You may not know which wild critters are roaming around out there in the dark, but somehow I don't think you're going to be alone in here this winter."

✳ 8 ✳

"Be careful what you wish for," Karen jokingly shook a finger at Melinda. "Or, more accurately, be careful what you *volunteer* for. How did your offer to help with the holiday celebration turn into you being named committee chair?"

She could only shake her head. "Well, at first I was just going to help out with marketing and publicity, like I did for the Fourth of July festival. That was supposed to be it. Or so I thought."

It was a damp, overcast day, and Melinda wished she'd driven the two blocks to the veterinary clinic to have lunch with Karen. Despite her thick gloves, her hands were still chilled from her walk.

She warmed them over her bowl of homemade chicken and noodles, silently congratulated herself for getting the dough rolled much thinner than last time, and filled Karen in on the details.

"There's five other people on the committee, so I thought I was safe from getting the top job. But then, Nancy's swamped with looming end-of-year paperwork at City Hall, and she's already leading the Christmas celebration plans at the Methodist Church."

"I don't know how she does it," Karen marveled, reaching for a potholder as the microwave chirped. "A single mom, doing two jobs for the city. Nancy is a planning machine."

"She's incredible, for sure," Melinda agreed. "So then, the elementary teacher on our board is also coordinating the school's soup supper that night. I hoped Mayor Jerry would ask Helen Mitchell to be chair. Helen's retired, she used to run a beauty shop here decades ago, she knows everyone in town. And she's worked on this event before. But Helen broke her hip and is laid up at a nursing home over in Charles City for six weeks, so she can't help out at all."

Melinda paused for a hearty slurp of her soup. "That meant it had to be me or Jake Newcastle, the guy on the City Council who's always getting everyone stirred up."

Karen snorted. "Wow, I guess you didn't have a choice, then. Jake's a character, the one guy everyone loves to hate. Every small town has one. How does he keep getting elected to the council, anyway?"

"No one else runs, I guess," Melinda shrugged. "I mean, look at Uncle Frank. A few write-in votes, and he's a council member, too."

"So Jerry begged you to do it, and you couldn't turn him down," Karen nodded understandingly as she joined Melinda at the break room's laminate-covered round table. "Doc says things start to slow down at the clinic this time of year, so let me know what I can do to help. And being new to town, this could be a good way for me to meet more people, other than just crawling around in their barns."

"We can use all the help we can get. Here's an early thank-you gift." Melinda opened a container of cranberry shortbread cookies and passed them across the table.

Doc was out on a farm call, but anyone wandering in during the lunch hour would know to ring the bell on the front counter.

Melinda and Karen weren't alone, however. Karen's regal collie, Pumpkin, snoozed on the rug by the refrigerator. Pumpkin was a sweet-tempered dog and, other than her instinct to want herd some of the clinic's feline patients, enjoyed coming to work with Karen rather than staying at their house just down the street.

Karen popped open her heated dish and snapped the tab on her soda can. "They've been having this Christmas event for decades, from what Doc says. Hopefully, you won't have to take on too much. Many of the activities should be on autopilot, right?"

"Technically, yes," Melinda replied. "The handful of businesses in town will stay open until eight that night, and everyone's going to decorate their store windows as usual. There's the supper at the school, the same as every other year and, well, that's it so far."

Prosper's Christmas celebration was a rather simple affair, compared to the dozens of activities included in Swanton's annual event.

The county seat's town square was always aglow, its dozens of businesses packed with customers. Thousands of colorful lights would be draped on the towering evergreen next to the restored bandstand, and Santa always arrived at the end of the evening. Carolers in period costumes strolled the streets, and vendors sold popcorn and hot chocolate.

Tiny Prosper couldn't match Swanton's big show, but maybe there was a way to freshen up the event. And as far as Melinda could tell, no other area community had a celebration planned for the same night as Prosper. If the weather cooperated and the committee could add a few more activities to the evening, they might draw larger crowds to Prosper's four-block Main Street.

"There's not much time to plan," she admitted, "since the event's barely four weeks away, but I hope I can come up with something new we can offer. It just seems like we can do more."

A brisk northwest wind slowed Melinda's walk back to Prosper Hardware, so she let her mind wander. Maybe some wonderful idea for the festival would appear if she stopped trying so hard to come up with one. Instead, she admired the metal-framed snowflake and tree decorations now installed on Main Street's lamp posts and had to smile in spite of her stiff, wind-blown cheeks.

As promised, Uncle Frank had donated the green and white paint and helped her give the frames fresh coats, while Bill changed all the bulbs and replaced much of the wiring.

Many customers coming in the front door of Prosper Hardware commented on the refurbished lights and how amazing they looked. A few residents even asked if the decorations were new. All of them beamed with pride when they talked about how the lights brought the holiday spirit to little Prosper, and their enthusiasm inspired Melinda to make this year's festival as special as she could. There had to be some way to give back to this friendly community that had given her a new start.

A splash of cold rain stung her right cheek, and then a few tiny, tentative snowflakes appeared on the back of her black gloves, spurring her imagination.

The holiday event should remain more commercial than religious, she suspected, to appeal to as many area residents as possible. But what activities might speak to people's hearts as well as their wallets?

All of the sudden, she had it. The idea was perfect.

She stopped short on the sidewalk, raised her fists and did a quick happy dance that was hindered by her puffy parka, glad that no one else was out along Main Street to witness her awkward celebration. Then she spotted Glenn Hanson, the town's postmaster, draping a garland of tinsel in the post office's front window and giving her a strange look. Melinda grinned, offered Glenn a big wave, and hurried the last few steps to Prosper Hardware.

Aunt Miriam was sorting returns at the counter when she burst through the front door, gasping with excitement. "Whatever is going on?" Miriam gave Melinda a quizzical look. "Did you run all the way back from the clinic? You look like you're about to burst."

Melinda hurried past, yanking off her knit cap as she headed for the stairs leading to the second-floor office.

"Let me get my coat off and text Karen," Melinda called over her shoulder when she reached the landing.

"I've got a fantastic idea for the holiday celebration. But Aunt Miriam, I need your help. I think it will take a pan of your maple-pecan rolls to get things off the ground."

Uncle Frank arrived at Prosper Hardware the next morning with a carefully wrapped tray that brought the conversation around the coffeepot to an abrupt halt. Auggie's eyes widened as he set his mug on the sideboard and eagerly took the pan from Frank's hands. "Miriam's famous maple-pecan rolls! Is today some kind of special occasion?"

"Beats me," Frank shrugged as he tussled with his coat and wool cap and added them to the hall tree by the cabinet. "Miriam was up earlier than usual, said she just felt like baking this morning. That's all I know."

Doc pulled a roll from the pan before Auggie could even get one for himself. "Well, I'm happy to eat them and not ask any questions," Doc said as he returned to his seat, not bothering with the stack of napkins on the sideboard.

The rolls' cream cheese frosting was drifted and thick, but Doc made no pretense of trying to wipe any of the calories away. He had a tall, wiry frame that didn't seem to be affected by all the sweets he consumed, despite being well into his fifties. Melinda marveled at his metabolism, but decided she'd rather watch what she ate than tussle with angry livestock to burn off extra calories.

She busied herself with wiping down the counter, trying to keep an indifferent smile on her face. Aunt Miriam, as always, had come through. Once the guys each had a roll in hand, Melinda came around the counter and pulled up a chair. She helped herself to a maple-pecan bun and a cup of coffee and waited for a lull in the conversation.

"So, some of you know I'm the new chair of the holiday event committee," she began in a casual tone as she pulled apart her roll.

"And I can't thank you enough for taking that on," Jerry said quickly between satisfied bites. Uncle Frank, who was already indulging in his second treat without Miriam there to stop him, nodded in agreement.

"I'm glad to help," Melinda shrugged, "and I've got some ideas on how we might draw more visitors. Doc, I think I could use your help on something. Karen says she'll do most of the work, but I wanted to run it by you."

"Sure thing, Melinda," Doc took a hearty gulp of his coffee. "We business owners need to do all we can to make this event a success."

"I'm glad you feel that way," she smiled. "Because I think it would be wonderful if we could add something special this year. A manger scene."

"Sounds good, people will like that," Doc answered as the other men nodded in agreement. But then Auggie raised a cautionary hand.

"Wait just a minute. I like that idea, but won't there be that nice manger display in front of the Catholic Church? The one they've put out for decades? Do we really need two?"

Auggie was right. The Catholic parish had a stunning antique nativity set. Melinda recalled viewing it several times as a child.

"Well, yes," she said slowly, "because this one would be much different. It would be a bigger scene, more ... lively. A live nativity, actually." The men stopped chewing and looked at each other in amazement.

"As in, live animals." Melinda gave Doc a hopeful look. He sat back in his chair, but she could see he was curious about the idea. "As in, on the vet clinic's front lawn."

Doc nearly dropped his roll.

George gasped and bounced out of his seat, then deposited his mug on the sideboard before he could spill his coffee on his wool cardigan. "What? You're serious, aren't you! There'd be real cows and horses and sheep and, oh, what am I forgetting?"

"That's right, George." Melinda answered, then glanced warily at Doc. He looked stunned.

She should have talked to him first, shouldn't have raised Karen's hopes and assured her Doc would love the idea. Everyone turned to look at Doc, who was running his fingers through his close-cropped gray hair, seemingly considering his options.

"Let's do it!" Doc at last slapped a palm on his faded jeans. "Why not? I don't think a live nativity's ever been attempted in this town. Melinda, if you're looking to generate buzz for our event, I think a herd of farm animals might be the way to go."

"It'll be the talk of the county for sure," Auggie smirked as he wiped the crumbs off his hands and his jeans. "Especially when those *live* animals get too lively and break away down Main Street."

Doc was quiet for a moment.

"It's true, we'll have to keep them under control. Whatever livestock we bring in must be good-natured, and comfortable being around crowds of people."

Suddenly, everyone was talking at once. Melinda was relieved. If Doc was on board, she and Karen would find a way to make it happen.

"A donkey," Doc nodded, his seriousness bringing the chatter to a halt. "We really need a donkey. Or we could get by with a mule, if we get desperate."

Auggie turned to Melinda. "The real question is, which of your barn cats will get in the manger and play Baby Jesus?"

"They should be more easygoing since they had their little surgeries," George put in, refilling his cup. "I bet they're staying closer to home these days."

"Sunny and Stormy are just now speaking to me again," she replied, "and it's been a week. I'm sure they have no interest in coming back to town, for any reason. Sorry, Auggie, but I think we'll have to get by with a doll."

"A cow shouldn't be hard to find," Doc reached into his back pocket for his phone and began to scroll through his contacts. "We should get some sheep, maybe a goat or two."

Uncle Frank gave Melinda a big thumbs-up. "I can't wait to see this. Wish I was strong enough to help out. There'll need to be several people there with the animals at all times, though. You'll need to fill out the rest of the cast."

Auggie, Jerry and George all immediately looked at Doc.

"Oh, no," Doc shook his head.

"I'll round up the animals. But I'm not playing Joseph, or wrapping a towel around my head to portray one of the wise men or something."

"But you'd be perfect for that, Doc," George said.

"Now, I'm trying to remember," Doc gave George a pointed look. "But weren't some of the wise men, you know, *wise* ... as in, *older?* You've got a few decades of experience on me, George."

"George can't be in the nativity," Melinda cut in quickly, her excitement growing.

"I've already got another assignment for him. George, how would you like to stand in for Santa? The real guy's pretty booked this time of year, you know."

George's blue eyes sparkled, then a big grin spread across his lined face. "Do you mean it? Why, I'd love to. Maybe Mary would want to play Mrs. Claus."

Melinda was touched that her new friends were so willing to help, to make an extra effort to spread holiday cheer. This Christmas celebration would be best one little Prosper had ever hosted.

"George, you're reading my mind," she jumped up and gave George's slight shoulders a quick hug. "Now I just need to find costumes for you and Mary. I better start a list." She hurried behind the counter and reached for a pad of paper next to the cash register.

"I almost hate to ask," Auggie lowered his chin. "But I don't have an assignment yet."

Melinda hadn't forgotten Uncle Frank's comment about Auggie's lack of Christmas spirit. She hesitated for a moment. The first request was easy, and he was sure to go along with it. But the other ...

"How about the co-op provide the feed for the animals in the live nativity?" Melinda knew this would appeal to Auggie's business sense. "I think we could set out a sign that mentions our fine sponsor."

"I can do that," Auggie replied, looking relieved. "That's easy. If I don't need to wear some sort of silly costume, I'm in." Doc nodded heartily at that last comment.

"And there's maybe something else." Melinda hesitated.

"Ah-ha!" Auggie studied her through his thick-rimmed glasses. "I should have known there'd be more. I was getting off too easy."

"I'd like you to get the lighted star out, Auggie. The big one that used to hang on the co-op's tower during the holidays." She rushed on before Auggie could react. "It would light the route into town for everyone turning off the state highway. It's perfect, it's ..."

Her voice died away in the awkward silence that settled over the group. Melinda saw Auggie's jaw tighten. The other men shuffled their feet and looked away.

"I don't know where it is," Auggie snapped, his brown eyes darkening. "Haven't seen it for years. And I don't have time to go looking for it, either."

Auggie abruptly stood and gulped the last of his coffee. He dropped his mug on the sideboard with a firm *thunk*, snatched up his coat and hurried to the door. Suddenly, he stopped and turned back toward Melinda.

"Put me down for the feed sponsorship." Auggie's tone softened, but he still bit off the ends of his words. "But that's it. I have to go. Dan can't run the shop without me."

The bells over the front door tinkled merrily as Auggie rushed out of Prosper Hardware. He jumped in his truck, gunned the engine, and roared off down Main Street.

"What was that all about?" Melinda looked around at the men, who had been laughing and enthusiastic about her plans just minutes before. Each was suddenly busy with something, sipping their coffee, scuffing their boots on the hardwood floor or searching in their pockets.

Doc turned back to his phone. Bill, who had just come in, snatched a maple-pecan roll off the tray and tied on his carpenter apron. "Well, I better get at those cut orders," Bill muttered as he hustled toward the safety of the wood shop.

Melinda waited for someone, anyone, to explain what just happened. No one did.

"What's going on?" She tried again, leaning against the front counter and studying the faces of her friends. None of them would meet her gaze. At last, Uncle Frank sighed.

"I'll probably get an earful," Frank muttered. "Auggie will guess right that I'm the one that told you about the star in the first place. He'll think I blabbed his business all over town."

Melinda wasn't sure how to respond, as Frank didn't elaborate. He suddenly was very busy stirring his coffee.

There obviously was a story to be heard. And beyond her curiosity was the fact that she considered Auggie a friend. He was always quick with a wise crack, the first to speak his mind on any topic, but she had just seen a glimpse of something else. Some sort of anger, or sadness.

And nervousness, as if Auggie was afraid someone might mention something he didn't want to remember.

Melinda decided whatever it was, she wouldn't get to the bottom of it that morning. It was five minutes to eight and the front door was already unlocked, so there wasn't time to do anything but straighten the counter. She stacked the gourds in their wicker basket, placing the green-and-white orb with the most bumps on the top of the pile.

Auggie's abrupt departure meant someone else needed to tidy up, and Uncle Frank was never in a hurry to head home. Frank at last rose from his chair and stacked the empty coffee cups on the metal tray.

"He can't be too surprised that it came up in conversation, seeing as you're chairing the holiday festival committee this year," Frank said, apparently trying to reassure himself as he gathered up the spoons and started for the utility room with the dishes.

Jerry quietly slipped away right after Auggie stormed out of the store. George, who had already shuffled to the hall tree and worked his arms into his coat, gave Melinda an encouraging smile as he made his way to the front door. "I'm proud to play Santa," George said as he pulled on his wool cap and adjusted its brown ear flaps. "Wait until Mary hears about this!"

Only Doc remained, and he was still hunched over his phone. Melinda gave the oak counter another quick buffing with a flannel cloth, then leaned over its gleaming surface in Doc's direction and waited.

"Don't ask," Doc answered her stare with a shake of his head. "I've lived here over twenty years, but even I don't know everybody's secrets. Whatever it is, I'm guessing Auggie wants to keep it to himself ... Yes! Here it is," Doc made a quick salute with his coffee mug and downed the last gulp.

"I think I've got us a donkey," Doc grinned as he reached for his coat, then filled a large thermos with the rest of the coffee from the pot on the sideboard.

"There's a guy up by Elm Springs that has unusual critters. I met him last year, when Doctor Winover was at a loss on how to treat some of the animals and asked me to stop by with a second opinion. This farmer's got two donkeys, and there's llamas, too. I'll let you know what I hear."

Doc was so distracted that he nearly bumped into the elderly woman coming in the front door as he was going out. Melinda knew her name was Gertrude, and she lived on the edge of town by the railroad tracks.

Gertrude fussed with the plastic bonnet that protected her white curls and stared after Doc in amazement.

"A donkey?" Gertrude gasped as she pulled a shopping list from her worn purse and set it on the counter. "Whatever does Doc want with a donkey? Or is it a llama he's really after? I don't know when I've seen that man so wound up."

For a moment, Melinda wondered if a live nativity was such a great idea. She assumed the display would be small and simple, maybe just a cow and a few sheep. But once he got over his shock, Doc became very enthusiastic. Maybe a little too much. Surely no one within an hour's drive of Prosper had a camel, but ... this could get out of control.

Gertrude sensed something was brewing. She was a kind woman, but there was a good chance she would pass on what she overheard. It was better to keep a lid on this live nativity idea until Melinda was sure it would happen.

"It's probably just some continuing education thing," she shrugged and gave Gertrude an understanding smile, reaching for the older woman's list.

"Now, let's get over to the pet aisle. It's so kind of you to feed those stray cats, Gertrude. We've got a special going on that kibble they like so much. I'll ring it up for you and we'll get Bill to load it into your car."

✳ 9 ✳

Melinda patted the leg of her jeans and called in the direction of the windbreak, which was one of Hobo's favorite snooping spots on the farm. "Let's go, Hobo!"

There was an answering bark and then Hobo, the white tip of his brown tail waving back at Melinda, dashed through the sleeping dirt of the garden and hurried to meet her by the back porch.

"Where have you been, huh?" She gave Hobo a quick hug and reached for the blaze-orange doggie vest resting on the top step. "But then, maybe I don't want to know. Let's go for a walk. We can explore together, going down the road in a civilized manner, not running around in all those downed twigs and dirty leaves in the windbreak."

Melinda was still amazed at how easily Hobo adjusted to walking on his leash, which before was only used for his annual visit to Doc's clinic. Horace moved too slow to take Hobo for walks, so they had simply enjoyed their daily rambles around the farm.

"Safety first, you know," she reminded Hobo as she snapped the nylon vest around his brown fur. "I'm wearing mine, too." She'd bought the neon-orange sweatshirt two sizes too big so it would zip over whatever coat the temperature required. Today, that was only a fleece jacket. The weather had been on a rollercoaster this past week, with autumn and winter fighting for the upper hand. But this Thanksgiving Eve was a beautiful afternoon, the skies a clear, deep blue and the harvested fields a golden carpet that rolled away from the farmhouse in every direction.

Prosper Hardware closed early, Aunt Miriam locking the door promptly at two o'clock and sending Bill and Melinda home. "If they don't have everything they need for dinner tomorrow, they're out of luck," Miriam had said. "The grocery store in Swanton's open until nine. Me, I'm going home to put my feet up before I start preparing the big feast. Melinda, just bring a salad and be at our house by eleven. You mom's bringing rolls and the pies, and I'll handle the rest."

Melinda was on deck to host the family's Christmas celebration, and her mind was already running with the possibilities. Her sister, Liz, and her family were coming from Milwaukee to stay at the farm for a few days. Mark, the youngest of the three siblings, had promised to fly in from Austin but called their parents just last night to break the news he was staying in Texas for Christmas. His girlfriend's family had invited him to join their celebration.

At first, Melinda wanted her parents and Frank and Miriam to come to the farm for Thanksgiving, but now she was secretly glad her aunt and uncle offered to host.

Sunday's trip to Minneapolis to empty out her apartment was already a blur, as if it happened weeks ago or to someone else, but there were still cardboard boxes stacked all over in the farmhouse's dining room and more in Wilbur's old bedroom upstairs.

Melinda tried to unpack a box or two each night, but the process was overwhelming. The rest of her possessions were now at a storage unit in Charles City, and would remain there until she and the Schermann family could sort out the farmhouse's contents in the spring.

She'd arrived at the farm in June with just the barest of essentials, and the cozy house seemed to have everything else she needed. All these extra things from her apartment, items that used to be part of her life, now just seemed like clutter.

Did she really need all of it? Why had she bought those clothes that she'd never worn? What was worth keeping? It was time to let go of so many things, but Melinda didn't feel like tackling that today.

"Let's see what's going on down at the creek," she said to Hobo, guiding him into the lane. "Wouldn't it be fun to see the wild turkeys? Maybe they are out and about, it's such a nice afternoon."

Her sneakers crunched out a rhythm in the driveway's gravel. She took a deep breath of the calm, chilly air, which was tinged with the smoky scent of a late-season leaf pile, and let her mind wander.

✳ ✳ ✳

"Are you ready to do this?" her mom asked as they stared at the front door of the grand brick apartment building. "This is a big day for you, honey."

"I think so," Melinda sighed as they picked their way up the sidewalk toward the carved oak front door. The three-story building already seemed strange and unfamiliar, as if someone else had lived here. Someone she sort of knew. Someone she no longer was.

They paused in the vestibule, enjoying a blast from the steam radiator as they removed their gloves and unbuttoned their coats. Diane patted down her short gray hair and gave her daughter an encouraging nod. It wasn't snowing, or even raining, but it was a damp, wild day.

Melinda tried to comfort herself that the stiff wind would sweep out the old and welcome the new. Her dad, Roger, was only a few minutes' behind, driving the rented moving truck. They had to get to work.

The hallway outside her third-floor apartment was warm and sleepy, the radiators humming under the leaded-glass windows at each end of the building. It was late morning and most residents were at brunch or church, or nodding over their Sunday newspapers. She clicked her key in the lock and stepped into what was rapidly becoming her past.

Everything was where she left it six weeks ago, when she came back to interview for the job at Susan's firm, the one she turned down. The apartment had a disjointed air, with half of its furniture missing and dust settling on the top of the built-in bookcases and the varnished window seat.

"Oh, my," Diane said as she set her purse on the floor. "I see what you mean. This place feels so different, especially with your couch gone. And also because ..."

Diane glanced toward the window seat that had been Oreo's favorite spot to soak up the sunshine.

Melinda felt the hot tears coming, then they were running down her face.

"Honey, you have to fully let him go," Diane whispered and put her arms around her daughter. "Oreo's been gone, what, eight months now? It was too soon, I know, but we never get enough time with the ones we love."

Diane rubbed Melinda's back. "Now you have Sunny and Stormy in your life. And Hobo. I know they can't take Oreo's place, but they're special, too."

"I know," Melinda sniffled. "I miss Oreo terribly, but that's not all. Who would have thought all this would happen? Sometimes, I still can't believe it. I can't believe I lost my job at WP&S. I can't believe I moved back home. But this, today, will really make it real. It's like I'm ripping off a Band-Aid I've been wearing for six months."

"Then do it quick," Diane gave her daughter an understanding nod. "Let's get these lights on, crank up the heat and get this place cleared out."

* * *

A gust of north wind slapped Melinda's cheek as she and Hobo reached the gravel road, bringing her out of her reverie. Stormy appeared a moment later, popping up out of the brown ditch grass and rubbing against her jeans.

She had to laugh at the amused glance Stormy gave Hobo. Both cats always looked rather smug when they saw her leash Hobo up for a walk.

"Don't worry, Stormy," Melinda reached down to pat his plush gray fur. "I'll never ask you to wear a harness."

She and Hobo turned into the breeze, keeping to the right-side track in the gravel. It would be a bit of a challenge to walk the half-mile to the bridge, but the trek home would be easy. Stormy, Melinda was glad to see, wanted nothing to do with this little parade and left the roadside for the autonomy of the ditch. He and Sunny were so independent, and she couldn't force them to stay in the yard, but she always cringed when she saw one or both of the cats strutting down the road as if they owned it.

A striped gopher darted out of the weeds on the side of the gravel, giving an indignant squawk when Hobo pulled tight on his leash and let out a warning bark. A pair of pheasants danced their way across the harvested field, their flash of green and gold feathers just visible among the stubble of shorn-off cornstalks. In a second the pheasants took flight, and Melinda slowed her step long enough to take in the graceful arc of their wings against the cobalt-hued sky.

"I never got to see that in the city," she told Hobo, who took advantage of their pause to investigate a hole in the dirt just off the gravel, surely the home of some burrowing animal. The opening was much larger than she would have liked it to be, and she gently pulled Hobo away to resume their walk.

Hobo always let her know when other critters were around. The other night, she was jolted awake during the wee hours when Hobo began a barking frenzy in the downstairs bedroom. She stumbled down the stairs, her phone clenched tight in her hand, scenarios from bad horror movies running through her sleep-fogged mind. Hobo guided her to the living room's picture window, where she could just make out a buck deer and two does snuffing through the discarded seeds under the maple tree's birdfeeders.

These fields might be vast and the houses far apart, but there really was so much life out in the country, Melinda mused as she and Hobo passed the yellow "one lane bridge ahead" sign. She couldn't believe how worried she'd been about feeling alone out here. And she was amazed at how quickly her old place started to feel empty.

* * *

A few trips down the service elevator in the back of the building, and the rest of the furniture was already loaded in the rented truck.

"Stairs are for young people," Roger joked as he and Melinda lifted her desk and set it on the rolling cart that came with the moving van.

Her dad's sandy hair defiantly showed only hints of true gray, and he stayed surprising fit playing golf with his retiree buddies, but Melinda was relieved there was an elevator in the building. Uncle Frank's heart attack had been a grim reminder that no one in her family was getting any younger. That included herself.

She remembered the day she moved in six years ago, how she'd been too impatient to wait for the elevator and lugged boxes up the front staircase, literally climbing toward the new life she would create in this building.

More memories waited for her in the second bedroom's closet. Shoved far in the back was the box of personal items she carried home on her last visit to WP&S. She put her hands on the box's surface to steady herself for a moment, then took a deep breath and lifted the flaps away.

In a second it all came back, the too-cheerful phone call asking her to report to human resources, the slow-ticking moments of shock in the conference room, the sad-faced woman who brought Melinda her purse as she stood there in the hallway, dazed, unsure of where to go or what to do.

"Stop it," she said to herself, gripping the edges of the cardboard box. "It's over. It's all over." She took another deep breath and closed her eyes.

"Keeping company with some ghosts?" It was her dad, with a fresh roll of packing tape in his hand.

"Ghosts of Melinda Past," she said, wiping at her eyes.

Roger carefully lowered himself to the hardwood floor next to his daughter and gently took the box from her hands.

"You have to just keep putting one foot in front of the other, Melinda. Remember how when I retired from the phone company, I wandered around the house for weeks? Drove your mom crazy. It was a big change, but I got through it and hey, golf swing's seriously improved. Now," Roger continued, "you want me to add this stuff to the box over there, the one that's going to the farm? I think I've got enough to fill the cart again."

She nodded and straightened up. "Good," Roger said. "There's some pictures and things in here you might want. You don't have to decide today."

And there were books. Too many, Melinda decided as she boxed them up and staggered with them to the cart. But there also was her Christmas tree, and totes filled with ornaments. She imagined how beautiful they would look in the farmhouse, and that idea inspired her to keep moving.

The apartment soon was a shell of what it used to be. The round wall clock, which had been at Grandma and Grandpa Foster's farm for decades, soon turned its hands toward two. Melinda set aside a few towels to carefully wrap the clock for its ride in her car's backseat, and she and Diane and Roger began to pack in earnest. The day was sliding away from them, and she wanted to be home by dark.

Home, she thought as she pawed the bathroom cabinet's contents into a plastic bin. *It's not here anymore.*

* * *

Melinda paused for a few minutes on the bridge, letting Hobo sniff the faint tracks in the gravel dust and inspect the metal guardrails. She had to roll her eyes, though, when Hobo lifted a back leg and added his scent to whatever else was there.

The creek was drowsy, lower than it had been the week before, the sun glinting off its shallow surface. She scanned the trees and bushes along the waterway, but saw no sign of the wild turkeys.

"When I want to see them, they're never here," she told Hobo as they turned back south. "But in the mornings, when I'm running late, they like to be right out here on the shoulder, strutting around in the road."

The wind was at her back now, and the late-season sun bathed her face with warmth. She should have worn her sunglasses, but no matter. There wouldn't be many more golden afternoons like this one.

They passed the wild plum thicket, its bare brambles stark against the wire pasture fence. When the plums returned late next summer, Melinda would still be here. She'd pick two full buckets next time, and make more jam with the recipe tucked away in the antique box hidden in one of the top kitchen cabinets.

The farmhouse seemed to expand as she and Hobo drew closer, its faded clapboards turning from a faraway gray to a soft white. Melinda had so much to be thankful for, and she sent up a quick prayer. How different her life was, how difficult the past year had been. Somehow, she landed here, in the last place she could have expected. But it was the right place for her.

There was the rumble of tires on the gravel, a vehicle advancing from behind, and she guided Hobo to the road's shoulder and slowed her step.

It was the mail carrier, and he offered a quick wave before stopping in front of the metal mailbox at the end of her drive. The dusty metal plate etched with "Schermann" was still bolted to the box's top, as Melinda didn't yet have the heart to take it down. Besides, her mail was delivered by the Prosper post office, and Glenn Hanson knew her address.

The mail car pulled away, faded into a fog of gravel dust. Melinda still got a tingle of curiosity when she approached the box. What might be inside today? The idea of someone driving these gravel roads in all kinds of weather, just to place those few envelopes in that metal box, was a fascinating one.

* * *

The mailbox in her apartment building was empty. Melinda knew she shouldn't be surprised, as she'd forwarded her mail months ago and her subletter moved out in late August. But she'd had a little hope that even one flyer would be in there, something that carried her old address one last time.

She hurried back upstairs, where Diane was sorting the kitchen cabinets' contents by what was expired and what could be set out on the little table in the building's laundry room, offered free to the other residents.

"You know, we haven't looked under the sink yet," Diane said as she filled a plastic sack with canned goods. Roger was loading the cart with more boxes from the bedroom.

"Oh, yeah, I need to check there." Melinda crouched down on the rag rug and reached for one of the cabinet doors. She suddenly recalled the morning after she lost her job, how she cried on this floor with Oreo's collar in her hand. How hard it had been to get up, get on her feet. But she knew that day that whatever happened, she needed to keep moving forward.

I did it, Melinda thought, feeling a jumble of emotions. *Somehow, I made it through.*

There wasn't much left, some forgotten washed-out cans to recycle and a half-empty box of trash bags. And in the back, her old coffeemaker.

She pulled it out and, for just a moment, held it in her hands, remembering how she'd decided that May morning to save money and make her own brew, rather than running to the trendy coffee shop on the corner. How that simple choice had been the first step to paring down her life.

"We need to pack this," she said to Diane. "I want this."

She didn't realize she was staring out the window over the sink, watching the last of the brown leaves dance on the trees along the edge of the parking lot, until she felt her mother's hand on her arm. "I think we'll head out soon, if there's not much else you need help with," Diane said gently.

"That'll give you a little time to lock up, honey. We'll just bring the truck over to the farm in the morning, we don't have to return it until tomorrow afternoon."

Roger appeared in the archway from the dining room. "Well, that the last of the boxes. If you want, we can swing by the farm and do chores. It's been a long day."

Melinda had to smile at the wistfulness in her dad's voice. He grew up on a farm, and never missed a chance to come to her acreage and toss some hay bales around.

"No, that's OK," she gave each of her parents a hug. "I can manage it when I get home. I won't be here long."

The empty apartment fell into a deep stillness after Diane and Roger left. Melinda took out the last of the trash. She made one more pass through the bare rooms, checked every closet and cabinet for anything she might have left behind.

She couldn't put it off any longer. It was time to go. She gently laid her two sets of apartment keys on the kitchen counter, noticed how insignificant they looked on the now-empty surface.

The building manager would take care of the rest. There was nothing left to sign, nothing left to do, her long-ago deposit would be mailed out by the end of the month. It was all so simple, too simple. All she had to do was lock the door behind her and walk away.

But there was one more stop to make. Melinda paused outside of 8A and thought of Charlie. The cheerful widower was always ready for a quick chat when she met him in the hall, or by the outdoor rack where he kept his bicycle next to those of tenants less than half his age. Sometimes he dropped in for a cup of tea and a snuggle with Oreo.

The tears threatened to return as she recalled how Charlie collapsed in his apartment, unable to reach the phone on the kitchen counter. Someone discovered his body the next day. Melinda was already gone then, learned what happened after it was too late.

And now, standing outside of 8A, she could hear the blare of football on the television, the hoots and claps of a few young men enjoying a Sunday-afternoon game. It would do no good to knock. She'd just look foolish, a crazy woman crying about some old guy they didn't know.

"Goodbye, Charlie," she whispered and wiped at her cheeks with the back of her hand.

Then, one by one, she followed the steps to the lobby and out to her loaded-down car, out to where the blustery north wind would push her south toward home.

* * *

It took a strong tug to get the rusted mailbox door to creak open. Hobo waited patiently at her side while Melinda reached in with her free hand.

A few advertising circulars, the free weekly newspaper that still came in Horace's name. There was her internet bill (it was still a thrill to see her name at this address!) and then, tucked inside the flyers, a tan envelope. She immediately recognized the careful writing on its front, and the postmark from Elm Springs.

"Hobo, look," she crouched down and tucked the rest of the mail under her arm. "I think we got something special today." Inside was a greeting card with a sepia-toned scene of two turkeys strutting along a rustic fence while a faded barn rested in the background.

Melinda, I hope you have a wonderful Thanksgiving. Kevin and Ada are coming here for dinner Thursday. I hear the meal is pretty good and we don't have to wash any dishes. It's been too long since there has been a big holiday gathering at the farm. I am glad you plan to host Christmas this year. Tell Hobo I love him. – Horace (and Wilbur)

"You mean the world to Horace," Melinda whispered as she held Hobo close, the rough gravel poking at the knees of her jeans. "And you mean the world to me, too."

Hobo gave a happy whimper, wagged his tail, and touched his nose to her face.

There was a chorus of bleats from the front pasture, and she looked up to see five wooly faces clustered at the fence.

"Yes, ladies, you're special, too," she waved at the sheep. Annie was the first to shuffle over to the adjoining length of fence, the one that bordered the driveway, as Melinda and Hobo began their walk toward the house.

The other four ewes followed Annie's lead, and the rest of the sheep soon hustled across the pasture to join them. There was little fresh grass left this time of year, but the sheep loved to forage in the crisp air as often as they could.

She unhooked Hobo's leash and he dashed off to join Sunny and Stormy, who had suddenly appeared out of the tall brown grass on the side of the driveway.

"I swear sometimes that all of you have a sixth sense," she told the sheep, reaching over the fence to rub the ewes' charcoal noses. "If you girls aren't tracking me, then Hobo's on guard duty. If he's busy, then Stormy and Sunny are supervising from the picnic table. The chickens don't pay me much mind, unless it's time for chores."

Melinda could just make out the hens in their run, their feathers aglow in the late-afternoon sun as they scratched for grubs and clucked at each other. She glanced around the farmyard, the same quick survey that had become second nature to her in the past months. The faded lawn was neat, all the outbuildings' doors were securely fastened. A few stray leaves, buffeted by the wind, had beached themselves along the machine shed's foundation.

The pumpkins were still stacked by the back porch and a cheerful fall wreath remained on the door. Two generous pots of magenta-hued mums now graced the wooden steps, riding home in the back of her car just that day after more than month of service in front of Prosper Hardware.

Melinda went inside, shook off her shoes and let herself into the kitchen. She piled the mail on the counter and took a lingering look around the farmhouse, a contented smile forming on her face.

All the clean dishes were finally put away, the counters wiped down, and the kitchen table relieved of its usual clutter of newspapers and magazines.

She gave a nod of approval to the dining room and the adjoining living room, where the oak woodwork gleamed. She overlooked the stacks of moving boxes and admired how some of her apartment's curtains were perfectly sized for the picture window.

All of Horace's tired red-and-blue checked panels were already pulled down, washed and stored in the downstairs bedroom's closet. Nothing in Melinda's stash of curtains could blend with the garish bluebird wallpaper in the dining room, but a few sets of soft sage panels from a discount store calmed the space.

The oak floors under the Schermann family's antique dining table remained bare, but the floral rug from her apartment softened the scuffed boards in the living room. Her overstuffed reading chair now held the angled post in front of the fireplace, facing the television, just as Horace's recliner once had.

Her coffee table was the perfect size for this room, and the small pot of orange mums on its surface echoed a larger display on the dining-room table. A gracious oval mirror that used to hang just inside the door of Melinda's apartment now graced the once-bare stretch of plaster over the fireplace.

Evening chores were coming on in only an hour, and she had to scrounge up something for supper. But all that could wait, if even for a few minutes. She shoved a cardboard box aside so she could stretch out on her beige sofa, the stylish one now covered with a Hobo-proof fleece blanket, and dozed off to the soft music made by the brisk wind as it danced around the corners of the farmhouse.

* 10 *

The eastern horizon was still a dark smudge when Melinda drove into Prosper Friday morning. She changed one of the car radio's pre-set stations to a channel rotating only Christmas tunes for the next four weeks, and soon a snazzy version of "Jingle Bell Rock" had her tapping her fingers on the steering wheel.

She didn't meet one car on the county blacktop. Kitchen lights were on in many of the farmhouses along the highway, and a warm light radiated out from a few barns' windows, but there was no indication that today was the biggest shopping day of the year. Aunt Miriam predicted Prosper Hardware would be busier than usual, but said there wouldn't be frenzied shoppers beating down the door. Even so, she canceled the coffee group just in case.

"The guys will just be underfoot," Miriam told Melinda. "And they'll hoard all the cookies and rolls I'm bringing in. We'll be festive, but it'll be business as usual. Our Black Friday-style sales will come the night of the town festival."

As her car bumped over the railroad tracks by Prosper Feed Co., she glanced up at the co-op's tallest storage tower. Every day, she watched to see if the lighted star would magically appear.

So far, she was disappointed. Auggie arrived at Prosper Hardware every morning as he always had, enjoyed his coffee and showed his usual good humor. And Melinda had asked no more questions.

But today, there was a small sign of Christmas cheer: A single strand of colored lights glowed in the co-op office's front window. Whatever might be weighing on Auggie's heart, he was at least trying to make a small effort. She had to give him credit for that.

Aunt Miriam was already behind the counter at Prosper Hardware, packing away the autumn gourds and wicker basket that had greeted customers since Labor Day. Her short gray curls were barely visible under a Santa hat. Bill, straightening up in the tools and fasteners aisle, pointed to his red-and-white cap and rolled his eyes at Melinda.

There was another hat waiting for her on the shelf behind the counter. Before she could say anything, Miriam reached in and pulled the cap out with a flourish.

"Yes, it's for you, Melinda!" Aunt Miriam trilled, giving her own hat's pom-pom a happy flip. "The holiday season is officially upon us."

Melinda tried to hide her revulsion. Did she really have to wear that thing?

"Marketing, my dear! As you say, it's all about the marketing." Miriam patted her on the shoulder, then hurried away with a stack of holiday sweatshirts in her arms.

"Bill," Melinda hissed. "Is she serious?"

"It's just for today and tomorrow," he grumbled as he passed by with a box of extension cords. "Just be glad we don't have to dress like Esther. She did that to herself."

Esther Denner, Frank and Miriam's neighbor, had rushed over to the store to help out when she'd heard about Uncle Frank's heart attack. Esther was retired and itching to get out of the house, and Miriam was grateful for her neighbor's help, so Esther soon became a paid, part-time employee.

She was indispensable to Melinda, filling her in on the back story of nearly every customer, but Esther was rather excitable and easily got carried away. All the holidays were celebrated with great gusto, and Esther's Christmas tree was already twinkling in her front window when inflatable ghosts still swayed on her front lawn.

"Melinda!" Esther came around the counter for an enthusiastic hug, although they had seen each other just two days ago. "Isn't this wonderful? Christmas is my favorite time of year. It was hard, but I waited until last night to break out my holiday attire. What do you think?" Esther gave a little twirl, and Melinda nodded appreciatively.

Three caroling kittens in sequined knit caps and mittens decorated Esther's forest-green sweatshirt, with the phrase "We Wish You a Meowy Xmas" embroidered below. Dangling snowflake earrings threatened to tangle themselves in the fluffy white band of Esther's too-large Santa hat.

"Esther, you look ... stunning," Melinda managed to say. "You're really getting into the holiday spirit."

"I think we need some music," Esther's blue eyes sparkled as she hurried away. "I brought in some of my own collection to get our customers in the mood to shop. Remember when Bill hooked up those speakers for the Halloween party? Might as well put them to use." A few moments later, Frank Sinatra's crooning filled the store.

"It's going to take something stronger than this cookie to keep up my holiday cheer if Esther intends to play DJ," Bill sighed as he passed by again. "If only we can make her stick to music that's ... tasteful. I fear Alvin and the Chipmunks could be on the playlist."

Melinda was pleasantly surprised to find five people waiting at the front door when she unlocked it at eight. Not everyone was off at the large retail districts and big-box stores, fighting other shoppers for a cheap television or another throw blanket they didn't need. Prosper Hardware was soon busy, but not hectic. Everyone was laughing and greeting friends, and the wonderful aroma of coffee and hot apple cider soon filled the store.

And really, the Santa hat wasn't so bad. She found herself humming along to the tunes, asking customers about their Thanksgiving celebrations and what they had planned for the

Christmas season. Several people mentioned they were looking forward to the town's holiday celebration, and that they'd heard rumors that something special would be added this year.

When Melinda first arrived in Prosper, she was quickly reminded of how fast news travels in a rural community. Now, she was using that to the holiday committee's advantage. She only smiled and nodded mysteriously as she was prodded for details, and encouraged everyone to check the city's website next Wednesday for a list of activities. Buzz was building about the event, and she was pleased with how her marketing skills were being put to use in her new life.

Saturday was also busy at the store, and Melinda was exhausted by the time she drove home, dusk already blanketing the countryside at five o'clock. Two days of holiday cheer had kicked her love of Christmas into overdrive, however, and that night she discovered her to-do list for decorating the farm was growing rapidly. Flash and sparkle would never do at the acreage; Melinda was determined to stick with a rustic, natural theme.

But time was running short, as Monday was her best chance to get all of her decorating done. Her idea to gather twigs in the windbreak and handcraft wreaths at the farmhouse's kitchen table was never going to happen.

So on Sunday, after church with her parents in Swanton, she decided to make a mad dash to the hobby and craft stores in Mason City.

Her sleigh was weighed down, and so was her credit card, by the time she started for home. A few flakes of snow skipped across the windshield just as she turned off the interstate and onto the state highway. By the time she reached her gravel road the snow had intensified, rushing right at the windshield.

"Our first real snow," Melinda grinned with excitement as she slowed the car and flipped the windshield wipers into a higher gear. "We're not supposed to get much. Just enough to get into the Christmas spirit, I guess."

She didn't feel very festive by the time she got the car unloaded, her nose chilled by the damp air. One-too-many sacks stuffed with Christmas decorations and wreaths waited on the floor of the back porch. She'd gotten carried away. But how could she not? This charming house would be stunning once she finished decorating. Besides, she comforted herself, everything had been on sale.

Melinda woke the next morning ready to decorate. After chores and breakfast, she lingered at the kitchen table with a steaming mug of coffee and a pumpkin-chocolate chip muffin left over from Aunt Miriam's spread of goodies at Prosper Hardware. The sun was shining, and the dusting of snow had turned the farm into a winter wonderland.

"Let's see," she scanned her list. "Every room downstairs needs something. I've got those red-and-white towels to put out here in the kitchen and in the downstairs bathroom. There's a pine-cone garland for the mantel, and a string of colored lights for the front porch. I can't wait to get those up. They'll be visible from the road."

The snow had melted off the sidewalk by late morning, and Hobo was sprawled out in the sunshine. He looked up in surprise when Melinda came down the steps, balancing a three-feet-wide faux evergreen wreath on her right arm. It was loaded down with red plastic berries, gold ball ornaments, and a generous plaid bow. Hobo sniffed the wreath, his tail shaking out a questioning rhythm.

"I know, I know, it's probably too much," she admitted as Hobo followed her across the yard toward the barn.

"But this is our first Christmas together, my first at the farm. If all goes well, it won't be my last. And Hobo, I'm not going to tell you how much all this cost. I'm considering it an investment, OK?"

The sheep rushed across the pasture when they saw her coming, crowding at the fence with sniffing noses and questioning eyes. "You ladies already have a very nice barn," Melinda said as she eyed the faded wood siding, considering her options.

"But who says you can't get a little holiday spirit, too? And I'll be able to enjoy this wreath from the kitchen. I just have to figure out where to hang it."

Should the wreath go to the left of the main door, or the right? Should she hang it in line with the small windows, or the door? That wasn't the only problem.

The fussy bow that seemed so charming at the superstore appeared silly and pretentious out here in the farmyard. The trailing ribbons were made of a weatherproof plastic, but they still looked like a dangerous temptation for two inquisitive cats and whatever wild critters might roam around out here at night. How high could a raccoon jump, anyway?

One of her dilemmas was soon resolved. She spied an ancient nail, covered with the same rust-red paint as the rest of the barn, driven into the wood siding just a few feet from the main door.

She stepped back, then clapped her hands in delight as she took in the full effect of the evergreen wreath. Maybe it wasn't too much, after all. The bright red berries and gold ornaments made for a nice contrast to the muted paint of the rustic barn. Even so, she reached over and unhooked the fussy plaid bow from the wreath.

"Even better," she said as she turned toward the sheep. "What do you think?" But the ewes, sensing Melinda didn't have any potato peels or other treats, had already wandered away across the pasture.

Hobo was sniffing along the barn's foundation, too intent on his detective work to notice how festive the barn had suddenly become. At least Sunny was crouched on the gravel, watching Melinda with his steady gold eyes.

"Look, Sunny!" she called to him and gestured at the wreath. "Isn't it perfect?"

Sunny blinked and rolled over to scratch his back. Then he rose to his feet and sauntered off toward the garage.

"What's the deal?" Melinda's arms fell, defeated, to her sides. "Don't tell me I'm the only one around here who is excited about Christmas."

Hobo looked up at the sound of her voice, then resumed his tracking. "That needs to change, especially since I've got more wreaths. You won't believe how many more wreaths."

She turned back toward the house, pausing for a moment to admire how the gigantic wreath stood out against the towering barn. It was worth every penny, well, every dollar. The barn was so large, Melinda told herself, that a skimpy little decoration just wouldn't do.

She returned with two more wreaths, each less than a foot wide and with only pine cones nestled in their branches. One went over the entrance to Sunny and Stormy's hideout in the barn, and the other next to the chicken coop's front door.

The last outdoor wreaths were lush and full but also understated, with iced branches and berries peeking out of the greenery. Melinda removed the fall decorations from the front and back porches and hung the new wreaths on the hooks, then sliced the softening pumpkins and tossed them in the windbreak for the wildlife to find.

She had just settled in with her lunch and the latest newspaper when she heard engine gears shifting and the rumble of heavy axles. She looked out just in time to see a tanker truck pull past the kitchen windows, angle over by the barn and, inexplicably, back toward the house.

"The picnic table!" Melinda shrieked, dashing for the porch door and her boots. By the time she got her coat on, the truck was already tucked between the house and the oak tree, missing the picnic table by mere inches.

"What the ..." she gasped, both shocked and impressed by the finesse of the truck's driver.

"Good afternoon." A young man in a navy cap and canvas jacket climbed down from the rig, which continued to growl. "You must be Melinda. Got your delivery here."

Melinda just stared at him. "I haven't ordered anything."

The man smirked and there was a spark of amusement in his brown eyes.

"No, you didn't. But it's that time of year again. I'm here to give you a refill."

Melinda didn't respond, and he laughed and adjusted his cap. "Ma'am, I'm Steve Baker, propane provider for this area. That gray tank there, around back of the house ..."

"I know what the tank is for," she snapped. That was true, but she'd also been in such a whirlwind the past few weeks that she hadn't bothered to check the gauge. The tank was full at the start of the summer, and Melinda hadn't given it another thought. Until now.

"Actually, I'm surprised to find you here, ma'am," Steve said in a tone that told Melinda he was fighting to keep a smirk off his face. "I mean, that you're still out here."

"Why wouldn't I be?" She put her hands on her hips. Hobo rushed around the garage and ran right for Steve, obviously spotting an old friend. But Melinda felt differently.

Steve turned his back to her and unlatched a heavy hose from the back of the rig.

"I know Horace went for a trial run at the nursing home with Wilbur. I heard he got a renter in June, but you were supposed to be gone by now, headed back to the city for some new job. Horace sometimes calls me, but I hadn't heard from him yet this fall. So, I decided to stop by."

What else had this stranger heard about her? And it was obvious that Steve was as intent on gathering fresh gossip as he was delivering propane. Anything she said would be passed around the rest of the township, and probably twisted around, too, by the end of the week.

"Thanks for coming," she said simply, then turned on her heel to go inside and finish her lunch.

Steve didn't appear to notice her departure, as he was so engrossed in looking this way and that, evaluating the acreage's appearance, as he dragged the hose around to the north side of the house.

It was a relief when the rumbling stopped. Soon, Steve banged on the back door.

"The tank was getting a little low, but now you're good." He ripped a ticket off a large notepad, and handed it to Melinda with a smug grin.

Her heart nearly dropped at the amount scribbled on the bottom. Propane was *how much* a gallon? But Steve was watching her closely. She couldn't let him see her surprise.

"I appreciate you stopping by." She smiled, trying to keep her voice even. "Happy holidays."

"Same to you," Steve replied. "You just mail that in with your payment," he gestured at the paper in her hand, then gave the farmyard another searching glance as he turned for his truck. Melinda heard him snicker when he looked toward the barn.

"Nice wreath." Steve called over his shoulder and opened the rig's door. "Well, hope you can manage things out here this winter. I'll be back in the spring."

"I'll be here," she responded, but her words were drowned out by the roar of the tanker's engine. She remained rooted to the back step, her hand protectively wrapped around Hobo's collar, while Steve maneuvered his massive rig out of the yard and roared back down the drive.

As soon as Steve was out of sight, Melinda let out a groan of frustration. She went inside for a plastic bag and marched down to the barn, Hobo right behind.

"What was I thinking?" she muttered, snapping the shiny gold balls off the wreath one by one. "There, so much better." But the thought of the propane bill, waiting for her on the kitchen counter, made her shoulders sag.

"Oh, Hobo, the expenses never end out here," Melinda gave him a comforting pat on the back, trying to make herself feel better.

"It's too bad I already took the tags off all those wreaths and brought them outside. If you're going to live in the house until spring, I might need to charge you rent."

Melinda stashed the propane ticket with the rest of her bills, then tried to push the thought of Steve's smugness away so she could focus on one of her favorite decorating tasks: setting up her artificial tree.

Its cardboard box waited in the corner of the dining room, right where the tree would look best. But her ornaments were upstairs, their totes tucked inside the door of the storage room so she couldn't break their delicate contents.

The chilly air in the closed-off bedroom hit her nose as soon as the paneled door creaked open. The floor vents inside were always closed, the air scented with dust and memories. Someday, when this farm became Melinda's, she was sure Horace, Ada and Kevin would sort out what was family heirlooms and what was junk.

But for now, the room was an obstacle course of stuff. In some places, boxes and crates were stacked as high as the angled eaves that met the outside walls. The gable nook with the triple-paned window, the one that looked out over the front yard, held only one layer of boxes to let a little sunlight into the room. The lone window in the north wall was covered with cardboard to block drafts, and the walls were painted an odd shade of aqua green.

Melinda brought down her decoration boxes and placed them on the dining room table, out of Hobo's curious reach, then set up the tree. Its strings of clear lights were soon glowing in the waning afternoon light. The berry garland that once graced the built-in bookcase in her apartment was a good fit for the top of the dining room's buffet. She added another garland across the cased opening into the living room. But she hesitated to set out a trio of modern-shaped crystal trees and returned them to the tote.

"Not everything from my old life is going to fit in here," she reminded herself as she reached into a box and felt something soft. It was her tree skirt, a cream felt with red berries and evergreen branches embroidered along its hem.

She tried to brush away what appeared to be trails of dust on the fabric, then realized they were fine black hairs. Her eyes filled with unexpected tears.

"Oh, Oreo," she whispered. "So much has changed. How was it only a year ago that you helped me set up this tree? I miss you so much. In a few days there'll be someone new in our old home, as if we were never there. How did the years fly by so quickly?"

She knelt on the oak floors and carefully arranged the tree skirt around the base. "You always liked to sit under our tree, didn't you, Oreo?" She laughed softly, remembering.

"And that one year, you went in the bedroom for a nap and I took the tree down when you weren't around to help. When you woke up, you stopped short and glared at where it had been. How you howled! I wasn't sure if you were mad that the tree disappeared, or that I took it down without you."

Melinda gently patted the stray black hairs back in place on the tree skirt. "There'll always be a spot for you, right under this tree. Although Hobo might decide he wants to sprawl out here, too."

Then she unwrapped her ornaments, recalling where and when she acquired them over the years, hanging only the unbreakable ones on the bottom rounds of the tree just as she had when Oreo was alive. The porcelain nativity display found its new place of honor on the buffet, and she was done. There were more decorations in the last box, but the house didn't need them.

Melinda gathered the totes and returned them to the storage room. She slid some old crates over and stacked more boxes to the side, trying to find a place for her containers that wouldn't block the door.

Then she spotted an odd shape nearby, wrapped in a sheet of plastic that looked like two garbage bags hurriedly taped together. The tape tore loose as she moved the bundle out of her way. It was a tabletop Christmas tree, tucked in a frayed basket. She recognized Horace's slanted scrawl on a nearby cardboard box and, setting aside the uncomfortable thought that she was being as nosy as Steve, carefully pulled away the flaps.

Melinda expected to find a few battered cartons of dime-store ornaments and some strings of tired lights. Those were just inside the box's rim, but there was so much more.

She lifted out a crocheted doily, its once-white fibers now a dull cream, that someone had cut partway through so it would wrap around the little tree's wicker base.

In the very bottom was a wooden box, its top scuffed and its dark varnish chipped on the corners. She hesitated for a moment, then popped the latch. The aroma of cedar tickled her nose.

"Look as these!" she gasped.

Huddled in a nest of muslin fabric were some of the most ornate Christmas ornaments Melinda had ever seen. There were several cut-glass balls in a rich shade of amber, their ribbed surfaces sparkling even in the dim light of the storage room. She unrolled a tissue-paper bundle and discovered a pair of ruby-red glass cardinals, poised to take flight.

She admired the ornaments for another moment, then reluctantly returned them to the wooden box and repacked the cardboard carton. She cleared a special place for it inside the door, then carefully re-wrapped the tabletop tree.

As she closed the storage room's door and pushed the faded towel back along its bottom, trapping the cold drafts inside, Melinda was already coming up with a plan.

"I know who needs these decorations," she said, a smile forming on her face. "And I've now got the perfect excuse to do something I've been thinking about for days."

✳ 11 ✳

Twilight was already falling over the vacant fields as Melinda reached the county highway. Hobo, his leash securely fastened to the bottom brace of the passenger seat, leaned forward to take in the strange sights he discovered out the car's windows.

"It won't take long to get there," she soothed him as they turned west toward Elm Springs. She left work early that afternoon to hurry home and brush the weed seeds out of Hobo's coat and clean his sometimes-white paws. "I can't wait for you to see Horace, Hobo. He's counting the minutes until we get there, I know he is."

Hobo was restless, as the few car trips in his past always ended at the vet clinic, but the white tip of his tail beat a rhythm of excitement at the sound of Horace's name.

Melinda had no idea how Hobo would react to the strangeness of the nursing home, with wheelchairs humming down its hallways and the odd mix of smells, from the odor of antiseptic cleansers to the tantalizing aromas drifting from the dining hall. She was grateful Kevin and Ada were meeting her at Scenic Vista to get in on the holiday fun. That, and to help keep Hobo under control.

Other than a tote bag carrying a pouch of doggie treats and a water bowl, the back seat of the car was crammed with a selection of Christmas decorations Melinda hoped would make Horace and Wilbur's small apartment bright and festive. The three-foot-tall basket tree rested against the seat cushions, still wrapped in its plastic bags. There was the cardboard carton filled with modern ornaments and lights.

The box of antique glass figurines was bundled in clean towels and packed in a plastic tote. She had added a stretch of holly-and-berry garland from her own stash of unused decorations, and a snowflake-and-red tablecloth discovered in one drawer of the farmhouse's dining room buffet.

It was only a twenty-minute drive to Elm Springs, but Melinda couldn't wait to get there. She hadn't seen Horace since he visited the farm in October, and had never been to his new home.

Although they were fifty years apart in age, she and Horace had so much in common. Both had faced a series of changes in the past year, ones that made this holiday season a time for both deep reflection and new hopes for the future. Melinda wanted Horace to feel at home in his new place, just as she now did. And as she set up her own Christmas tree and draped garland over the farmhouse's oak woodwork, she found herself wondering about past holiday seasons at the farm. Horace could be quiet but he also loved to tell stories, and Melinda hoped to hear some of them that evening.

"Hobo, I'm sure you'll be the center of attention," she told him, then grimaced. "I made some vague promises when the director of Scenic Vista asked if you had obedience training. Try to be a good boy, OK?"

Houses began to congregate along the road, and she slowed the car as the outskirts of Elm Springs came into view. Hobo whimpered at the sight of the care facility, where strings of clear lights and evergreen garland twirled around the front entry's posts. Electric candles flickered in some of the windows on the front of the three-story brick building.

"It's OK, Hobo. We made it!" Melinda sang as she pulled into a parking space just outside the entrance.

It was a weeknight, and there seemed to be few visitors. She was glad, as there would be fewer distractions for Hobo once they got inside. "I know this is all very strange for you, but we're going to have fun. And look who's here!"

Kevin Arndt stepped down from his navy truck, which was parked just a few spaces away. He gave Melinda an enthusiastic wave, then hurried around to help his mom down from the pickup's cab. Ada and Kevin both lived in Mason City, about a half hour north of Elm Springs.

Kevin taught at a community college, and Ada had sold her farm near Eagle River and retired several years ago when her husband passed away. She was the youngest of the eight Schermann children, separated by nearly twenty years from Wilbur and Horace, who were the oldest, but never failed to be there when her brothers needed support. And Kevin had always been devoted to Horace and Wilbur, driving to the farm several times a month to do whatever was needed so his uncles could remain at their home as long as possible.

It was Kevin who advertised the acreage for rent last summer, when Horace finally agreed to an extended stay with Wilbur at Scenic Vista. Horace had intended to return home, and refused to leave the farm unless they could find someone to care for Hobo and the sheep and chickens in his absence.

"Turns out, that person was me." Melinda rubbed Hobo's shoulders. "A year ago, I never would have believed my life was going to turn out like this. But I'm so glad it did."

Ada was hurrying toward them now, tugging a thick-knit cream cap over her cropped white hair. Her arms were loaded down with tote bags. Melinda barely got out of the car before Ada gave her a warm hug.

"This was a wonderful idea! No reason all those decorations should be stuffed up there in the front room, gathering dust, when my brothers can put them to use here."

"My uncles will have the best-decorated room at Scenic Vista," Kevin laughed. Behind his glasses, Kevin had the same striking blue eyes as his mother and uncles. "How did the trip go? I see Hobo's waiting patiently in the car."

"I think I held my breath the whole way," Melinda glanced cautiously at Hobo. "You know, it's too bad Jack had to work late. I was looking forward to meeting him," she gave Kevin a teasing jab with her elbow. "But then, I feel like I know him already. You talk about him all the time."

Kevin beamed at the mention of his new boyfriend. "Maybe after the holidays, we'll have to get down to the farm. He's fascinated with the idyllic life you have out there. I almost think he wants to live in the country someday."

Melinda laughed. "I'm sure I can find some chores that'll change his mind in a hurry, if you like."

Hobo began to bounce in his seat when he spotted Kevin and Ada. He greeted Kevin with a happy bark and tried to leap into his arms.

"Hobo! Hey, bud! I haven't seen you in so long, like, six weeks! You were so brave to make the trip today." Kevin carefully loosened the leash and, after a few encouraging words, Hobo stepped down to the pavement. He sniffed about for a moment, then went into a sit and remained still.

Kevin raised an eyebrow. "That's good, Hobo." He turned to Melinda, a look of amazement on his face. "I didn't know Hobo was so well-trained. Does he do tricks, too?"

Melinda could only roll her eyes as she handed a box of decorations to Ada. "I have no idea. He does as he pleases. Let's just pray he's a good boy once we get inside."

Kevin guided Hobo to the evergreen bushes clustered just past the entrance, then turned and gave his mom and Melinda a grinning thumbs-up.

"Good," Melinda sighed. "Maybe this will work after all."

Hobo's appearance in the care facility's lobby brought gasps of delight from the residents gathered around a puzzle near the fireplace. Holiday music drifted down from the nurses' station.

Two women shuffling by, one with a cane and the other with a walker, debated what flavor of ice cream would be served at dinner. "It's Thursday," the first one said, "you know that means mint chip." The other woman only shrugged and inched toward Hobo, who hesitated and gave Melinda a questioning look.

"It's OK," she whispered. Hobo had never visited a nursing home before but thanks to Wilbur and Horace, he was familiar with the halting movements of elderly people. He accepted the woman's tentative pat on the head and then turned on the charm, his red collar and his brushed brown coat glowing in the soft light of the lobby. Ada grasped Melinda's arm with her free hand.

"Look at that," Ada beamed. "He's the life of the party."

Kevin handed Hobo's leash to Melinda and relieved her of the box she carried. "Horace and Wilbur are just down the hall. But you better take Hobo. He knows you best."

They had barely rounded the final bend when Horace appeared in one of the open doorways. His purple-and-green plaid shirt and khaki pants were a significant improvement from the ragged-yet-clean overalls he was wearing the day Melinda first visited the farm. Horace gasped when he saw Hobo, and Hobo pulled so hard on his lead that Melinda almost lost her footing.

"Hobo!" Taking his time, Horace kneeled down to hug his friend. "Oh, it is so good to see you, buddy!"

Horace's voice caught with emotion, and he wrapped his arms tighter around Hobo.

Melinda felt a momentary pang of guilt seeing Hobo and Horace together. How they must miss each other. Hobo loved her, she was sure of that, but she wondered how often he thought of Horace. She decided she was willing to share. Hobo's heart was big enough to love two best friends.

"Come in, come in," Horace gestured to his guests, shyly accepting the hugs offered by Kevin and Ada, then turning to give Melinda's hand a still-firm squeeze. "We've been looking forward to this since you called. What's in that box you've got there, Ada?"

"Christmas," she crowed. "There's more out in the car. And Melinda's brought eight jars of corn relish, too!"

"Oh, I've been looking forward to that," Horace beamed. Melinda suspected he was as thrilled about the pungent relish as he was the Christmas decorations.

Wilbur was napping in a lift chair next to Horace's well-worn leather recliner. There was a red fleece throw tucked over Wilbur's thin legs and a navy cardigan wrapped around his shoulders. When he opened his eyes, he seemed confused by the sudden commotion and gave Ada and Kevin a searching look. But his face lit up at the sight of Hobo.

"Does Wilbur know you?" Melinda whispered to Kevin.

"Not really," he sighed. "His dementia is progressing, of course. Sometimes he recognizes Horace, but it's been some time since he's been sure about Mom and I."

Horace settled in his recliner and leaned down to stroke Hobo's nose. The friends were already lost in conversation.

Melinda was pleasantly surprised by the coziness of the small apartment. The large triple window in the living area looked over the care center's courtyard, where a birdfeeder swayed in a nearby tree.

A compact table and chairs waited in one corner of the room, and there was a short counter with a sink, quarter-size refrigerator and microwave. Two single beds were visible through a doorway, with a handicapped-accessible bathroom beyond. Everything was neat and clean, even if the rooms and furniture were coated in shades of beige and lacked character.

"This is really nice," she told Kevin.

"It faces east. Perfect for two old farmers used to getting up with the sun," Kevin replied as he set a box on the floor by Horace's chair.

"Wilbur got lucky getting into this suite last year, it was a last-minute opening. So when his roommate moved out, we thought Horace might be willing to come up here. They've got everything they need."

Horace suddenly looked up from talking to Hobo. "Where are my manners? Everyone, pull up a chair. Kevin, there's another one in the bedroom. I wish I had some coffee to offer everybody. But there's always a pot on down at the cafeteria."

"I'll get some," Kevin offered. "And when I get back, Uncle Horace, I'll go out to Melinda's car and bring in your tree."

Horace grinned. "You have it? The one in the basket?"

"Oh, yes!" Melinda reached over and patted Horace on the arm. She couldn't wait to see how the little tree would look on the small cabinet next to the television. "And your ornaments, too. You tell us where you want everything to go, and we'll decorate while we're here."

Kevin brought in coffee and the rest of the decorations, then made sure the apartment's door was securely closed behind him. Ada folded the snowflake tablecloth to a better size, spread it on the cabinet's surface and displayed the small tree on top.

Hobo rose only once from his spot by Horace's recliner, coming to Melinda's side to inspect a twist of lights she pulled from a box. He accepted a handful of treats from her tote bag, then settled back on the carpet at Horace's side.

Kevin produced a pack of thumb tacks from his coat pocket, and used them to swag a string of colored lights and Melinda's donated garland above the picture window. Melinda circled the small tree with a strand of clear lights. Ada reached into a bag and pulled out a snow globe of a farm scene that she placed on the shelf under the television, then rummaged in her canvas tote for a plastic container.

"I couldn't resist baking up a batch of Mom's sugar cookies," Ada said as she passed them around. Wilbur's blue eyes shone with interest and he reached for a cutout in the shape of a snowman. He took a small, reverent bite, and a contented grin spread across his lined face.

"Mom," Kevin mumbled around a mouthful of cookie, "it's not the holidays until you make these. They're so soft. What's the secret?"

"Sour cream," Ada replied. "It's my grandmother's recipe. There's a copy in the recipe box out at the farm, Melinda, if you're interested."

"I certainly am," she took another bite of her star-shaped cookie. "These are amazing. And is that almond flavoring in the frosting?" Ada nodded.

Melinda now knew which recipe she would take to her neighbor Mabel's cookie-baking party in just a few weeks.

What better way to honor the Schermann farm's Christmas traditions than to bake these delicious cookies?

They passed the treats around a second time before Melinda reached for the antique ornament box. "I found this upstairs," she said as she carefully handed the container to Horace. He raised the latch, peeked in, and gave a satisfied nod. Ada hurried over and lifted one of the amber glass balls so it glowed in the soft light of the room.

"I knew these had to still be out at the farm," Ada said. "But I haven't seen them in years. Melinda, I'm so glad you stumbled across them. One side of the family brought these over from Germany, but I don't recall the exact story."

Ada traced the delicate ribbed glass with a careful finger. "I wish I had paid more attention to things like that, when Mother and Father were still around to tell us."

Horace gently pushed Hobo's curious nose aside and reached into the box, lifting out another glass ornament.

"We always put these on the tree last, after the popcorn strings and paper chains and such," he explained to Kevin and Melinda. "And we didn't cut our tree until just a few days before Christmas. Usually we got one out of the windbreak, or down at the creek. Had to take a sled to haul it home."

Wilbur had set the rest of his cookie aside and seemed to be listening intently, as if the past was so much closer to him than the present. Kevin noticed Wilbur's interest, and turned to his mom and Horace.

"I'd love to hear everything you know, at least. What else is the box? What else do you remember?"

"Now these," Ada reverently lifted out two more clumps of tissue paper, "these I know the story to." She handed one to Melinda, who unwrapped it and admired the beautiful ruby hue of the glass cardinal perched in her palm.

"Father bought this set for Mother the first Christmas they were married," Ada continued as she helped Wilbur remove the second bird's protective paper.

"That would've been, oh, let's see, 1922. He found them at a little five-and-dime store over in Swanton."

Wilbur tentatively touched the bird's glass feathers, the light of memory appearing in his eyes.

"Mother always added these to the tree at the very last," Horace recalled as Melinda passed the other glass bird his way. "She put them together on the top of the tree, just under the star. You know, we always put the tree in what I call the inside corner of the dining room," Horace turned to Melinda. "We had an iron tree stand, a fancy thing that Grandpa bought way back when times weren't so hard. I don't know what happened to it."

"I put my tree in that very spot!" Melinda exclaimed. "Seemed like the place for it."

"That's right." Horace was pleased. "I loved Christmas, looked forward to it for months. But this was during the Great Depression, you see. Our gifts were always homemade. We were lucky to get an orange in our stocking, maybe a bit of penny candy. Our parents probably purchased it at Prosper Hardware." He raised an eyebrow at Melinda.

"The Christmases I remember weren't quite so lean," Ada added, "but then, I was the tail end of us eight kids. That would have been in the forties, when things had turned around a little. One year I got a new doll. Not a hand-me-down from one of the other girls that Mother cleaned up and sewed a new dress for. A brand-new doll. That was a big day for me."

Kevin reached over and straightened Wilbur's blanket. "What was your best Christmas, Uncle Wilbur?"

Wilbur still held the glass cardinal gently in his grasp, as if afraid it might fly away. He didn't answer at first, and Melinda wondered if he was following the conversation. But then Wilbur raised his chin.

"Best Christmas ... that was when I came home from the war. Said I'd never leave the farm again. And I never did."

"That was 1945," Ada wrapped an arm around her oldest brother. "I remember that one, too. It was the best, you're right about that." She turned to glance at Horace, and then at Kevin and Melinda.

"Wilbur's train came into the Prosper depot late the afternoon of Christmas Eve. Father went to town with the truck to bring him home. I can still see that old truck bouncing up the lane, Father tooting the horn. Mother ran out into the snow, didn't even pull her shawl on. She all but dragged you out of that truck, Wilbur, crying and laughing so hard that she could barely stand to let you go."

"I was home," Wilbur whispered, a look on his face that made Melinda's heart ache. "So glad to be home."

"It was a wonderful place to come back to," Horace said quietly as he looked down, fiddling with the latch on the ornament box. Melinda couldn't read emotions.

"I was fortunate that I never had to leave. With Wilbur gone, I was needed even more at home. By the time I was eighteen, the war was almost over. Even then, I was lucky that I didn't get drafted."

Everyone was silent for a moment, lost in their own thoughts. Horace's comments surprised Melinda, as that was the most she'd ever heard him say about his personal life. She had often wondered why neither Wilbur or Horace ever married. Ada told her Wilbur's girlfriend jilted him while he was overseas, and Horace was so shy that he never dated much. Kevin mentioned once that Horace was smart enough to attend college at Iowa State, but hadn't wanted to leave the farm. Melinda always suspected there wasn't enough money for Horace's tuition.

But now, she saw that Horace may have never considered leaving his birthplace. The farm was such a big part of both Wilbur and Horace, and Melinda understood how they felt. She, too, felt she was at last at home.

"Well," Horace said briskly, looking up again, "let's see what else you found."

"There's some modern decorations in this other box," she answered, lifting its flaps. "The usual stuff, like strings of colored lights and metallic balls. Horace," she hesitated, "if the glass ornaments are so special, why did you stop putting them out?"

Horace was silent for a moment, then sighed. "The year Mother died, we didn't get a tree. Seemed like too much work for just the two of us. We just let it go, I guess."

Melinda's heart hurt to think of these two elderly brothers, the last ones left on the home place, quietly marking the holiday season with no Christmas tree, no decorations. She remembered Horace's Thanksgiving card, his excitement that, at long last, another big Christmas gathering was planned at the farm. Melinda was even more determined to make it special, to bring back some of the holiday spirit that the house apparently hadn't enjoyed in decades.

"Well, I let that slide for one year," Ada said, shaking a finger at Horace.

"Christmas without a Christmas tree? I never. Next December, I showed up out there with this basket tree and some simple ornaments, set it up myself there on the buffet."

"Now, Ada," Horace gave his little sister a level stare. "We always spent the day with your family, it's not like we were alone. Besides, we always kept up with one very important holiday tradition, tree or no tree."

Ada rolled her eyes. "Oh, Horace, if you mean that nonsense with the hay and the frost and whatever, I don't know if that's a Christmas tradition. Always seemed a little pagan to me." She turned to Kevin and Melinda. "Grandpa Schermann swore by it, said his father and grandfather always did it. Father believed it, too."

"As do I," Horace was adamant. "Or at least, I'm not about to break the tradition. A farmer needs to use all the tricks he has up his sleeve to keep his animals healthy."

"What are you talking about?" Melinda interrupted.

"See here," Horace leaned over the arm of his chair. "On Christmas Eve, you set out some hay. In a bucket if you need to, if there's snow on the ground. It picks up the frost overnight. The Christmas frost is supposed to be special. Then Christmas morning, you feed a little of the hay to each of your animals. It's good luck, you see. It will protect them through the coming year."

Ada snorted and rose from her chair, reached for the carton of modern ornaments and turned to the little tree. "Bunch of silliness if you ask me. Grown men, running around, setting out buckets on Christmas Eve. We were always in a hurry the way it was, to get to church on time."

"So, did it work?" Kevin beat Melinda to it.

"Well ... I don't know," Horace crossed his arms. "We lost a few over the years, of course, but that's to be expected. But not many. Farming's a gamble for sure. I say, anything that might tip things in your favor is worth it."

Ada knew Horace was subborn. She just shook her head and added the last of the modern ornaments to the little tree.

Melinda thought in turn of her dear animals: the chickens, the sheep, Hobo, Sunny and Stormy. They had been Horace's, but they were hers now. That October day when she had a change of heart and wouldn't allow Nathan and Angie to take the sheep to the sale barn, she made a commitment.

She understood what Horace meant: She'd do everything she could to keep her animals safe. Especially with winter on its way, and a few of the sheep surely pregnant. It would be weeks yet before she could be sure how many, but Melinda was determined to not let her little flock down.

Horace returned to his cookie and looked on while Kevin picked up the box of antique ornaments and joined Ada at the tree. There was a knock at the door, and two elderly men shuffled into the room.

"We're heading down for some checkers before supper," the one man said. The other smiled at the little tree and gave a low whistle of appreciation.

"Looks like you're busy, Mr. Claus."

"Count me in for tomorrow," Horace replied. Melinda could see how pleased he was with the decorations. The place was brighter, more festive. "I've got company just now."

After his friends left, Horace leaned her way. "Now, if there's not any snow and it's a calm night," he lowered his voice, "the best place to spread out that hay is on the concrete slab where the windmill used to be. Otherwise, put it in a bucket right by the barn door. If it's windy, tuck the bucket on the east side of the garage."

Melinda hid her smile and nodded, filing away that bit of information. "I'll do it. You can be sure of that."

"Glad to hear it," Horace whispered. "Might as well because ... Hobo, what is it, buddy?"

Hobo was up on his haunches, his ears alert. Wilbur suddenly grinned and pointed toward the apartment's door. Before Wilbur could say anything, before Horace could reach for Hobo's leash, Hobo let out a happy bark and dashed toward the hall.

"Cat!" Wilbur shouted. "I saw the cat! And so did Hobo!"

"*Cat?*" Melinda leaped from her seat, nearly bumping into Kevin as he also rushed for the entrance. "Those guys left the door open! Oh, no ..."

The chase was already on. They entered the hallway just in time to see a fluffy calico cat land on the nurses' station with a yowl, the sign-in clipboard flying to the floor with a "*whap!*" that only seemed to fuel Hobo's excitement. Hobo rounded the desk and tried to climb over the nurse working at the computer.

"Princess Puffypants, look out!" the woman shouted. She tried to take hold of Hobo's collar, but he darted off.

The cat leaped away and skittered down the hall. Hobo again was in pursuit, and suddenly deaf to Melinda's pleas to *stop, halt, stay!*

"The dining room's that way," Kevin groaned as he and Melinda ran after Hobo, dodging residents and their canes and walkers. "This could become, well, catastrophic."

Princess Puffypants, her ringed tail flicking in fear and irritation, dashed into the dining hall and launched herself into a startled woman's lap. Hobo suddenly slowed, his interest now divided between the howling cat protected by the arms of a stranger and the wonderful aromas coming from the care center's kitchen.

Hobo's moment of hesitation gave Melinda and Kevin the chance they needed.

Kevin dived forward and grasped the end of Hobo's leash, lost his balance and landed on the rug. The seniors already gathered in the dining hall began to clap their admiration for Kevin's athletic save.

"Merry Christmas, everybody!" Kevin panted as he got to his feet, adjusted his glasses and waved awkwardly to the group. The applause grew louder. Melinda was mortified but she smiled, added her greeting of "Happy holidays!" and took Hobo's lead from Kevin. Out in the hallway, an administrator was trying to keep a straight face as she admonished Horace to "keep control of your guests at all times."

Hobo settled down quickly once they returned to Horace and Wilbur's apartment, but Melinda knew the sooner she got Hobo out of the building, the better. Ada offered Hobo a drink of water while Melinda and Kevin took the empty decoration boxes out to her car.

It was long past dark, and Melinda couldn't face the leftovers waiting in the refrigerator at the farm. She pulled through the drive-up at Elm Springs' lone fast-food joint, and splurged on a fully loaded cheeseburger and fries for herself and a plain cooked patty for Hobo. She settled Hobo in the now-empty backseat with the crumbled beef in his dish, and started for home.

"I don't know who was more out of control, Hobo," she sighed as they rode through the darkness, a few snowflakes dancing in the car's headlights and holiday tunes humming on the radio.

"You, or me and Kevin. Or Princess Puffypants." Melinda snorted, then giggled, then laughed so hard she nearly choked on her cheeseburger.

✻ 12 ✻

The Prosper post office's modest lobby was packed, with four people already in line, when Melinda elbowed through the door during her lunch hour. Postmaster Glenn Hanson, Auggie's closest competitor for the local title of Biggest Gossip Hound, was quick to weigh parcels and slap them with postage stickers, but slow to let patrons out the door.

"Well, now, Beatrice, how's your daughter doing down in Ames? Is she bringing her family home for Christmas?"

Glenn leaned on the counter, fitting most of his protruding belly under the ledge. Through his wire-rimmed glasses, he gave the woman a look that told her he was hanging on every word.

"So glad to hear it," Glenn mused. Melinda hoped he would move on to the next customer. He didn't.

"Tell me again where your son lives these days. Why, it's been years since I saw him last. How's he doing, anyway?"

Melinda shifted her two parcels from her left side to her right. They weren't large, but they would get heavy if Glenn kept on like this.

One was gifts for Susan, and the other was for Cassie. Melinda's Christmas gifts for her two best friends were simple and useful this year; no more expensive perfume or random candles. Not only had Melinda's day-to-day life changed in just a few months, but her shopping habits had, too.

There was one jar each of the wild-plum jam Melinda canned back in September, following the Schermann family recipe, with fruit she picked from the brambles alongside her gravel road. And both friends would get a plush, hand-knitted scarf, Cassie's in shades of green and Susan's in a palette of soft blue and gray.

Melinda had hoped to knit the scarves herself, imagined how cozy it would be to sit by her fireplace with skeins of yarn and metal needles clicking in a soothing rhythm. But time got away from her, and she'd never had a chance for her mom to show her how to knit. Diane took up the hobby when she retired from the Swanton school district a few years ago, and gleefully agreed to create the scarves for Susan and Cassie. Melinda was a bit disappointed in herself, but vowed that she'd learn the skill next year.

Beatrice was at last allowed to leave the post office. The man next in line, somebody named Ronald, was quizzed about his general health, the temperament of his family's new dog, and if the Iowa State football team had a chance at winning their bowl game later that month. The woman just ahead of Melinda, her arms laden with parcels, gave Melinda an exasperated look and set her packages on the floor.

Melinda watched the minutes tick away on the square clock just behind the counter and tried to be patient. With her background in marketing, she understood what Glenn was doing: In addition to gathering as much local news as possible, his aim was to provide first-rate customer service.

If little Prosper wanted to keep its post office thriving, residents had to feel welcome and that their packages were handled with special care.

Just when it seemed Glenn had harvested all of Ronald's useful news, Ronald offered another juicy tidbit: His neighbors up on Oak Street were moving to Mason City and their house had sold.

Glenn raised his eyebrows. "Really? Why, Ronald, I hadn't heard that. Is that the tan one with the green shutters? Who bought it? Any word on what the house sold for?"

Ronald shared what he knew, including a rumor about the property's sale price that he'd heard from another neighbor. Glenn abruptly turned toward Melinda.

"You heard anything about new residents over at the store? Anyone new been in lately?"

"Huh? Oh, sorry, Glenn. Nope, I haven't noticed anyone." She had zoned off, thinking about all the lovely things she would knit once she found the time to learn.

Maybe this winter, when the snow was flying and she couldn't take long walks down to the creek. But then, she'd have to shovel all those paths to the barn and chicken coop, her chores would take forever and ...

"Oh, you haven't seen anyone." Glenn was disappointed. "Oh, that's too bad."

At last, it was Melinda's turn at the counter. No one else was in the post office. Glenn pressed her for fresh details about the holiday festival, and said he was planning special activities for the post office that night. As he finally set Cassie's box on the scale, he seemed to be turning something over in his mind. Melinda waited, wondering what the next discussion topic would be.

"Well, I have to tell you, Pete saw something strange on his route yesterday." Pete was one of the three rural mail carriers based out of the Prosper post office.

"He's got the roads north and east of town. I really don't know what to make of it, I really don't. I keep turning it over in my mind. Makes no sense, you know?"

She didn't. Glenn was usually the one pumping other people for gossip, but now it seemed he wanted to share something with her. Melinda wasn't sure if this was some sign she'd been fully accepted by the Prosper community, or if Glenn just couldn't bear to keep it to himself.

Either way, showing interest might be her ticket to getting back to the store. "So, what happened?"

Glenn frowned. "Well, Pete was out on his route, a few miles northeast of where the county blacktop crosses the river there at the old iron bridge. Just past that T intersection and up the big hill." Melinda had no idea where that was, but nodded encouragingly.

"So, Pete's just dropped the mail at the Johnsons' place," Glenn leaned over the counter, "and as he passes the lane for the Benniger farm, he could have sworn there were lights on in the kitchen. It was just after four-thirty, but you know how early it gets dark these days. No mistaking, Pete says, that someone was in the house."

She tried to feign interest for Glenn's sake and held back her laughter. Glenn always had to know everything going on for miles around Prosper. But had he stooped so low as to clock what time people arrived home from work?

"Do ... do the Bennigers normally not get home until five or later?" .

He gave her an incredulous stare, then shook his head. "Oh, if only it were that. I forget that you haven't been around here all that long."

Glenn paused for dramatic effect, then continued.

"See, Melinda, no one's lived at the old Benniger farm for, oh, at least two years now. But Pete swears he saw lights on. And ... there was a strange car parked right there by the house, just like nobody's business."

"Someone owns the place," she reasoned. "Maybe they were just checking on the house or something?"

"Could be," Glenn sounded skeptical. "But here's the kicker: Pete swears the car had Wisconsin license plates. The owner lives in Dubuque, he's some nephew of the previous residents. He rarely comes back here."

Glenn paused. "But he's a doctor, I suppose he could have moved and started a new practice, but ..."

"You probably would have heard about it," she couldn't help but finish Glenn's thought.

Glenn laughed. "Now you're catching on, Melinda. Anyway, here's what little I know."

What followed was an abbreviated history of the Benniger family since the end of the Civil War. They were some of the earliest settlers in the area and were already wealthy by the late 1800s. One son took over the farm and raised a heritage breed of cattle that only increased the family's fortune. He built the sprawling brick house that now stood on the property. "A real showplace," Glenn called it.

"I don't really know much else," he sighed, "but there was an elderly man and his wife living there last. They retired and moved closer to one of their kids, I heard. The fields are rented out, but the house has been empty since they left. A sad sight to see, I always say, but it happens too often."

Melinda thought of Horace and Wilbur and their farm. Her farm.

If she hadn't come home when she did, if she hadn't seen the "for rent" sign guiding her off the county highway that memorable day back in early June, her charming farmhouse may have suffered the same fate.

She glanced at the clock, its hands pointing close to one, and saw her chance to escape. "Looks like I should get back to the store," she said. "What's Pete going to do now? Did he call the county sheriff?"

"We talked about that," Glenn tapped his fingers on the counter. "But Pete's not sure it's criminal, if you know what I mean. If someone broke in, why would they turn the lights on and attract notice like that? Pete's going to check again today, then maybe track down the owner and give him a call."

The day had started out sunny, but turned gloomy while Melinda was at the post office. Heavy clouds were lowering over the co-op's tower and a biting wind now blasted down Main Street, flinging about tufts of yesterday's snow. She pondered Glenn's story as she hustled back to Prosper Hardware, her chin tucked into the collar of her parka.

If Glenn's hunch was correct, something strange was indeed going on at the Benniger farm. Melinda found it odd that he and Pete hadn't notified the sheriff right away, but people around here liked to handle things on their own when they could. Maybe there was a good explanation for what Pete saw. Prosper Hardware was unusually busy that afternoon, and she quickly put the mystery out of her mind.

But that night, as Melinda curled up on the sofa watching holiday movies with Hobo, she found her mind going back to Glenn's story.

She listened to the wind driving around the corners of the farmhouse and gazed into the dining room where her Christmas tree glittered proudly in the corner. The beautiful tree's lights glowed, and the furnace let out a gentle hum as warmth pushed up from the ironwork floor vents.

"None of this would be happening right now, like this, if I wasn't here," she whispered to Hobo. "If we weren't here."

She thought of the Benniger farm, of an old brick house sitting alone in the snow and the dark. What was it like inside? Glenn said it was a fancy place, so surely more ornate than the simple, comforting lines of the Schermann farmhouse. She imagined a formal parlor, intricate grates adorning the fireplaces, stained-glass designs in the top layers of the picture windows. Was there an open staircase with a hand-carved banister? Molded plaster medallions wrapped around the ceiling's pendants?

Melinda shivered and pulled her fleece blanket closer. It would be so cold in that house tonight, even if the furnace was up just enough to keep the pipes from freezing.

Was the furniture still there, maybe covered in ghostly sheets, or did the bare rooms echo with loneliness? And the barn ... crouching there across the yard, full of deep shadows. When the animals were gone, and the people moved away, it was as if a farm's very soul went with them.

She comforted herself with the thought of the dozing sheep sheltered in her own snug barn, of Sunny and Stormy curled up in their hideout under the heat lamp. Of the hens, their feathers fluffed, resting on the perches in their cozy coop. And she knew that Horace, lounging in his recliner at the care center, could rest easy knowing his former home wasn't dark, cold and empty.

What Pete saw was still on her mind the next morning. All the regulars were at Prosper Hardware, enjoying their coffee and the blueberry muffins she brought in.

What if they knew something Glenn didn't? It wasn't likely, but Melinda decided she had to find out.

"I went to the post office yesterday to mail some packages," she said as she poured a mug of Auggie's strong brew and generously added sugar and powdered creamer. George, noting Melinda's delight when he shared a canister of pumpkin-spice powder back in October, had taken to supplying the group with seasonal varieties along with the plain creamer Auggie preferred. The current flavor was peppermint mocha, and while the guys gave George a hard time about his "fancy drink mix," Melinda noticed the canister was surprisingly light.

"I bet it was busy," Jerry replied. "It's the first week of December. If you've got packages to mail, now's the time."

Melinda took her usual seat. "It was. And I heard something interesting while I was there. Glenn told me what Pete noticed the other day while he was out on his route."

She shared what she knew, trying to remember exactly what Glenn said about the farm's location. If she was going to spread gossip, she would do her best to be accurate.

"It's up on a hill," she told the guys, who were now hanging on her every word. "A fancy brick house. Glenn said it used to be in the Benniger family. I'm not sure if I'm pronouncing that right, but ..."

Auggie froze, his coffee cup halfway to his face. The other men, caught up in the mystery, didn't seem to notice.

"Wonder what's going on?" George shook his head. "Sounds awful odd to me. And I remember that house. Mary and I used to live out that way, drove by it all the time. Glenn's right, it's been vacant for a few years."

"That house is something special," Doc chimed in. "It's rundown these days, of course. I always like to admire it when I'm out that way. But that hill is nasty when it's icy. Downhill all the way to the river. I've heard those heritage cows the Benniger family raised were quite the breed."

"The 'g' is almost silent," Auggie suddenly interrupted the conversation. "That's how you say it."

Everyone turned to stare at Auggie.

"Look at you, Auggie, you're a walking encyclopedia today," George chuckled.

"My grandma on my mother's side was a Benniger," Auggie continued, his voice low and halting. "They go way back around here, although the surname has sort of died out. One of my nephews over in Decorah owns the place now."

"Really?" Melinda gasped, then decided she shouldn't be surprised. In a community this small, it was common for many longtime residents to be distant relatives.

"But, Auggie, Glenn said the guy was from Dubuque, that he's a doctor."

Auggie shook his head. "Right occupation, wrong place. I didn't know David was back visiting. Seems odd. Christmas is a few weeks off yet, and he always drops in at the co-op when he's in town."

"Oh, and there's something else," she added. "How could I forget this part? Pete told Glenn the car in the yard had Wisconsin plates, he was sure of it."

Auggie didn't respond, but she saw his knuckles turn white as he tightened his grip on his coffee cup. Uncle Frank and Jerry exchanged worried looks.

Melinda was about to ask what was going on, but stopped when she saw Auggie had turned pale. With one last swig of his coffee, he was up and out of his chair. Auggie's mug hit the sideboard's metal counter with a clang and he grabbed his coat and hat. Was it her imagination, or were Auggie's hands shaking just a bit?

"Well, gotta get down to the co-op," he said briskly, pulling his brown knit cap down to the top of his glasses. "Should be busy today. Got a grain shipment coming in at eleven." Avoiding the concerned glances of his friends, Auggie hustled for the front door. The tinkling bell above it broke the group's stunned silence.

"What was that all about?" Bill came up the aisle from the back room, pulling off his coat along the way. "I don't think I've ever seen Auggie Kleinsbach speechless."

"I have," Melinda's voice wavered. What had she done? What had she said? "But only once. That morning a few weeks ago, when I asked him to put the Christmas star up on the side of the co-op. He did the very same thing, clammed up and ran out of here like his grain elevators were on fire."

She looked around at the guarded faces of her friends. "Last time," she said gently, "everyone in this room claimed to have no idea what was going on, yet at the same time told me to leave it be. I did ... that time."

"I still don't know what the deal is, honestly, Melinda," Doc said earnestly.

She gave him an understanding nod and looked at Bill, who just shrugged.

"Anyone else got anything to say?" Melinda tried again.

More silence.

"Auggie is our friend," she said urgently. "If there's some sort of trouble, if he's hurting in some way, we need to help him. And if that wasn't his nephew's car out at that farm, someone needs to tell the authorities."

Finally, Uncle Frank sighed. "If it's who I think ..."

"Frank," Jerry said sharply. "Drop it. We don't know ..."

"Know what?" Melinda was exasperated. These men chattered all morning, every morning about anything that happened within twenty miles of Prosper Hardware. Now they were suddenly quiet. And hiding something.

"It's bound to get out, if it's true," Frank pointed a finger at Jerry, who finally threw his hands up in a weak defense. Frank pivoted in his chair to face his niece.

"Auggie's got some kids, as you know. There's the son that lives over in Swanton, and a daughter up in Rochester. But he's got another boy, his oldest."

Melinda frowned. "Really? I've only heard him talk about those two."

"And there's a reason for that," Jerry gave Frank a worried look. "Evan is ... well, he's got problems. Can't seem to hold a job, I guess. He's married, but I hear that's not going so great these days."

Jerry didn't continue. Before Melinda could push him on where he was getting all this information, George piped up.

"He and Auggie don't speak," George put in gently. "About five years ago, they got into it at Christmas dinner. Things were on thin ice already, then something else happened, Auggie never said what. Evan got in his car right then and there and headed back ..."

"To Wisconsin," Jerry finished. "He lives over in Madison, or at least he used to."

"Why would he come back here if he and Auggie are estranged?" Bill asked. "And why would he be at that farm?"

"Well, if the guy who owns it is Auggie's nephew," Doc spoke slowly, piecing things together, "that makes him Evan's first cousin. They surely know each other. Still doesn't make much sense, though. But then, there's also no reason why some random person from Wisconsin would drive all the way out here to break into an old house."

"Could it be someone else?" Jerry wondered. "Anyone else? Could it still be someone in the family?"

"That's possible," Uncle Frank admitted. "There would be cousins all over."

Frank rose from his chair and put his paper plate in the trash can by the sideboard, signaling the debate was over, at least for now. The other guys took their cues, and gathered up their coats and folded their chairs back against the wall. Melinda picked up the rest of the coffee cups and stacked them on the metal tray, then snapped the lid back on the muffins, her mind swirling with curiosity and confusion.

"We don't know what the deal is," Frank reminded his friends. The men nodded, and Melinda saw there would be no more theories offered that morning. "Maybe this has nothing to do with Evan. But I have to say, Auggie's face clouded over in a hurry. He may know more than he's willing to share."

* 13 *

Melinda tugged on her gloves and quickly pulled Prosper Hardware's front door closed behind her, trying to keep the cold air from rushing into the store.

The skies were heavy, the air thick and damp. She could almost smell the snow expected to fall in a few hours, a quick-moving system that was to drop only a few inches and clear out by morning. Melinda hoped that forecast would hold, as the town's holiday festival was tomorrow night.

A light dusting of show would enhance the tiny community's charm and add to the festive feel, but a blizzard would cancel the annual celebration and wipe out everyone's weeks of hard work. With so much going on in the weeks leading up to Christmas, Mayor Jerry and the planning committee had already agreed that it might not be feasible to reschedule the event.

Melinda tried to take comfort in the fact that Auggie's prediction was in lock-step with the forecasts from state meteorologists and the Mason City television station. The snow would come and go, then clear skies and calm winds would arrive just in time for the festival.

"I just hope they are all correct," she muttered as she tucked her clipboard under her arm and glanced up and down Main Street, which was nearly deserted at this hour in the early afternoon. "There's enough things up in the air as it is."

This was her last chance to check in with all the business owners, make sure everyone had what they needed for the celebration. As she crossed Main Street to reach the library and City Hall, she marveled at how many volunteer hours were needed to put on an event that came and went in the blink of an evening. Years ago, she'd been tapped to serve on the holiday party committee at WP&S. The group held a few bagel-fueled meetings in a conference room, made a few phone calls, and were done.

This was so different and so complex. Although the festival was steered by Melinda's committee, every business owner and organization had their own activities, ideas and volunteers. And visitors from several miles around would be streaming into tiny Prosper in less than twenty-four hours. It was almost too late to change the plan, she knew, but her walk through the small business district would at least make her feel like she had a handle on things.

Prosper Hardware, thankfully, was all set for tomorrow night. Diane and Miriam were busy baking cookies to serve to guests, and Roger was coming with Diane to help at the store during the event.

George and Mary had their Claus costumes. Bill, with a little assistance from Uncle Frank, moved featured inventory items to more visible spots toward the front of the store and near the cash register. Esther, as she excitedly told Melinda just that morning, had at last decided which Christmas-themed sweater she would wear during the open house.

Melinda's contribution to the store's plans arrived just yesterday: A shipment of forest-green knit caps, with "Prosper Hardware Est. 1894" embroidered on their brims in crisp white thread. The hats were thick and soft, just as promised on the apparel company's website.

They were beautiful, comfortable, and the perfect way to advertise the store. The first one hundred customers would receive a cap, the inside stuffed with a pair of hand-warmer packets. Melinda couldn't have been more pleased with her purchase, and Miriam and Frank were also impressed.

The city's only Christmas tree was set up in the library lobby, its multi-colored lights sparkling by the check-out desk. City Hall, which Nancy said saw far less foot traffic, had to be content with several ropes of evergreen garland and clear lights in its front window.

Nancy saw Melinda wiping her boots on the library's mat, waved to her from City Hall's front desk, and motioned for Melinda to come on through.

"Making the rounds?" She gestured at Melinda's clipboard with her pen. "The two city buildings are ready. I've rounded up all the scissors and paper I can find for the snowflake crafts, and the volunteers on the library board are all lined up to bring cookies and punch for the kids."

"Thanks, Nancy, I knew I could count on you to have it all under control." With a small thrill of relief, Melinda crossed off the first line on her notepad. "I've got my list, I've checked it twice. But who's been naughty, and who's been nice? That has yet to be seen."

"Who's making trouble?" Nancy gave Melinda a searching look over the reading glasses tacked on her nose.

"Let me guess. Auggie still doesn't have that star up on the co-op, does he? I come in from the other side of town, as you know, so I haven't been by there lately. But I know how difficult Auggie can be."

"I hated to bring it up again, and I hoped it would just appear." Melinda threw up her hands, then helped herself to the candy canes on the counter. "When it hadn't by this morning, I had to say something. He just grunted and changed the subject."

"That man's normally never at a loss for words," Nancy rolled her eyes.

Melinda hesitated, choosing her words carefully. She liked Nancy and wanted to confide in her about Auggie's strange behavior. Melinda knew Nancy was discreet, and she might have some insight into the situation. But Melinda kept silent. She wished she'd never brought up Glenn's gossip at Prosper Hardware.

Something was bothering Auggie, that was for sure, but he never mentioned it again. She wondered if Glenn had any more information to share, and knew she'd get an earful when she stopped in at the post office in a few minutes. But part of her hoped there wasn't anything new to hear.

"Well, Auggie did put up one string of lights in the co-op's window," she said at last. "He keeps reminding me of that. His wife's been kind enough to make netting packets filled with a birdseed mix they sell at the co-op, so he's got something to give away, and he's providing the feed for the live nativity. I finished the little sign for that last night, and Auggie gave his nod of approval this morning."

"Sounds like that's as good as it will get," Nancy shrugged. "I don't know how Jane puts up with him sometimes. He's as stubborn as they come. Anyway, I talked with Tony this morning. The fire department's all ready to escort Santa from the elementary school's soup supper to the hardware store."

Melinda crossed another item off her list. "Wonderful! We might pull this event off after all."

"Anyone gives you any grief, you just wave that clipboard in their face," Nancy suggested. "It literally takes a village to host a festival like this. Everyone needs to do their part."

Melinda's next stop was Sam Holden's insurance office. Sam, who was in his late sixties, was a quiet man who never drew attention to his storefront except for one pot of flowers in the spring and summer.

His office had been closed during past holiday festivals, and it took a pep talk from Uncle Frank to get Sam on board for this year's celebration. Melinda smiled triumphantly when she saw the toy train and ceramic village now on display in his front window.

Sam was glad to see her, and excitedly explained how he'd tried to set up the village to echo Prosper's own Main Street.

"It's too bad our train tracks run at that odd angle. My display window's not deep enough." He shook his head, but Melinda could still hear the pride in his voice. "So, I rearranged the town a little to make it fit."

"Sam, it looks terrific," she assured him. "Did you get those calendars in?"

"Got them last week. They weren't that expensive, really, and you know, people will turn to them all year long. Glad you recommended them, Melinda."

"Not a problem," she replied and checked Sam off her list. "See you tomorrow night!"

Father Perkins at the Catholic church assured her the carolers had their final practice the night before, and were determined to stroll Main Street whatever the weather. The parish's vintage nativity display was set up on the front lawn weeks ago, and Father Perkins said all the spotlights were checked over and new bulbs installed.

"Don't want a sudden blackout on the biggest night of the year," Father Perkins chuckled, then amended his statement. "Well, I mean, other than Christmas Eve."

Doc and Bill were hard at work on the front lawn of the veterinary clinic, the ring of their hammers echoing through the still air as they pieced together the manger scene for the live nativity. Melinda had to stop at the curb and take it all in. The display was even better than she had imagined.

A simple frame of two-by-fours supported a twelve foot-wide back wall and sides that were nearly three foot deep, making a structure just large enough to anchor the scene. Discarded pallets from the co-op provided the rough wood slats for the walls. The humble shelter's peak was clad with plywood, and Bill had tacked chicken wire over it and tucked in fistfuls of hay to create a thatched roof.

"This looks amazing!" Melinda hooted and clapped her hands. "I'd seen the pieces in the back of the store, Bill, but here, all together? It's beautiful."

He grinned with satisfaction, then reached into his parka pocket for more screws. "Let's just say I got a bit carried away. I've got it in sections. It'll be easy to put away for next year."

Doc straightened a panel and held it square for Bill. "We've got to get through tomorrow night first," he said. "But I think we've got a new tradition on our hands here."

"True words, spoken by the head wise man himself," Bill smirked. Doc, after much prodding by Karen and Melinda, at last agreed to dress up for the display. Karen would also serve as a wise man, and Melinda's neighbor, John Olson, would round out the trio.

Three of John's sheep, all 4-H champions comfortable in the show ring, would hang out in a small pen next to the manger. John had roped his son, Dylan, and Dylan's girlfriend into playing Joseph and Mary. Tyler, John's other son, would serve as shepherd. With the help of two veterinarians and three skilled sheep farmers, Melinda hoped the live nativity would run smoothly.

Doc turned toward the small barn behind the clinic, which housed two stalls for the occasional large livestock patients needing closer observation. "I'll get those extra fence panels out of the barn, Bill, and I think we'll have everything we need," Doc said. "Melinda, can you give me a hand?"

"Sure can." She wrapped her scarf tighter as a gust of wind rushed down Main Street. "I know you've got this nailed down," she joked, "but I'm just making the rounds to be sure. Anything else I can do to help?"

"I think we're set," Doc unlatched the barn door. "John's bringing some straw bales along with his sheep and Auggie's got the feed, as you know. I've got plenty of water buckets for the animals. One of our clients has a half-grown calf he'll bring in, another 4-H pet, and a woman from over by Swanton volunteered some of her goats."

"And the donkey?"

"Yep, we've got us a donkey. Name's Gus. I hear he's quite the character, but his owner's offered to stay on-site in case we need help. He's willing to take questions about Gus from the crowd, even." Doc grinned as he sorted fence panels. "The sheep will go in this pen, the other animals we'll picket on leads around that rustic manger Bill put together. I recruited one of my daughter's old dolls to play Jesus."

"Good thing the littlest actor won't give you any trouble, then," Melinda tucked her clipboard under her arm to help

Doc lift a fence panel out the door. "Let's hope the animals are as complacent as the baby doll."

The fried-food warmth of the Watering Hole welcomed Melinda after her block-long walk from the vet clinic. Only a few men leaned over the bar at this hour, while two tables of lunch customers still lingered over their meals.

"What's all that goin' on up at Doc's?" a man with a heavy beard called from his bar stool as she came in the door. "I hear he's bringing in a whole circus for tomorrow night."

"Only a few sheep and goats, and a few other critters," Melinda said evenly. She didn't recognize this guy, but it was obvious he was fishing for any eyebrow-raising tidbits he could pass on to his buddies. While many people told her they were excited about the live nativity, she'd heard more than a few grumbles that the idea was silly, even dangerous. She wasn't about to hand the man any gossip he could use.

"Karen and Doc will be on-hand at all times. It's going to be a great addition to the festival."

One of the other men let out a disbelieving snort. "It's a wonder Doc ever brought on that lady vet in the first place. And she oughta stay there in the office, giving rabies shots to cats and such. Why, she's so tiny there's no way she could wrangle a mad bull."

Jessie Kirkpatrick, who owned the Watering Hole with her husband, Doug, was on her way back from clearing a table. She gave Melinda a friendly nod before turning toward the guys at the bar. Jessie was petite and pretty, with dark, curly hair and blue eyes, but she could hold her own with any opinionated customer.

"Karen did an amazing job setting a lame horse's leg out at my parents' farm," she said matter-of-factly. "He healed up wonderfully. No reason Karen can't handle the job."

Jessie deliberately turned her back on the men, who were momentarily silenced.

"Melinda, I've got great news," Jessie set down her tray of dirty dishes. "Doug finally got that doughnut recipe from the daughter of this place's former owner. We're going to fry them up tomorrow night. The Watering Hole's famous cinnamon-sugar doughnuts are back!"

"I can't wait to sample those," Melinda returned Jessie's excited smile, then gave the men at the bar one more glance and raised her voice. "I hope we see all of you at the festival tomorrow night."

Melinda's list was getting shorter and her spirits were soaring. So far, everyone seemed on board and ready. A few snowflakes drifted down and stuck to the sleeves of her parka as she crossed Third Street. Soon, it would be snowing in earnest. She could just call the Methodist Church and check on plans for their dessert buffet, and she knew Auggie and Jane were set down at the co-op. Her only other stop was the post office.

The lobby was surprisingly quiet. Glenn sat at the front counter, engrossed in the latest edition of the Mason City newspaper. He didn't even make an effort to shove the paper aside and appear busy as she came in the door.

"That's quite the write-up, Melinda," Glenn gave the newspaper an approving shake. "We got nearly a quarter page this year. And your quotes from Jerry make him sound, well, really mayor-like."

"The photos I shared from last year's event might help our cause. They'll draw people's attention to the article, I hope."

Melinda eyed a bowl of foil-wrapped chocolate kisses on the counter. She already had candy canes from City Hall in her pocket, and a container of Esther's chocolate-star cookies had been calling her name all day from the sideboard at Prosper Hardware. She'd better not.

"And, by the way," Glenn leaned over and lowered his voice, even though he and Melinda were the only people in the post office.

"I gotta tell you. Pete's struck out on that stuff going on at the Benniger farm. Last two days, when he's gone by? No car in the yard." Glenn sounded disappointed. "There's still a faint track in the driveway, but we haven't had fresh snow for several days. Nothing new to report."

Melinda disagreed, thinking of Auggie's reaction the other morning at the store. But she wasn't about to share that with Glenn. "Good to know," was all she said. "Well, are you all set for tomorrow night? Is there anything you need?"

"I got my second shipment of holiday stamps just today, so we won't run out," he replied, then reached under the counter. "I'd been thinking about what you told us business owners about marketing, making sure we had something to hand out to people during the festival. And I got these."

With a smug grin, Glenn plopped down a stack of shrink-wrapped stationery.

"Thank-you notes! This is brilliant. What a great way to get people to stock up on stamps."

"The first fifty people in the door get a dozen cards with envelopes," he said. "Kids these days, they need to learn to say 'thank you' for stuff. And an email's just not the same. That got me thinking about Christmas when I was a kid. So, I've got something else planned."

Melinda glanced at her clipboard. She didn't have anything written down next to "post office" other than "freebie TBA by Glenn." That was now covered, apparently.

"We're going to have taffy!" Glenn all but shouted. "Won't that be great?"

"Oh, so you'll hand out candy, too," she nodded encouragingly. "That's good."

"No, no, Melinda, it's way better than that," he rapped his knuckles on the counter. "See, we're going to make the taffy right here, my wife and I. Mix it, cook it, pull it ... every step of the way! Marie will cut it up, and our sons and their kids will wrap it and hand it out to everyone."

Melinda had never made taffy, but recalled Grandma and Grandpa Foster talking about it. It was messy, and it took patience and a great deal of time to make. "Glenn," she tried to keep her tone as gentle as possible, "isn't taffy a lot of work? And, well, don't you need a stove?"

"Oh, we've got one in the back," he waved Melinda's concerns away. "We'll cook it there, then bring it up. Why?"

"Well," Melinda hesitated. "I don't know for sure, but maybe you'd need a ... permit for that? If you're making food, and in a public building ..."

"Oh, nonsense," Glenn shrugged. "It's just some candy. It could get messy, but that's part of the fun, right? Don't worry, we'll make sure all the kids and grandkids scrub their hands before they start." He paused. "Look, it'll be a last-minute surprise. Who's going to find out? I mean, who would care?"

Melinda suppressed a sigh. She could think of a few people who might care. Like the county health inspector. Or Mayor Jerry. But Glenn obviously had made up his mind. And there was a woman loaded down with packages about to come in the door.

"OK, just promise me," Melinda whispered before she turned to leave, "plastic gloves all around. I think we've got a few boxes in stock next door if you don't have any here."

"This conversation never happened," Glenn whispered back, then switched to his usual booming voice. "Thanks for coming by, Melinda, we're all ready for tomorrow night!"

She didn't add Glenn's latest idea to her check-off list. But it wasn't likely anyone would complain, and he seemed determined to see the idea through. If pulling taffy put Glenn in the Christmas spirit, who was she to judge?

She'd been overwhelmed when the committee chair's reins were first handed to her, then got caught up in the million little details that could make tomorrow night special. What if the Catholic church's choir donned vintage costumes as they strolled along Main Street? Would George like to ride on top of the fire truck those few blocks from the school to Prosper Hardware, rather than inside?

Melinda had soon decided she needed to check her expectations. It was cold, and the holiday tunes would be just as meaningful if the singers could bundle up in heavy hooded coats and boots. George was eighty-two, and the shuffle in his step had become more noticeable in the past few months. It would be just as exciting for the kids if Santa stepped down from the fire truck's cab as its roof.

And now, her work was done. Anything else anyone did, or whatever else anyone planned, wasn't her responsibility.

As for the co-op's missing star ... She would see Auggie in the morning, of course, but as Melinda came back into the warmth of Prosper Hardware and removed her gloves, she made a decision. Not one more word about the lighted star and its whereabouts. Maybe it was really missing, or maybe not. Auggie apparently had something weighing on his mind, if not his heart. She was going to let it go.

"And there's plenty to do around here," she reminded herself as she set her clipboard behind the counter and took off her coat. "Esther, I think it would be a good idea to make one more pass through here and tidy up. Who knows what tomorrow will bring?"

"Isn't that the truth," Esther shook her head, setting her snowman earrings to dancing. "Today's been busier than I expected. I was just thinking that the front door needs a wreath. I've got another one at home just the right size. The store looks nice, of course, but it's a little bare. We could use some more decorations, don't you think?"

Melinda glanced at the lighted evergreen garlands draped above both front windows, and another section that graced the top of the sideboard. More glowing strands twisted around the railing to the upstairs office and storeroom. The Christmas tree sparkled in a front corner, its branches loaded down with dazzling ornaments.

She hesitated, then remembered the promise she made to herself only minutes ago to just get out of the way. "Esther, I think that's a lovely idea."

✳ 14 ✳

Just as predicted, the skies cleared a few hours before the holiday celebration. Melinda rushed through chores, changed her clothes, and hurried back to Prosper Hardware in time for the official five o'clock start of the evening's activities.

The sunset was brilliant, one of those paintings of vibrant reds and oranges that was all the more breathtaking thanks to the thin dusting of fresh snow. It was nearly dark by the time she turned onto the blacktop and drove back to town. She had looked forward to this night for weeks, but her last-minute preparations put in her a sentimental mood.

Her red cardigan, white tee and black pants were cheerful and comfortable. But as she dressed, Melinda had suddenly missed the whirl of parties that used to be the foundation of her holiday season.

WP&S always footed the bill for a lavish formal dinner at an upscale club. Next came a weekend lunch to catch up with old friends from college. There was also a cozy afternoon of tree-trimming at Susan's house, and a few rounds of cocktails with other groups of friends. The grand finale was an all-out spectacle of a New Year's Eve bash at Cassie and Jim's old-money mansion, complete with a balloon drop at midnight.

Melinda was at the bathroom mirror, working her brown hair into waves with a curling iron that had been tucked away for months, when she caught a glimpse of her former self.

For just a moment, she yearned for the carefully chosen trio of cocktail dresses that used to hang in her closet, her sparkly sandals and the lovely cream wool coat she always reached for on special nights out. They were long gone, dropped off at a trendy consignment store in Minneapolis.

Tonight didn't promise that level of excitement. But as she drove along, the sunset deepening into twilight, Melinda decided she was fine with that.

This celebration would still be filled with friends, and family, too. Her newfound connections to the community, to the store's customers and Prosper's residents, would still make this event memorable. There would be wonderful food, even if it wasn't catered. And best of all, she'd be home at a respectable hour, her toes unpinched and her head clear, and snuggled under her down comforter long before the clock struck midnight.

Several vehicles were already turning off the state highway toward the soft smudge of street lights on the eastern horizon. Melinda felt her spirits lift as she traveled the last mile into Prosper. And then, she saw it.

Far above the fields, on the side of the co-op's tallest storage tower, a breathtaking star shone strong and steady, its outline of clear lights welcoming visitors to the town.

"He found it!" She shouted and gave the steering wheel a triumphant slap. "Auggie did it! It's so beautiful! But simple, too. No wonder everyone was asking if the star would reappear this year. Oh, it's perfect!"

She craned her neck for a closer look as she approached the co-op. The star's frame was larger than she expected, but its actual size was impossible to determine from the ground. There looked to be a dark-railed catwalk under the star, and she shivered to think of Auggie and Dan, his assistant, wrestling that heavy metal frame out of storage and onto such a narrow ledge.

"He must have set it out before dark, that's for sure," Melinda decided. "I wouldn't get out on that balcony, even in the middle of the day." The star would have been over her shoulder when she left town, and probably not lit, so she didn't notice it. "And anyway, I'd given up on Auggie, and stopped watching for the star to appear."

She swallowed a twinge of guilt. Auggie was opinionated and sometimes downright cranky, but he had followed through, at last.

The light dusting of snow made Prosper's Main Street look like a scene out of a Norman Rockwell painting. Clusters of people bundled in down jackets and wool coats wandered the sidewalks, waving and calling to friends and neighbors. The snowflake and tree decorations on the light posts glowed and glistened, the high-gloss paints Melinda and Frank sprayed over the metal frames adding to the magical effect.

The front windows of the occupied buildings along Main Street sparkled with clear and colored lights, and the arched stained-glass window on the front of the Methodist church, lit from the inside, nearly took Melinda's breath away. A line of cars snaked their way toward the soup supper at the elementary school, just a block off Main Street, and many of the parking spaces along the thoroughfare as well as the side streets were already filled.

She didn't turn on Third Street to reach Prosper Hardware's back lot as she usually did. Two more blocks down Main, she could just make out the spotlights in front of the live nativity on the vet clinic's front lawn. She had to go there first. Once she got behind the counter at the store, Melinda knew, she wouldn't get a chance to see the display in all its glory.

Two stock trailers were double-parked on the corner of Main and Fourth streets, and about a dozen people were already milling about. As she pulled up to the curb, a wise man flagged her down. Melinda nearly doubled over with laughter as she climbed out of the car.

"Greetings! I bring you tidings of great joy!" Karen shouted as she wrestled her robe's hood away from her face.

"Oh, Karen! You look fabulous! Is that a parka you've got on under that getup?"

"You bet," Karen said defiantly. "And long johns, two pairs of socks ... you name it and I'm wearing it. Remind me why I volunteered for this?"

"Because you're a pillar of the community," Melinda said. "And, oh yeah, Doc and I put you up to it. I just hope your professional expertise isn't needed tonight."

"Me, too," Karen turned toward the display, gathering her robe in her right hand as her boots crunched across the snow, Melinda right behind. "Especially since I'm wearing so many layers. I don't think I could run down a crazy farm animal tonight if I had to. Well, would you look at that." Karen pointed toward the corner.

A pickup pulling a small trailer had turned off Main just after Melinda. A man and a woman, bundled up in coveralls and thick knit caps, were now leading three goats on harnesses down the sidewalk.

"I get that it's a little cold out," Melinda gasped, "but do the goats need coats?"

The fleece blankets tied over the goats' brown backs were patterned with unmistakable colors: Two of the critters sported red-and-gold prints, and the larger animal, surely a male, sported a yellow-and-black wrap.

"Doc's not going to like this," Karen shook her head. "We're both Iowa State grads, and he's got a serious grudge against the U of I. That big goat better expect some teasing about his sweater."

The woman waved to Melinda and Karen as she steered the two smaller goats toward the nativity display. "Flossie and Florence always root for the Cyclones," she said.

Melinda wasn't sure how to respond. Karen, known for being unflappable in unusual situations, didn't miss a beat. She just smiled at the woman and reached for one of the harness leads. "So do I. Let's get them over to the manger scene. I think the rest of the animals are here."

"Biscuit always brings up the rear. He likes to really make an entrance," the woman gestured back at her husband and the male goat, who were just crossing the street.

Melinda hoped that meant Biscuit was used to crowds, as a small traffic jam was setting up on Main Street and the sidewalks were filling in with more visitors.

Most of the nativity's participants were already in place. John Olson, not yet in costume but bundled into his chore coveralls, hovered next to the small pen that enclosed his three prize sheep. Pumpkin, Karen's collie dog, was tethered to a corner of the manger, her watchful eyes trained on the ewes in the corral. There was no doubt which critter was Gus. The gray donkey, his lead secured to the corner post of the stable, was heartily enjoying the snack of stale grass he could reach on the display's thatched roof, rather than the pan of fresh hay at his feet.

Dylan Olson, dressed as Joseph, was tossing a bundle back and forth with his brother Tyler, the shepherd. To her horror, Melinda realized it was the doll that would soon star as Baby Jesus.

"Put that down," she hissed at the boys, glancing nervously up the street toward the Catholic church, where the choir members were gathering on the front steps. "All we need is one of the church ladies to see this."

The shepherd laughed and pitched the blanket-wrapped bundle to Melinda.

"Aw, the carolers haven't come by yet. Besides, it's not like Mary cares where her baby is."

Melinda turned to find Lauren, Dylan's girlfriend, taking a selfie with Gus, who let out a raucous "hee-aw" when the flash snapped on Lauren's phone. Melinda took a deep, calming breath and settled the poor doll in the manger, fixing its blue blanket and straightening the tinsel-garland halo on its bare head.

"Excuse me," Melinda approached Lauren, who was now adjusting her veil. "No smartphones, OK? It's not authentic."

Lauren rolled her eyes but tucked the phone in her robe.

"I already warned them about that," John leaned over the fence, "and I also said, absolutely no PDA. People don't want to see Mary and Joseph making out."

"Thanks, John," Melinda gave her neighbor a thumbs-up. "Where's your costume?"

Then she spotted Doc coming across the yard of the clinic, his steel-toed work boots visible under the hem of his robe. He had a bundle of cloth over his arm.

"Here, John, I deputize you as a member of the royal trio," Doc handed over the robe. "The guy with the calf called and says he's got the flu. The owner, I mean, not the calf. But that's fine, as we've got quite the menagerie as it is."

Doc grinned as he glanced around at the display. "Melinda, I think we're about all set. What the ..." His jaw dropped when he saw the goats.

"They don't like the cold, she says," Melinda whispered as Karen helped the man and woman tether Flossie, Florence and Biscuit to the ground pickets next to the manger.

Doc let out a quiet groan. "They're just a little nuts," he told Melinda in a low voice. "I mean the people, not the goats. The goats seem well-mannered enough, I've been doctoring them for years and never had a pinch of trouble with any of them. Figured I'd get the sanest animals I could find, and deal with the crazy people that come with them," Doc muttered out of the corner of his mouth. "Oh, no offense, John."

"None taken," John gestured for Melinda to hold his gloves while he adjusted his robe. "There. I'm ready. Wait now ... who's this?"

Melinda smothered a laugh inside her thick scarf as a young man with a professional-grade camera around his neck approached from the curb. "That, you guys, is a reporter from the Mason City newspaper. I'll just get out of the way." She started for her car as her friends groaned. "Remember, it's for the good of the community!"

Bill met her at the back door of Prosper Hardware, wearing one of the Santa hats Miriam first pressed upon them for Black Friday.

He had another one in his hand. "Here, put this on."

"I was foolish to think I'd get out of wearing some sort of costume myself," Melinda slapped the hat on her head.

"Everyone's wearing one," Diane trilled as she popped through the door that went into the store, the hinges letting out their usual screech. "Even your dad."

"That I have to see." Melinda gave her mom a quick hug. "I'm glad you could help out. If even a fraction of the people outside come in here, we'll be swamped tonight. Nice sweater, by the way." Diane's top showed a trio of felt evergreen trees on a tan background.

"Didn't want to get too crazy, but we have to get into the holiday spirit," she gave the pompom on her hat a flip, then settled her cap more squarely over her close-cropped white hair. "Why don't you get your coat upstairs and we'll set out the cookies and cupcakes on the sideboard?"

The store was already buzzing with holiday guests, but Melinda paused on the stairs to take it all in.

Prosper Hardware's pressed-tin ceiling glowed and the oak floors gleamed. The Christmas tree was filled with colored lights and glittery ornaments, and she saw Roger and Frank arranging an antique padded rocking chair between it and the window. She recognized the burgundy-and-white braided rug now set before the rocker as the one that normally anchored her parents' dining room table. Soft strains of classical holiday music drifted from the speakers Bill re-arranged in the corners of the store that afternoon.

The store's decorations were festive, yet simple. Everything looked perfect. All the effort, all the planning was paying off. "There's nowhere I'd rather be, right now," Melinda whispered.

"Isn't it lovely?" came a woman's voice from the top of the stairs. "I think we're almost ready."

She turned to see Mary Freitag step toward the landing, her white curls covered by a floppy red cap trimmed with crocheted white lace. The full skirt of her candy-striped dress came nearly to the tops of her black orthopedic shoes.

"Oh, Mary! I love it!" Melinda gave Mary a round of applause. "I'm so glad you agreed to play along. And where is Santa, by the way?"

"Oh, you know Santa, he shows up in the funniest places," Mary winked and set a pair of wire spectacles on her nose.

There was a rustling downstairs and the shuffling of boots on the oak floor. "Ho ho ho!" George's voice boomed out from the alcove that hid the store's restroom. "A Merry Christmas to all, and to all a good night!"

George turned to Bill, switching back to his usual soft tone. "How's that sound?"

"Perfect pitch, George. You sound like you stepped out of a cartoon. And I mean that in a good way."

"Excellent," George replied. "I've been working on it at home, you know."

"I've got my sleigh pulled up out back," Bill grinned and rubbed his hands together. "This is way too much fun. The heat's blasting in the truck, if you and Mrs. Claus are ready for transport over to the soup supper."

Melinda, Miriam and Diane arranged the platters of homemade cookies, cupcakes and candies on the sideboard. Esther, sporting a sweater embroidered with poinsettias and a Santa cat, helped set up a small table nearby offering coffee, warm cider and hot cocoa. The treats were soon snapped up by the crush of visitors already swarming the store's aisles.

Uncle Frank beamed at Melinda as he adjusted his new red suspenders. "Never seen a crowd quite like this. The weather turned just in time, it's not twenty below zero ... I think we'll have one of our best holiday open houses in years."

Roger stayed busy at the front door, handing out the Prosper Hardware stocking hats and hand-warmer packets. Diane and Esther watched over the refreshment tables and Bill and Frank wandered the aisles, helping shoppers pick out just the right gifts. Aunt Miriam's last-minute idea to set up a gift-wrapping station proved popular, and Diane soon had to join her sister there to keep the line moving.

Melinda stayed at the register, counting change and swiping credit cards as fast as she could. But no one seemed to be in a great hurry, as the long checkout line provided a chance to meet and greet both friends and strangers.

Melinda was touched by the thoughtful gifts that were slid her way across the counter: cozy hats and gloves, wrench sets, sweatshirts, and choices from the small selection of toys Frank and Miriam ordered especially for the holiday season. Packages of candy, the perfect way to top off a Christmas stocking, were also popular.

None of the gifts were fancy, or frivolous, or expensive. Instead, many were useful, and all chosen with care.

The first hour of the open house flew by in a flash. Soon, a siren sounded outside, its wail growing in volume until Prosper's only fire truck pulled up to the curb in front of the store. Frank hurried to the door, his excitement drawing the attention of the children already inside Prosper Hardware.

"I think someone's coming!" Frank shouted. The chatter in the line by the cash register died away and the store fell into an expectant silence. "Who could it be?"

Tony Bevins, wearing a green elf hat, hustled around the front of the cab and helped Santa and Mrs. Claus down from the truck. Screams of delight came from the children clustered by the store's front windows.

"Ho ho ho! Merry Christmas, everyone!" George stomped his shiny black boots on the mat just inside the door, pausing long enough to let all the children get a good look at Santa. Mary came in behind him, and Melinda heard excited gasps from customers of all ages.

"Well, look at all these wonderful children gathered here tonight," Santa exclaimed, his kind blue eyes sparkling.

"As soon as I get settled, I want to hear what everyone wants for Christmas! Mrs. Claus will take good notes, so I won't forget," he added, which brought giggles from many of the children.

The line to sit with Santa soon snaked around the front of the store. The sight of the fire truck, decorated with evergreen wreaths and garland, parked in front of Prosper Hardware drew more families to the building's front door.

Roger joined Melinda at the register, as all the knit caps were given away faster than expected. When it became clear that Roger couldn't keep up with sacking purchases, Bill came over to help.

"Is there a maximum occupancy in here?" Melinda asked as she slid a stack of purchases in Bill's direction.

"As a member of the fire department, I can confirm that number is one hundred-fifty," he shouted over the chatter and laughter echoing through the high-ceilinged store. "I'm sure we've had far more than that come in the door already, but people eventually move on down the street."

Melinda had just finished another sale when her phone vibrated in her pocket. "Just a second," she told the next woman in line.

Karen's number flashed on the screen. "This can't be good," she muttered, but gave the people waiting to check out a cheerful smile. "Bill, how about you take over the register for a second?"

"Melinda!" Karen shouted over the noise swirling around her. "Get your dad and Bill, go to the front door!"

"What?" Melinda put a palm over her other ear, trying to drown out the laughter and music. "What's wrong?"

"It's the goats!" Karen gasped. "The big guy, in the Hawkeyes' blanket? He got his lead off the picket, somehow. Pumpkin started barking and tried to herd him back to the manger, but he spooked and took off through the crowd. He's coming your way!"

"Stay at the register," Melinda told Bill, who gave her a confused look. "Dad, Mom, come on!"

"He's coming!" Melinda heard a man shout just as she and her parents made it out to the sidewalk. "That big goat's running down Main! He's a sneaky one, they tried to catch him but ..."

A murmur of excitement rippled through the crowd. Some of the revelers pushed themselves back against Prosper Hardware, while others, many of them teenagers, dashed off toward the live nativity.

"That's all we need," Roger groaned to Melinda. "A bunch of boys thinking they're going to be the big heroes. Hey!" he called to the bystanders. "Everybody, just step to the side, out of the way, it'll be fine."

The crowd in the next block started to shift. Melinda heard screams and laughter, then spotted a flash of black and yellow in the crush of people in front of the Watering Hole.

Biscuit dodged left and right, staying just free of the outstretched hands trying to slow him down. He bumped into one startled woman and Melinda saw a small paper bag soar into the air, then several doughnuts rain down on the crowd. Just as Karen feared, Biscuit was running straight toward Prosper Hardware.

"Biscuit," a woman's voice wailed. "Baby, come back here. Mama says it's OK. Biscuit …"

Melinda spotted the goat's owner running only a few feet behind, waiving her arms so frantically that if Biscuit happened to look back, her panic would probably cause him to increase his speed.

"Do you think we can take him?" Roger called to Melinda.

"*What*? Dad, are you serious?"

"Well, you outsmarted that ram last summer out on the road," Roger shouted, rubbing his hands together. "And he was three times this guy's size."

"He wasn't on a dead run," Melinda gasped. "And I just squeaked back into my car. I hid inside until Ed and Nathan came. They're the ones that got him in the trailer."

"I know this wasn't what you had in mind when you moved back here, honey," Roger rocked on his heels, craning his neck to peer up the street. "But if we don't grab him, he could tear all the way down to the co-op. Someone could get hurt. OK, here he comes. Get ready."

Biscuit dashed across Third Street and barreled into the crowd in front of the post office. One man tripped and fell to the sidewalk as he attempted to snatch Biscuit's lead, which was dragging on the ground and rattling, further spooking the poor animal.

He was charging right toward Roger. At the last second, Melinda pushed her father aside, hoping the frantic goat wouldn't get either of them with a direct hit from his horns. She felt the halter slide under her palm, and latched on. Biscuit let out an angry bellow and tacked to the right, pulling Melinda off her feet.

I'm glad I wore my puffy parka, she had time to think just before her backside hit the pavement and she started to slide. *I have to hold on, I can't let him get away ...*

"Whoa!" a familiar voice yelled. Then came a whooshing sound. Biscuit jerked to a stop, and so did Melinda. She glanced up to see a wise man running toward them, his robe flying behind him and a loop of rope in his hand.

She looked over at Biscuit, who was huffing and puffing but still on his feet. The lasso end of the rope was looped around his neck.

"Good toss, Doc!" someone shouted. Then everyone began to clap and cheer.

"Melinda, are you OK?" Doc handed the rope to Roger and helped her stand. She managed to answer with a nod. "That was quite a tackle! Maybe you could sign with the Vikings and go pro next year."

There was a gasp from the crowd and Melinda turned to see George running out the front door of Prosper Hardware, his Santa beard hanging at a precarious angle.

"I've never seen anything like it in my eighty-some years!" George shouted.

"I looked out just in time to see that goat come barreling down the street. I was going to run out here and nab him, but Mary stopped me." George sounded disappointed.

Melinda started to laugh, then couldn't stop. The idea of George, bundled up as Santa, taking down a crazed goat in a fleece sweater was just too much. "Well, I'm glad I could stop you from hurting yourself ... ummm, Santa."

George's eyes widened. "Thank you, my dear girl!" he boomed in his Santa voice. He discretely adjusted his fake beard, then turned to face the strange looks coming from a cluster of nearby children. "We have goats at the North Pole, you know, not just reindeer."

That seemed to pass muster with all but the oldest kids. Santa gently shooed all of them toward the front door of the store. "Well, everybody, let's get back inside to those cookies! I think there's a few little children I still need to speak with tonight."

Roger gave Melinda a thumbs-up and helped Santa with crowd control. Doc, with his wise man robe still tied over his coveralls, gave Biscuit a quick pat down. "He should be OK. Just a case of stage fright, is all."

Biscuit's owner caught up to the group, puffing with exertion. "My husband's bringing the trailer around," she told Melinda, then turned and threw her arms around Biscuit. "Oh, my baby! Are you hurt? Thank goodness you're safe. I've got some carrots for you." Biscuit stamped a hoof and grunted, then eagerly accepted the snack.

The woman's husband emerged from the crowd, gave Doc a sheepish look, and guided Biscuit to the trailer. Karen had already helped the man load the other two goats at the live nativity, Melinda learned later, gently suggesting they start for home before the traffic heading out of town increased.

"Well, we almost made it to the end before chaos broke out," Doc said as the truck and trailer pulled away. "Another half hour, and it would've been a raging success."

"It still was," Roger clapped Doc on the shoulder. "Prosper's never had a live nativity before that anyone can recall. I think you've got yourself a new tradition, Doc."

Doc shook his head as he rolled up his lasso. "It's been a few years since I've needed this thing. Last time, it was a bull that wouldn't cooperate. As for next year's nativity, we'll drive the pickets down sooner, before the ground gets so frozen. And I might have to expand my search for some show goats."

The last customers trickled out of Prosper Hardware just before nine. Aunt Miriam lowered herself to a folding chair next to the cookie table with a satisfied sigh.

"Another holiday open house under our belts," Miriam reached for a thick square of walnut-cranberry fudge and took a generous bite. "Thank you, everyone, for your hard work.

Let's get things settled and go home. We can tidy up in the morning. Santa, I expect your reindeer will be itching to take off soon?"

George chuckled and removed his fake beard. "This was the most fun I've had in some time. The suit's a little cumbersome, but what a hoot. You won't believe the requests I got, all these smart watches and tablets and such. I just smiled and nodded, hoped the parents were listening and knew what their kids were jabbering about."

Mary removed her Mrs. Claus bonnet and sighed. "I just feel bad for that one little girl. She said all she wanted for Christmas was for her dad to find a job."

"What?" Diane exclaimed. "Oh, that's so sad."

"I asked her what else she wanted," George shook his head. "Maybe a doll, or some coloring books, at least. But she insisted she didn't need anything for herself."

"We sometimes forget that others are far worse off than we are," Aunt Miriam gave Uncle Frank a meaningful look, then rose from her chair to give her husband a quick peck on the cheek before she boxed up the few cookies remaining on the trays.

Bill pulled out his wallet and stepped over to George. "Looks like I need to pay up, Santa."

"Oh, yes, that's right," George snickered. "There's that little wager for us to take care of. I guess you're on the losing end, Bill."

"What's all this about?" Melinda looked up from behind the counter, where she was rubbing first-aid ointment into an asphalt scrape on her wrist.

"Now, no offense, Melinda," George replied gently. "But when you get a bunch of farm animals together, especially ones that don't know each other and aren't used to crowds, you're bound to have an escapee or two."

He gave Bill a wink. "I guess all my decades of experience helped me place my bet."

"I had my money on the donkey," Bill said, then sighed as he handed George a five-dollar bill.

* 15 *

Melinda was very proud of herself. So far, she had only snitched five chocolate stars out of the package beckoning to her from the kitchen counter.

It wasn't even nine in the morning, and she had hours of cookie baking and decorating ahead of her. But this time, as she passed the spot by the kitchen door, she reached for a different zip-top bag.

"These walnuts are a good source of protein, so they're OK," she explained to Hobo, who had his nose aimed high, sniffing curiously at the ever-growing stack of baking ingredients. "For me, I mean, but not for you." She gave Hobo an appraising glance and reached for the canvas tote bags hanging on a nail by the refrigerator.

"I think it's best if these goodies head out to the back porch until I'm ready to leave for Ed and Mabel's."

Hobo's brown eyes lit up at the mention of their closest neighbors, a couple in their early seventies who were Melinda's first call when she needed someone to do chores if she was going away. Or for just about anything else, for that matter. Mabel was a childhood friend of Ada's, and she and Ed knew their way around the Schermann farm as well as Melinda did.

"I know, they're two of your favorite people," she gave Hobo a reassuring pat on the head. "Mine, too. Ed's shown me how to wrangle the sheep and outsmart the chickens, and Mabel's passed on her love of canning and gardening. But I'm sorry, they're not coming here today. I'm going there."

Angie was meeting Melinda at Mabel and Ed's, along with the Bauers' old friends Will and Helen Emmerson, who lived over on the blacktop.

The Emmersons' home was seriously damaged during the July tornado that ripped through the rural neighborhood, and they lived with their son's family for several weeks until their house was repaired. Helen had only superficial injuries, but Ed's right leg was in a brace for several weeks due to a compound fracture. Melinda had met the Emmersons just once, at Angie and Nathan's September workday to finish their new barn, and was eager to get to know them better.

She sacked up the chocolate stars and the walnuts, and added a tub of sour cream from the refrigerator. It was cold enough on the unheated back porch to keep the sour cream fresh until she was ready to leave. A plastic tote already out on the bench held several bags of powdered sugar, along with a copy of the Schermann family's sour-cream cookie recipe. She was too afraid to take the original out of the house, worried she might lose it.

The other ladies would bring recipes to share, along with many of the other ingredients. Mabel would provide the flour, butter and eggs, and Ed and Will had appointed themselves to the quality-control committee.

Melinda knew she would do plenty of taste-testing as well. She changed into a clean sweatshirt and her nicest sweatpants, then loaded her contributions in the car. Hobo lost interest in the preparations once she moved the food to the back porch, and was already snoring away on the crazy quilt in Horace's old bedroom by the time she left.

"It looks like a Christmas card out here," she marveled as she glanced around the sleepy farm yard, where a few snowflakes dusted the maple and oak trees' bare branches and settled on the massive evergreen wreath still anchored next to the barn door.

There was the faint, comforting aroma of wood smoke in the air, and she spied a gray plume rising from the southwest, where someone was burning a late-season brush pile on this calm, cold day.

As she drove down the lane and turned north on the gravel, Melinda wondered who lived at that farm. Several stalwart rows of evergreens sheltered its north and east sides, making it difficult for her to get a good view of the house and outbuildings. That acreage was the opposite direction from the way she always traveled, so she had never driven by the place. Still, it was less than a mile from her farm, and she should get to know all of her neighbors better.

"Maybe I'll remember to ask Ed and Mabel today," she said as her car glided over the one-lane creek bridge and approached the crossroads just south of the Bauers' place.

"I really need to meet more people. What am I supposed to do? Call people and invite myself for dinner? Maybe, when spring comes, I'll make an effort reach out more."

Angie's car was already in Ed and Mabel's yard when Melinda turned in the drive. Their square, gray farmhouse was set off with fresh cream trim and rested comfortably close to the road. Sammy, their golden lab, hustled over and barked her welcome before Melinda could even cut the engine.

"Hey, there!" Ed waved from the back door, a bulky cardigan covering his thin, wiry frame. He made his way down the back steps and started for Melinda's hatchback with the stride of a farmer half his age.

"Sammy, let Melinda out of the car, my goodness! Here, hand me that tote."

"I'm sort of surprised you've hung around for this," she teased Ed. "You'll have no peace today."

Ed only laughed and reached for the sacks of powdered sugar. "Are you kidding? I wouldn't miss this for anything. It's my job to sample everything and make sure it's made just right. And Will's coming to help me with that."

The Bauers' kitchen already smelled wonderful, thanks to a pot of freshly brewed coffee and something savory bubbling away in a slow cooker. The room was spotless but comfortably dated, decorated in shades of rust, brown and cream. Short evergreen garlands were tacked over the windows' ruffled valances, and a ceramic village glowed on a narrow table by the walk-through to the living room.

"Come in, come in," Mabel looked up briefly from reaching into the refrigerator. Her white hair was carefully curled and styled as usual, and she had a holly-print apron tied over her sweatshirt and jeans. Angie sat at the kitchen table, pouring peanuts and dried cranberries into bowls. She paused long enough to give Melinda a quick wave.

"We're going to set up assembly lines," Angie tipped her auburn curls toward the adjacent dining room. "We'll do some almond-bark candies first while the cookie dough sets up in the fridge. Did you bring Horace's mom's recipe? I can't wait to try it."

"If you want to get the mixer going, I've got the margarine sticks out there by the stove," Mabel called over her shoulder as she pulled a stack of mixing bowls from a high cabinet.

"And help yourself to the coffee. There's bran muffins, but they are in the refrigerator. We need all the counter space we can get."

Before Melinda could get the bowl of sour-cream cookie dough sealed with plastic wrap, a truck arrived in the driveway. "There's Helen and Will," Mabel called toward the living room, where Ed had his feet up in front of the television. "Dear, how about you help them get inside?"

Melinda was pleased to see Will's easy stride, rather than the painful gait he struggled with at Angie and Nathan's just a few months before. But he was still in great spirits at the potluck, eager to reconnect with neighbors and friends, and was that way today as well.

"We're loading down with goodies, just like Santa's elves," Will joked to Ed as he handed over a plastic sack of supplies. He was much shorter than Ed, and had a portly frame that indicated he was an expert eater. Melinda recalled how Will asked her to fill his plate at Angie and Nathan's potluck, then made quick work of two kinds of potato salad along with an assortment of desserts as well as a hamburger.

"What's in here?" Ed's brow furrowed as he set one sack on the counter. "Helen, do you need bricks to make cookies?"

"That's almond bark," Helen answered, then lifted a plastic container out of her tan canvas bag. She was a petite woman, with kind brown eyes and iron-gray hair.

"Cornbread to go with the chili," she told Mabel. "Where should I park this?"

"Anywhere there's a clear space," Mabel shrugged.

The women soon had cookie sheets covered in wax paper set around on the kitchen table. Mabel melted batches of almond bark in the microwave, then hurried them over to the assembly line before they cooled.

"Thank goodness we don't need to get out the old double broiler," Mabel said to Helen while lounging against the counter, occasionally popping the microwave open to give a bowl of vanilla almond bark a quick stir.

"Oh, what a pain that used to be," Helen shook her head, then turned to Angie and Melinda. "Back in the prehistoric era, girls, candy making was a touch-and-go business. You had to get the water in the double boiler hot, but not too hot. Then wait for the candy coating to warm. Then make sure you didn't burn it. This is so much easier."

"Sounds complicated." Melinda took a warm bowl of candy coating from Mabel and quickly dumped in several cups of peanuts. "Helen, what kind of cookies are you making today? I hear you have a family favorite to share."

"Will's grandmother made these wonderful molasses cookies," Helen replied as she added generous cups of dried cranberries and walnuts to a bowl of vanilla almond bark.

"One of his great aunts taught at the little country school just down the road many years ago, and she always handed these cookies out at the Christmas program. The school was just past the crossroads," Helen added, noticing Melinda's interest in the topic. "On the east side of the road, just north of the creek."

"I had no idea." Melinda knew there was a field driveway there, but never suspected it was ever used for more than tractors. What else didn't she know about her neighborhood?

"They had a school every two miles," Angie was saying. "The next one to the south was across from our church. Well, I brought along my mom's recipe for peanut butter cookies with chocolate stars. Today will give me a head start on the ten dozen I need to have made by next week."

"Ten dozen?" Melinda's spatula froze in midair. Mabel made a shooing gesture with her hands, and Melinda doubled her speed before the almond bark could harden.

"Yeah," Angie sighed. "I'm on the committee for the children's program at church, and we're having a cookie walk to raise money for the Sunday School. I'm running out of time, as somehow I ended up directing the pageant ... again. My Joseph isn't the most pleasant kid to work with."

Melinda shook her head in sympathy. She knew how stressful it could be to find yourself at the helm of a large community event. And Angie and Nathan had two little girls, as well as a full-scale farm to manage. "Does this boy not know his lines?"

"Worse," Angie rolled her eyes. "He knows them. And those for every other kid. A few are still learning their parts, and he said he didn't want to work with these amateurs. That's the very word he used, by the way. And he's ten."

"Sounds like he's trying too hard," Mabel brought Helen another bowl of almond bark and whisked an empty dish over to the sink, where she put it to soak. "That boy is probably more critical of himself than he is of anyone else."

Helen reached over and patted Angie on the arm. "I used to teach Sunday school, dear. Just ignore his rants. He'll see he can't get a rise out of you, and he'll knock it off." She then turned to Melinda. "So, tell me about these sugar cookies you're making, Melinda."

By the time they paused for a late lunch, the dining room table was filled with rows of candies set out on waxed paper and cooling racks stacked with cookies.

"All that's left is the fun part," Mabel said as she set out bowls of chili. "We'll whip up the frosting after we eat and get those cut-out cookies decorated."

Ed and Will joined the women at the kitchen table, bringing hearty appetites despite the all cookies they snitched throughout the morning. Talk quickly turned to everyone's Christmas plans. Angie was the only one not hosting overnight guests that year. Will glanced at the calendar on the kitchen wall and reminded Helen they should get their packages to the Prosper post office as soon as possible.

"It's been busy, I know," Melinda said as she reached for another piece of Helen's spicy cornbread. She wanted that recipe, too. "I had a long wait in line one day last week."

"Glenn Hanson's an old buddy of mine," Will replied as he added more chili powder to his bowl. "I saw him at church yesterday. That post office has been a zoo. And man, the stuff he hears. It sounds like people feel the need to unload all their grievances and gossip along with their packages."

Everyone laughed, except Melinda. She dreaded what might come next, and she was right. Will repeated Glenn's story about the mysterious car at the Benniger farm.

Ed dropped his spoon into his chili. "You don't say? My mother was tied into that Benniger clan."

He turned to Melinda and explained. "You know Auggie, of course. He and I are second cousins. Haven't seen him lately. Wonder if he knows what the deal is?"

Melinda took note of yet another connection in this rural community. Her family had also lived there for generations. What were the odds she was distantly related to at least one of her new neighbors?

Before she could make a joke about long-lost cousins, though, Will pressed on.

"Well, sounds like it might be some relative staying at the house," he continued in a hushed tone. "Glenn's carrier saw a car with Wisconsin plates out there again on Saturday. Took the info down and ran it through some database. You'll never believe who the car's registered to."

Mabel put up an interrupting hand. "OK, OK, stop this. You two are worse than some old biddies at a church social." She turned to Melinda. "My dear, are you all right?"

Melinda swallowed and tried to steady her voice. The story had already spread, but at least she could warn her neighbors to be sensitive to Auggie's feelings.

"Glenn told me all about it last week," she admitted. "I didn't know Auggie's connection to the place, but he got very upset when I brought it up at the store. I wished I hadn't. He left the store in a hurry, he wouldn't talk about it."

Some kind of understanding look passed between Ed and Mabel. Mabel shook her head and sighed. "You don't think?" she said to her husband.

"Yep, it's Evan's car," Will chimed in. "No wonder Auggie got upset. Either he's heard the gossip, or he's already talked to Evan, which would be a step forward given how things are. But Glenn said it had to be Evan Kleinsbach's car, no doubt."

"Who's Evan Kleinsbach?" Angie interrupted, waving her spoon. "Is he a fugitive or something?"

Ed quickly explained the situation. He knew more about the rift between Auggie and his son than what Melinda had heard at Prosper Hardware.

"Has anyone tried to contact David yet?" Ed asked Will. "He either knows all about it, or he should."

"Glenn heard David is looking after the place these days, but didn't know how to get ahold of him. And since this Evan guy is family, Glenn hesitated to call the sheriff."

Will paused. "Ed, do you have David's number?"

Ed was already up from the table and hurrying into the den. "You bet I do."

Melinda heard the snap of a drawer latch and a rustling of paper, then a mumbled conversation. Everyone waited.

"Yep, it's Evan all right," Ed nodded as he came back to the kitchen. "David said Evan called him a few weeks ago, said he needed a place to stay for a while. David thought it was odd, but he wanted to help. He told Evan where to find the key that's hidden out there."

Ed was about to sit back down, then stopped.

"Will, it's too cold for us to putter around out in the barn while the ladies finish up these cookies. Maybe we should take a little drive."

"I don't believe this," Mabel huffed as she gathered up the chili bowls. "Ed, what exactly are you going to do? Head over there and knock on the door?"

"Well, yes," Ed shrugged. "What if Evan needs help, or just a listening ear? He's my cousin, after all."

"Distant cousin," Mabel snapped.

"I'm about all the close relation he's got around here," Ed persisted, crossing his arms.

"Other than his parents, of course," Mabel gave her husband an exasperated look, then rolled her eyes. "Ed Bauer, you always go ahead and do whatever you want, no matter what I say. I guess this time's no different."

"I take it you're staying home," Ed muttered.

"Of course I am," Mabel gestured at the dining-room table stacked with cookies. "I've got better things to do."

"I'll go," Melinda said, then almost wished she'd stayed quiet. She had to admit, she was curious about both the once-grand house and its mysterious visitor. And if Ed and Will were so determined to drive over there …

"Maybe that's not such a bad idea," Will suggested before Melinda could excuse herself from Ed and Will's plan. "Melinda, you know Auggie. And Evan's around your age, and so is his wife. They have a little girl. Things might be more social if it's not just us two geezers coming around."

Mabel's stance softened. "Well, I don't know if it's our business, but I guess it can't hurt."

"I don't recall asking," Ed countered, but gave his wife a quick peck on the cheek before he went to find his coat.

Mabel reached for a plastic serving tray decorated with a snowman, quickly rinsed and dried it, then turned for the dining room.

"If you're going to make a house call," she said over her shoulder, "you don't want to show up empty-handed."

* 16 *

Melinda sat quietly in the backseat, the plate of cookies and candy in her lap, while Ed and Will debated several theories about Evan Kleinsbach's sudden return to Prosper.

"I know he's had some troubles in the past," Ed mused as he steered his car east into town. "But I don't know all the details. Haven't seen him in years."

"Wonder what he's doing here?" Will shook his head as he messed with the radio to find a country station he liked. "Something must have happened. Or maybe he's just here for the holidays?"

"Little early for that, especially for someone with adult responsibilities," Ed responded. "He's, what, thirty-eight or so? It's not like he's a college kid."

Melinda wrapped her arms around the treat plate and pulled its plastic wrap tighter as Ed took the bend in Main Street next to Prosper Feed Co.

She cringed as she thought of Auggie, processing orders in the co-op's office, while she and her neighbors drove out to the Benniger farm to stick their noses into his personal affairs. Ed was Evan's family, too, but Melinda had to agree with Mabel. Maybe this wasn't such a great idea. And when Melinda first came back to this area, hadn't she rolled her eyes at how nosy people could be, even if it was well-intentioned?

But this was different, Melinda told herself. She knew how hard it was to face sudden changes in life. And how tempting it was to return home so you could start again. Maybe she could offer encouragement to Evan and his wife, Melinda reasoned, be a friend when they needed one most.

Main Street reverted to a county highway once it passed the water tower behind the veterinary clinic. There was a short stretch of homes pressed close together, and then the road was back out in the country.

Just past where the blacktop bridged the river, Ed took a quick left and started down a gravel road as curvy as Melinda's way home was straight. Thick clusters of trees blocked the river on the left, and pastures studded with trees fronted the other side of the road.

She couldn't believe how ruggedly beautiful the terrain was in the river bottom, and how everything sparkled in the fresh dusting of snow. She again chastised herself for rarely leaving her well-worn path from the farm to Prosper Hardware to her parents' place in Swanton and back again. When Ed said, "well, this is the corner," she felt her pulse pick up and she leaned forward to get a better look at the three-way intersection.

It was just as Doc described it, a right turn into another gravel road that rose away from the river. They passed an unassuming farm, then a stately windbreak soon appeared on the left at the crest of the hill, growing larger as the car pulled up the steep grade. Through the protective trees, Melinda could just make out the shadowy outlines of a barn and outbuildings. The house, however, had yet to show itself.

A battered metal mailbox, its nameplate brackets long ago rusted away, slumped across from the driveway. Will gave a low whistle when the car turned into the lane.

"Better give it a little gas there, Ed," he suggested. "No one's cleared this drive, there's just these tire tracks. Maybe we should have brought my truck."

"The snow's not so deep," Ed replied. "Besides, we've got a strong young person in the back, I'm sure she's handy with a shovel." He glanced in the rearview mirror and gave Melinda a big grin.

"My coveralls are at home," she gave Ed a pointed look. She would be forty in a few months, but age was always a relative number, especially in a community with so many senior residents. "Besides, Mabel said my job is to guard the cookies from you two so there's some left to share."

The view from the lane was magnificent, with the left-side pasture stretching down to the snaking dark line of trees along the river. Off to the northwest, the grid of Prosper's few streets and buildings was but a small island in the expanse of gently rolling, snow-covered fields. It was no wonder that, more than one hundred and thirty years ago, someone had chosen this very spot for a homestead.

The farm's outbuildings, however, were breathtaking for another reason. Their cracked boards were a weathered brown, any red paint long since worn away. A caved-in roof topped what might have been a chicken house. The barn, while still on its feet, had a definite southward slump to its shoulders. While the scraggly dead grass between the house and barn may have been mowed during the summer, the weeds and native plants had long ago reclaimed the rest of their territory.

"That house is still standing tall," Ed shook his head in amazement. "But then, it was built to do just that. I haven't been over here in, what, ten years? When I was a kid, a great-uncle and aunt lived here, and we came over for a big family reunion every July."

"Just look at that trim work," Will marveled. "And those walls must be thick. It would take more than a few years of neglect to topple this house."

The historic home was sturdy and proud, its red brick walls set off by the heavy white casements that outlined its tall, narrow windows.

Generous gables punctuated the steep slate roof that crowned the two-story home. Sturdy columns supported a turned-post porch that wrapped around two sides of the house. Melinda glimpsed what appeared to be a glass-walled solarium gazing out over the river valley.

The gravel drive made a grand, circular sweep through the yard. She could imagine high-stepping horses pulling shiny black carriages up to the home's wide porch steps, and men and women in elegant Victorian dress sweeping their way into a grand hall. The house was impressive, but there was something odd about it. Melinda decided it was simply out of place in the middle of these farm fields, like an overdressed lady showing up for a barbecue.

A faint glow radiated from one of the front windows, but the rest of the house appeared dark. A relatively new car huddled next to the porch, as if seeking shelter from the winds that would race across this hilltop on stormy nights.

"Wisconsin plates," Will pointed, excitement rising in his voice. "Looks like they're still here. Ed, how about you take the lead, being you're family and all."

"Sure thing," Ed pulled up next to the other car, then reached around to take the plate of treats from Melinda. "Well, let's see what's going on."

A few footprints broke up the skim of snow on the brick sidewalk, which was laid out in an elaborate herringbone pattern. It was clear that no detail, no expense, had been spared when the house was built.

But the home's tumble-down condition was unmistakable the closer the vistors came to the veranda. The railings' white paint was cracked and faded, and some of the spindles were broken. The porch floor's wide wooden boards had a distinctive slant, and Melinda cringed when her next step released a protesting creak.

An elaborate iron plate surrounded what may have once been a button-style doorbell. Ed grimaced at the dirty black wires that snaked up from the contraption, and instead rapped a staccato on one of the two paneled front doors. There was no sound or movement inside, but they waited. Melinda was studying a cardboard-covered crack in one of the entry's frosted windows when the door suddenly flew open.

"Can I help you?" The man hesitated and shifted his feet, as if trying to politely greet his guests and still block their view into the house.

He was the right age to be Evan, with soft brown eyes and short brown hair flecked with a few hints of gray. Melinda decided Evan had been handsome once, but his face was now drawn and pale, and there were heavy bags under his eyes. His jeans were creased and his sweatshirt faded.

"Evan ... is it you?" Ed began.

The younger man's eyes widened and he pulled back. "Who are you? I'm sorry, I ..." For a moment Melinda was afraid he might shut the door in their faces.

"I'm Ed Bauer," Ed tried gently. "If you're who I think you are, I'm your distant cousin. We're not here to make trouble. I talked to David this afternoon." The man's shoulders suddenly relaxed. "We just wanted to come by and see if you needed anything. That is, if you really are Evan Kleinsbach."

"Yes," Evan gave a sigh of relief and traces of a smile appeared in the sad lines around his mouth. Now that he was a little more at ease, Melinda could not miss the obvious resemblance to Auggie.

"Yes, I am. Sorry, you just startled me. I ... we ... haven't had any company yet. Dave said we are OK to stay as long as we want, and ... wait. You're Ed Bauer? Do you live over west of town, in a gray house?"

"I sure do," Ed offered a handshake and Evan accepted it. "Haven't seen you in years, Evan."

"We were out to your place once for a family thing, when I was a kid," his tired eyes lit up over some pleasant memory. "I remember your house. And your wife, she was so kind. Carol, maybe? Or ..."

"Mabel," Ed nodded. "Her name's Mabel."

Evan paused and looked past Ed, as if he just noticed Will and Melinda. "Oh, sorry, where are my manners? Please, everyone, come in out of the cold."

Evan's gaze fastened on the tray of cookies and candy with a yearning that suddenly made Melinda sad. It was

Christmas, after all, an especially hard time of year for anyone struggling in life and living in such a desolate place.

The vestibule was stuffy with dust. A tired hall tree leaned in one corner, its fourth leg broken. "Here, you can take off your coats," Evan offered graciously, then hesitated.

"Or, maybe you'll want to leave them on. It's a bit chilly. I kicked up the furnace but, you know old houses ..." his voice trailed off as he put a shoulder to the heavy interior door and motioned them inside.

It took Melinda's eyes a moment to adjust to the gloom. The brocade curtains blanketing the tall windows were pushed wide, but the ceiling was high and only one floor lamp was switched on in a corner. A blaze burned merrily behind the tiled fireplace's elegant grate, and a worn couch and chair huddled close to the fire. Two air mattresses napped near a large heat register in the floor, their surfaces unmade tumbles of pillows and blankets.

The plaster walls, once painted an elegant shade of sage green, were depressingly bare. Lighter patches indicated where artwork and photos once graced the cavernous space. Despite the fire, the former sitting room's boundaries remained dark and chilly. A lump of dusty white sheets in one corner indicated the room's few pieces of furniture were here when Evan arrived. Imposing oak pocket doors closed off the rest of the house, and a dreary hallway wandered off in the other direction.

The house was ... she could think of no better word for it ... forlorn. And Evan's spirits seemed to match the house's mood, no matter how he tried to put on a smile for his guests. Will gave her a worried look then glanced at Ed, who was focused on Evan's attempt at social chatter.

"Well, we got into town just two weeks ago," Evan was saying as he snatched a tiny sock off the parquet floor. "Not sure how long we'll stay, but it's a fine place for now. Thought we'd come home for the holidays, you know."

Evan paused and Melinda saw the slump in his shoulders, even as he tried to keep his tone light.

Ed seemed to be searching for the right words. "I know you don't always see eye-to-eye with your parents, Evan," he offered gently. Evan stiffened a bit, but made no attempt to deny it. "Do they ... do they know you're here?"

"I talk to Mom once in a while." he turned his back to Ed and reached for two dirty plates stacked on a side table. "Let me get these into the kitchen. I'll be right back."

Ed gave Will and Melinda a cautious look. "He didn't answer me," Ed whispered. "I don't know what to think."

Evan returned, rubbing his hands on worn dishtowel, his expression more cheerful. "Here, everyone, have a seat," he gestured to the sagging olive-green couch, then settled on the ratty, overstuffed brown chair nearby.

"I'm Will Emmerson," Will said suddenly. Melinda realized that, with the strangeness of the situation, she also hadn't introduced herself.

"And I'm Melinda Foster," she tried for an encouraging smile. "I live just south of Ed and Mabel, about a mile. Will, here, is also their neighbor."

"It's good to meet you," Evan extended his hand to first Melinda and then Will. His grip was weaker than Melinda expected, and his skin felt thin and cool.

"We're having a baking party at our house today," Ed quickly added in the awkward silence that followed. "In case you're wondering why half my neighborhood came along."

"We brought treats," Melinda lifted the tray off the side table and handed it to Evan, who took only one molasses cookie but seemed inclined to grab a handful. "We wanted to welcome you to town, Evan."

"I'm sure you're wondering how we knew you were here," Ed took a peanut cluster off the tray and passed it to Will.

"Well, yes," Evan admitted. "We haven't been out and about much yet."

The snacks lowered the tension in the room, but Evan didn't rise to get napkins or offer his guests anything to drink. They had surprised him, that was for sure, but glancing around at the sparseness of the sitting room, Melinda wondered what Evan had in the house to eat. She had unzipped her coat, but wasn't sure if she wanted to remove it.

"Postal carrier saw your car last week," Will explained. "I'm afraid you've caused quite a stir in town, Evan. People know this place has been empty for a while."

"Oh, yes, of course," he said with a small smirk. "I forgot about how everyone in a small town knows everyone's business." He paused, looking at Will and Ed. "No offense."

"None taken," Ed just shrugged. "Post office ran your license plates, figured out it was you. When I heard, I called up David and confirmed it. Don't worry, no one's called the sheriff or anything."

"That's good to know," Evan said a bit wryly. "Especially since I got approval from Dave to be here."

Melinda saw a need to steer the conversation away from the fact that people were basically spying on Evan.

"So, what brings you back to Prosper?" she smiled and all but shoved the cookie and candy tray into Ed's hands, indicating he should pass it around again.

Evan took another bite of his cookie and took his time chewing. "Well, my wife and I ..."

"Your wife?" Ed sat up straighter and looked around. "Is she here? I've never had the chance to ..."

"No," Evan answered, almost in a whisper. "No, Carrie's not here, Ed. In fact, we're ... well, we're not together anymore. At least, we won't be for some time, if ever."

"I'm sorry to hear that," Will finally said, as Ed seemed embarrassed into silence.

"So, Evan, what do you do?" Melinda tried again. "You must have a good job over in ... Madison, right? Any place that gives their employees such a nice stretch of time off at Christmas must be ..."

"I lost my job," Evan answered through gritted teeth. "I got laid off six weeks ago."

He looked down, stubbing the parquet floor with the toe of his worn tennis shoe. "Then Carrie left a few weeks after that. December first came around, and I didn't have the rent.

Told the landlord I'd get it, somehow, to give us time. But when a week went by, well, he kicked us out."

"That's a tough break, Evan," Ed said quietly. "Sounds pretty harsh to only get a week's notice. I could see maybe a fine or something, but ..."

"Actually," Evan said bitterly, "we didn't have the money for November's rent, either."

No one said anything. Evan looked at the floor, then put his head in his hands.

"I didn't have anywhere for us to go," his voice wavered, then he sniffled. "Motels were so expensive, and ..."

Melinda saw movement out of the corner of her eye. A little girl with a red knit cap pulled over a mass of dark curls was watching them from a sliver of a gap between the pocket doors. Melinda smiled at the girl and gave her a little wave.

Evan looked up, then behind him. "Chloe, it's OK," he said in a soothing voice, then brightened a bit. "We have company. Why don't you come in and say hello?"

Chloe nudged the doors with her arm and slipped through. Right behind her was a stunning tortoiseshell cat with green eyes.

"Daisy and I were playing upstairs," Chloe told her father. "Daddy, this house is so big. You could get lost in it!"

"That's why I want you to stay down on this floor, OK?" Evan gave her a quick kiss on the forehead. The little girl, also in faded jeans and a sweatshirt, spied the tray of cookies and her eyes widened in surprise. Evan laughed and nodded his approval.

"Yes, you can have one. Just one, now. We'll save the rest for later."

Chloe smiled dreamily as she settled on the faded cushion of a nearby footstool and nibbled the chocolate star from one of Angie's peanut butter cookies. Daisy jumped up next to her, but Chloe pulled the cookie out of the cat's reach.

"You see why I had to come back," Evan nodded toward his little girl. "She'd be so scared in a shelter. And so many places wouldn't take Daisy, and she's part of the family, too.

None of our friends had room and, well, I don't know what I'm going to do. Chloe's only four, so she's not in school yet. Dave was kind enough to help us out. We'll stay through the holidays, I guess, and then, I just don't know."

Melinda looked around the shabby sitting room and peered into the empty dining hall. Deep shadows were already gathering there, only hazy light coming through the room's leaded-glass windows as the sun slid toward the west. Darkness came so early this time of year, with Christmas less than two weeks away.

Will was making small talk with Evan about the weather, trying to fill the awkward silence in the room. Melinda glanced over at Ed and saw the heartbreak on his face.

"Evan," Ed cut in kindly. "Might I trouble you for a glass of water? Is the kitchen ..."

"Sure, Ed," Evan pointed down the hallway. "Right through there. Help yourself."

Chloe savored her cookie one bite at a time. Melinda was about to ask Chloe what she wanted Santa to bring this year, then stopped when she realized Santa may not come at all.

"I really like your kitty, Chloe," she said instead. "Daisy is such a pretty name."

Chloe gave Daisy a soft pat on the head. "When I was a baby, she was a baby. Daisy really likes living here. Yesterday, she found a toy mouse to play with, it was in the kitchen behind the stove."

Melinda cringed, but only said, "Wow, I bet Daisy liked that. Does she sleep with you at night?"

"Oh, yes," Chloe nodded. "Right by me. And she loves to sit by the fire. Daddy says we're camping. But we are just indoors this time."

Ed returned from the kitchen, a strange tension in his shoulders. "Well, Evan, I'm glad we stopped by," he tried for a smile. "I suppose we'd better get back. You just keep the cookie plate for now."

"Thanks for coming," Evan stood to shake hands. How different he seemed from the hesitant man who answered the door less than an hour before. Melinda hoped the chance to share his troubles had brought Evan some comfort.

Ed reached in his coat pocket for a pen and scrap of paper. "Here, let me give you my number. You need anything, you call. We're just fifteen minutes away."

Evan gratefully took the note, glanced at it and put it in his jeans pocket. "I will, Ed. Thanks. That means a lot to me. Here, I'll show you to the door."

Chloe came into the vestibule with her father and waved energetically to her visitors as Ed's car circled the drive. Melinda and Will waved back, and Ed tooted the horn. Chloe's face broke into a big grin.

They started down the lane, Ed trying to keep the car in the snowy tracks. There was a moment of strained silence. Then everyone started talking at once.

"Good Lord," Will sputtered. "I didn't know what to expect, but ..."

"How are they going to keep warm?" Melinda exclaimed. "Did you feel that draft? Was it coming from the ..."

"I don't believe this," Ed groaned. "He's just squatting in there. It's getting way too cold for that. And with a little girl and a cat ..."

The car fell silent again. After it slid to a stop at the intersection with the river road, Ed glanced in the rearview mirror and put the car in park, trying to collect his thoughts.

"If you had told me this was going on, I never would have believed you," Ed slapped a hand on his leg.

"I checked that kitchen over. A bag of cat food and a bag of litter, some peanut butter and bread and cereal and a few cans of soup. There's some lunch meat in the fridge, and a little carton of milk."

"Chloe said Daisy found a toy mouse yesterday," Melinda said darkly.

"You know that house is full of mice, and very few of them are dead," Will interjected. "And who knows what else is living in there? I wouldn't want that little girl roaming around on her own, either."

"That kitchen was so empty and dusty," Ed muttered. "Who knows what the bathroom looks like? I almost don't want to know. I can't believe David allowed this."

"Maybe he was afraid what would happen if he didn't say yes," Will said sadly. "Evan's got nowhere else to turn. If he had other options, I don't think he ever would have come back here like this."

Melinda had quickly recognized the heartbreak in Evan's kind eyes. The despair, the struggle, the loss of direction. Not so long ago, she'd been wandering through her days, too, searching for her next step in life.

"And I thought I had it bad when I lost my job," she said softly, the tears starting to form in the back of her throat. "But they're so much more desperate than I ever was."

Will sighed. "Evan's in a tough spot, for sure. And with Christmas on the way, too."

"I don't know what we are going to do about this," Ed put the car into gear then turned to look at Melinda and Will, determination in his eyes. "But we are going to do *something*. We have got to do *something*."

* 17 *

The front lot at Prosper Feed Co. was empty except for a few pickups clustered near the main entrance. Melinda parked away from the front door and tried to collect her thoughts.

They had accomplished so much in just a few days. Helen, Angie and Mabel were shocked when they heard about Evan's situation, and the idea of alerting the authorities was briefly considered, then dropped. Evan and Chloe had food, and the furnace in the old Benniger home was working.

"And most of all, those two have each other," Mabel said with a sigh. "As long as Chloe's basic needs are met, we can't risk her being taken away from her father. She's been through enough. There's got to be other ways we can help."

Angie offered to sort through her daughters' extra clothes, and was sure she had a few discarded toys and stuffed animals that would make Chloe's Christmas brighter. Melinda rounded up food, litter and toys for Daisy. Ed got Evan's cell phone number from David, and Evan agreed to take Chloe into Charles City for a few hours later that week so Christmas decorations, toys and clothes could be delivered as a surprise for the little girl.

Evan insisted he needed nothing for himself, but that didn't stop Frank and Miriam from setting up a gift certificate to Prosper Hardware. Will and Helen donated their full-size Christmas tree and its decorations, as they had switched to a tabletop model years ago. Through friends at their church, Ed and Mabel found a toddler bed to provide Chloe somewhere to sleep other than an air mattress on the floor.

"We'd better stop there," Ed said to Melinda last night on the phone. "If we do too much, Evan will be embarrassed. His pride is about all he has left, other than his daughter."

"There's only one other thing that would make their Christmas special," she had replied. "I'll see what I can do."

"And here I am," Melinda gripped the steering wheel tighter, her stomach flipping over once, then twice. Auggie's truck was parked by the co-op's back entrance. He was usually in the office at this hour, sorting purchase orders and updating his business records. If she could speak to Auggie away from Dan, his assistant, and any customers that might be lingering in the lobby, maybe there was a chance ...

Melinda glanced at her phone. She had to be back at Prosper Hardware in forty-five minutes. She offered up a quick prayer, stepped out of the car and marched up to the co-op's front door.

The yeasty aroma of animal feed greeted her as she entered the building. Two men lounged in folding chairs next to the coffeepot and Dan leaned on the counter, flipping through a feed supply catalog. Auggie, Melinda was relieved to see, was nowhere in sight.

"Hey, Melinda," Dan looked up, his thick coppery beard nodding in greeting. "What brings you in today? We've got a special going on that dog food Hobo likes so much."

"Thanks, Dan, but we're all stocked up," she answered cheerfully. The two men continued to chat about crop prices, but she could tell they were listening. "Actually, I've got something here for Auggie. I keep forgetting to give it to him in the mornings down at the store. Is he in the office?"

"He was," Dan answered. "Just went up into the tower a bit ago, though, to work on his weather reports. Do you want to leave whatever it is up here?"

"Well, I really want to see his reaction," she said, then reached in her purse for the faded 1934 Prosper Feed Co.

calendar she discovered last fall while cleaning Horace's chicken house. She kept forgetting to give it to Auggie, and now saw why: It was her ticket to talking to him alone.

"Wow!" Dan gasped. "I've never seen anything like it. Where did you get that?"

"It was behind the chimney in Horace's chicken house. Fell out when I was cleaning. I can't wait for Auggie to see it."

"He's going to love that. Head through the door there," Dan grinned and pointed. "Down the hall you'll find the stairs. Go up three flights. There's a little cubbyhole to the left, he'll be in there."

The stairwell was dim and the steep metal steps echoed Melinda's footfalls as she climbed. She began to sweat in the close air, and paused at the second-floor landing to remove her parka and knit cap. At the next level, she could see into a dusty hallway where light leaked around a half-closed door.

On the other side was Auggie, planted in an old wooden roller chair, bent over a desk as he studied a thick ledger. He turned at the shuffle of her shoes on the concrete floor.

"Melinda! Whatever brings you up here today? I'm just updating my weather logs. Come in, come in."

The nook smelled like a library, musty and mysterious. Scuffed wooden shelves crammed with leather-bound ledgers filled two walls of the tiny office. Auggie's sleek laptop, set out on a scarred metal desk directly under a bare-bulb ceiling fixture, looked comically out of place. One of the room's two windows had a large pane that appeared to open inward. Outside, a line of weather gadgets was anchored to the wall and protected by a wire cage.

"Look at this," Melinda grinned, momentarily distracted from her errand. "Auggie, it's like your own little science lab up here. And that view!" She advanced to the windows, which kept their eyes trained on the west.

"Gotta see the weather when it comes in," he said. "Old McAlister, who owned the co-op back when this tower was built in the late 1940s, set up this room. The co-op's been tracking the weather for more than a hundred years, you know." Auggie gestured proudly at the ledgers. He seemed especially excited to have company, and Melinda soon found out why.

"I'm not quite positive yet," he said in an urgent whisper. "But we might get a big blizzard blowing through here right around Christmas."

Melinda's heart sank. "Oh, I hope we don't, Auggie. I've got everyone coming out to the farm, including my sister's family. They're driving out from Milwaukee."

"Well, I might be wrong. But we're overdue for a substantial snow. Usually have one by now." He seemed a bit deflated, then perked up. "So, what's going on?"

Melinda pulled out the fragile calendar and explained where she found it.

"Ooooh, let me see that." Auggie gingerly took the delicate item in his hands. "I can't believe it. 1934! You know, I've always heard the co-op used to give out stuff like this around the holidays. But in more than thirty years here, I've only ever come across one of these calendars in the storage room, and it was from the 1950s. This is ... well, it's astounding. Would you mind if I made a copy of this?"

"Oh, Auggie, no, it's for you to keep," Melinda insisted. "Just take it."

"Are you sure?" he was clearly touched. "It might be worth hundreds of dollars online or something. But then, no one has probably heard of Prosper, so I guess ..." He gave a determined nod. "After I copy it, I'll get this framed up nice and hang it downstairs. Thanks, Melinda."

"Well, I'm glad you like it," she said quietly, "but, well, there's something else."

His eyebrows shot up. "What is it? Got some good gossip? Settle in and spill the beans, kid." He gestured to a stool pushed against the wall.

Melinda sat, then fiddled with the drawstring on her parka hood. "Well, I don't know how many people know," she cringed, thinking of Glenn and Pete. "But, Auggie ... did you know Evan was back?"

Auggie's smile vanished. "What did you say?"

The little office was suddenly charged with something that made Melinda uneasy. "I think you heard me, Auggie," she said gently. "Do you ... have you talked to him?"

"What business is that of yours?" he snapped, his brown eyes flashing behind his glasses. But he was too curious to let it go. "What have you heard, anyway?"

Melinda swallowed and squeezed her hands together, then related all she knew.

For a moment, Auggie said nothing.

"So what you're telling me is," he said at last, his voice low and cold. "Everyone's been talking about me. Down at the store, even?"

"No, Auggie, it's not like that."

"But Pete and Glenn know Evan's out there," Auggie rolled his eyes. "Good Lord, that means half the county knows. I don't talk to Evan, as I'm sure you're heard by now."

"Can I ask why?" Melinda hesitated, then continued. "He seems like a nice guy. And that little girl of his, she's so sweet. They've fallen on hard times, sounds like. And it's almost Christmas, don't you think ..."

"Don't you tell me how to handle this!" Auggie raised his voice, his anger echoing around the little room. "He's my son, he's my problem! Did Jane put you up to this?"

"What?" Melinda couldn't believe it. She barely knew Auggie's wife, and she would never end-run him like that. "No, I haven't talked to her. Why are you so stubborn? Let me guess, Jane has enough sense to not totally cut her son out of her life. He's family, Auggie, surely ..."

Auggie leaped out of his chair, its metal wheels screeching across the concrete floor. He stomped past Melinda and, for a moment, she thought he would storm out of the room. Instead, he glanced down the stairwell and shut the door.

"So, you want to know what's going on?" he muttered through clenched teeth. "All right, I'll tell you. You promise, though, to keep your mouth shut about this. Evan's hurt his mother enough over the years."

Melinda nodded. Auggie lowered himself into his chair with a resigned sigh. "Now, don't interrupt me."

He leaned back and looked at the ceiling for a moment. "So here's the deal. Evan wasn't straight with all of you the other day. He and Carrie are separated, he called his mother last week to tell her that. It's been months since he's called. Carrie's gone, all right. But do you know where she is?"

Melinda, as promised, only shook her head.

"Rehab. She's in *rehab*, Melinda. For the third time. Carrie's addicted to painkillers. She was in a bad car accident eight years ago, right after she and Evan met. Things got away from her, I guess. She gets better for a while, says she's not using. Then Evan catches her hiding pills in her purse. He knows she's buying stuff on the street. Doesn't help that Madison's a college town."

"I'm sorry," Melinda whispered. "Evan only said she was gone, and that he lost his job and couldn't make the rent."

Auggie's mouth hardened into a frown. "Did Evan say why he lost his job? Because the last time that happened, he showed up to work drunk."

Melinda could only blink. She couldn't reconcile the kind, shy man she had met with the person Auggie described.

"Surprising, isn't it?" Auggie said acidly. "Evan looks so clean cut. We put him through college, the first in our family to get out of Prosper and get a fancy education. He's smart. Works in IT stuff, software engineering, that sort of thing. But he gets depressed, and then he drinks."

Melinda's mind was spinning. "Wait. Does Carrie drink, too? Poor Chloe ..."

"I believe she does, from time to time. They go in cycles, those two." Auggie's shoulders slumped. "I'm tired of the drama, of the calls in the middle of the night for money. So, how'd he look the other day?"

Despite his frustration with his oldest son, Melinda sensed Auggie was hungry for any tidbit she might share.

"Well, I don't know him, of course," she replied. "But he looked sober to me. Got big bags under his eyes, though, really tired. Exhausted. Seemed ... desperate, Auggie, despite trying to put on a good front for all of us."

"Maybe he's hit bottom this time. Maybe he'll kick Carrie to the curb for good," Auggie crossed his arms. "But I'm not holding out any hope. Not again."

They sat in silence for a moment. Auggie's chin trembled slightly, and he quickly looked at the floor. Melinda decided if she had any chance of convincing Auggie to open his heart to his son, there was maybe only one way in.

"Chloe's such a sweet little girl, Auggie," she whispered. "She was so happy to have company. If everything is as you say, the only friend she has left is her cat."

"It is how I say it is," his voice was ragged but hard. "And it's Evan's fault I never see my granddaughter. Last time I saw her, she was only six months old. We'd given them another chance, invited Evan and Carrie for Christmas. Jane was so eager to see that little baby."

Melinda could tell Jane hadn't been the only one, but stayed silent.

"So they come visit," Auggie began. "Our other kids were here, too. At that time, Chloe was our only grandchild. We're at the table, having a nice dinner, and I'm thinking, maybe they're turning things around because of the baby. They both were working ... But then, I'm on my way to the basement to get more cans of pop, and Carrie's in the bathroom. I hear all this rattling around."

He leaned back in his chair. "So I come back, and I've got the case of pop under my arm, but for some reason I stop and look in the bathroom. There's a bottle of aspirin on the floor. Seems odd. I step in and open the medicine cabinet, and it's like a raccoon's been pawing around in there. Stuff's falling into the sink, the shelves are a mess."

"So, Carrie was looking for drugs." Melinda knew it wasn't a question.

"Yeah," he said flatly. "We didn't have the kind she wanted. But that didn't matter. I could hardly see, I was so angry. I'd never felt so betrayed in all my life."

Auggie put a hand over his eyes. "I started yelling at them. I know, it was Christmas and everything, but I was done. Done with the lying."

"So what happened?"

"Evan defends her, said she's just got a headache. Carrie just sits there. Doesn't even try to make up some lie. The baby starts wailing. Then Jane starts crying. My daughter runs into the kitchen. My other son, he jumps up and starts shouting at Evan to grow up, to pull himself together because of that baby. Then they're shoving each other. It gets so ugly. I can't take it anymore. I order Evan to get out of our house, right now, and don't ever come back."

Melinda wants to go to her friend and put an arm around his shoulder, but she's afraid he'll push her away.

"So Carrie says nothing," Auggie is sobbing now. "She picks up Chloe and, doesn't even put on her coat, just goes out and sits in the car. Like none of it is her fault. I go in the bedroom, shut the door. I hear more crying and pleading, people shuffling around and the front door banging open, banging closed. I hear their car start up, then it's going down the driveway, then it's gone."

"I'm sorry, Auggie," Melinda wiped at her eyes. "I had no idea. And I'm sorry I pestered you to put up that star. Christmas must be so painful for you."

"You didn't know," he whispered. "Hardly anyone does, at least not all the gory details. And we don't talk about it, at home. We have Christmas like always, like it never happened. But there's more. We discovered Jane's mother's wedding ring was missing. My grandpa's pocket watch was gone, too."

"They stole from you? Oh, Auggie ..."

"We looked everywhere," he shook his head. "Never found them. Jane's jewelry box looked like someone had picked through it, moved things around. Now, I don't know that Evan did it. Maybe it was all Carrie's doing."

It was clear that, years later, Auggie still held out hope his son wasn't a thief.

Melinda didn't know what to say. Then she did.

"I feel like a fool. I marched up here like I was in some cheesy holiday movie, so sure I was going to reunite you with your son and granddaughter just in time for Christmas. But all I've done is rip your wounds wide open again."

"You didn't know," Auggie replied sadly. "You were just trying to help."

"I guess," Melinda sighed. Then she sat up straighter. "You know, though, that's not all I was trying to do."

"Oh, really? Let's hear it, then."

"I was trying to keep you from making a big mistake. One that you would always regret. Because Auggie, you did the same for me."

"I did?" Auggie frowned. "What? When?"

Melinda smiled and shook her head at her friend. "Don't you remember? Two months ago, when I was agonizing about whether I should take that job in Minneapolis? Everyone else was kind, of course ... too kind. But you didn't sugarcoat things. I was sitting there at the store, crying and exhausted, and you told me not to settle for something that didn't feel right. You just stepped in and set me straight."

"Well, I tend to do that sometimes," he admitted, then tried for a half-hearted smile. "When it's needed."

"It was one of the nicest things anyone has ever done for me," Melinda continued. "You said that job wasn't good enough for me. That I had options, that I could start over."

"And you have," Auggie said. "When you showed up at Prosper Hardware that first morning, I thought, 'give her a month and she'll be gone.' But you kept the store going when Frank was sick. You took in Hobo, and those nutty cats. You're running that farm, just like Horace did."

"You helped me find the confidence to make the right choice," Melinda replied. "And Auggie, I know you hate people telling you what to do, but I have to say it: This may be your last chance with Evan and Chloe."

Auggie shook his head and looked away.

"I mean it," she pointed a finger at him. "I thought that before. And now that I've heard the full story? I know it's true. If you turn your back on Evan again, he and Chloe may be out of your life for good. Don't blow it."

"I don't know, Melinda," he rubbed his face and sighed. "I just don't know if I can."

"I'm done," she said gently as she pulled on her coat. "I've said what I came here to say. Don't worry, this conversation will not leave this room. But you think about it, Auggie. It's not too late."

Melinda unlatched the door and turned for the stairs. Auggie swiveled in his chair, sighed again, and went back to his weather logs, where two and two always equaled four.

* 18 *

Auggie's prediction for a nasty blizzard right at Christmas lurked in the back of Melinda's mind while she ran through her list of everything she wanted to accomplish before the holiday. What if she served a rich root-vegetable soup as a special course for Christmas dinner? Where would everyone sleep? Would Hobo willingly share Horace's bed?

And it would be smart to have some seasonal craft ready to amuse her nephews, who were four and six. But what if they spilled glue or paint on the farmhouse's beautiful hardwood floors?

If she had time, there were these cute reindeer table favors she'd seen online, they would look so lovely on that antique dining room table. Did she have the right candles for the centerpiece? What about ...

"I'd like two bags of ice melt, too." The thud of soup cans on Prosper Hardware's oak counter startled Melinda out of her circling thoughts. "Does Bill have any in the back?"

"Oh, yes. Yes, he does," She rang up the man's purchases, tacked on the charge for the ice melt, then stacked his other items in the canvas totes he carried. Melinda was pleasantly surprised by how many customers brought in their own reusable bags. She should talk to Miriam about ordering their own. They could be dark green with white letters, like the knit caps that were so popular at the open house ...

"Guess we've got some bad weather coming," the man sighed as he pulled out his wallet. "*Bam!* Out of nowhere, just in the last hour, they changed the forecast. Six inches later tonight, at least." He sighed and picked up his tote bags, apparently oblivious to how Melinda was staring at him in surprise. "You ready for that?"

No, she wasn't. Auggie had said next week ...

"Sure am," she nodded and smiled as if everything was under control. "If you drive around to the back door, Bill will get that ice melt for you."

As soon as the man left, she reached for her phone. He was right, the forecast had changed. And there was a text from Angie. Ed had just called; their visit to Evan and Chloe's would be put off for a few days because of the chance of bad weather. "Ed doesn't like to text but wanted you to know right away," she wrote, adding a smiley face.

Melinda mentally cataloged her emergency supplies at home. The flashlights were stocked with fresh batteries, as was the weather radio she purchased after the tornado. There was a several days' supply of animal feed already at the farm. But one other thing hadn't been crossed off her winter preparedness list, and she decided to get Ed's opinion. He picked up on the first ring.

The skies were dimming with heavy clouds when Ed arrived at the farm later that afternoon. "Feel that damp in the air?" he told Melinda. "It'll snow for sure tonight."

They went into the barn, where Ed's arrival was greeted with an excited chorus from the sheep. He had been their caretaker in the days between Horace's departure and Melinda's arrival, and the sheep never forgot a friendly face. Or really, anyone who fed them their grain.

"Move along, ladies," Ed told the ewes as he and Melinda turned through the crowd, making their way to where the sheep's waterer crouched by the far wall. "We're going to get everything ready for you in case there's a storm coming."

The hulking metal box in the corner, by some magic Melinda had yet to fully uncover, provided the sheep with a constant, unfrozen water supply. It had to be several decades old, the red-and-white decal on its side long ago worn away. She had spent several minutes down in the straw the other night, peering at the shabby thing's corners and connections with a flashlight while Annie grunted for attention, before deciding she needed a veteran farmer's input.

"It seems fine to me," Ed said now as he gave the contraption a good-natured kick. "Water level's been steady, right? And no ice floating in the trough in the mornings?"

"So far, so good. But how will I know if something is going wrong with it?" Melinda skeptically eyed the thick black cord that climbed up to a dusty, cobwebbed outlet near the ceiling.

"Well, one of two things will happen," Ed nodded sagely. "You'll come out in the morning to find a bunch of angry sheep and an iced-over trough; in that case, a few whacks with a hatchet will do until I can come over. Or, you'll look out the kitchen window to find the thing sparked and the whole barn burned down while you slept."

"Ed!"

He chuckled at the horror on her face. "Now, now, I'm just joking. It's obviously been humming along for decades. I've known Horace and Wilbur for, what, fifty years? They'd never go cheap on something like this. It looks pretty rough, but it works just fine."

"But what if the water line freezes?" Melinda glanced this way and that. "Where is it, anyway?"

"That's buried way down, below the frost line," Ed explained. "Same for the pipes that run to the house from the well, which is out there under that concrete pad where the windmill used to be."

He gave Melinda's arm an encouraging pat. "Only worry there is when it gets to, oh, twenty or thirty below at night. That's when you'll want to run your house faucets at a little drip to keep the lines open, so you don't lose water to both the house and the barn."

Melinda filed that terrifying tidbit away for later use as they returned to the barn's main aisle.

"Let's see if there's a hatchet in the grain room, just in case you need it," Ed suggested. He paused long enough to give a few pets to Sunny, who had supervised the water tank's examination from the ridge of the aisle fence.

"How likely do you think it is that a storm's on the way?" Melinda asked. "Auggie's all wound up about a big blizzard for next week, but didn't predict one for tonight. In fact, he barely said one word this morning at coffee group, about the weather or anything else."

"I take it he's still not wanting to forgive Evan," Ed speculated as they sorted through the grain room's shelves and corners.

She just shook her head. "As far as I know, he hasn't changed his mind since I cornered him about it the other day. I don't think I should bring it up again."

"I think that's best," Ed nodded. "As for a storm tonight, let's hope the TV people are getting all excited for nothing. We might get lucky. Hey, here you go!" He held up a hatchet hidden behind a stack of scrap lumber in one corner.

As she waved from back steps while Ed's truck disappeared down the lane, a part of her almost hoped for a big blizzard. It would be a true test of her preparations and her abilities. Horace thought she could manage the farm on her own. She wanted to believe he was right.

Melinda was snuggled on the couch with Hobo, watching television and skimming through the newspaper, when the first flakes began to fall. By the time she went to bed, the snow was coming fast and thick and the wind was whistling through the windbreak. She set her alarm for a half hour earlier than usual, but found herself awake even before it sounded. It was as if a strange silence, a deep and muffled kind, had roused her from sleep.

She hurried to the west window and tried to peer out into the darkness, where a few tag-along flakes still drifted through the reassuring glow of the yard light.

Everything was covered in a fresh layer of white. It was hard to be sure in the pre-dawn gloom, but the white caps on the outbuildings' roofs looked to only be about four inches deep. Despite her anticipation for a big storm, Melinda had to admit she was relieved. Even so, this would be the first morning she had to shovel snow before chores. She'd better get outside.

"What do you think?" she asked Hobo when he met her at the bottom of the stairs, still yawning and stretching. "I think we got just enough snow for you to have a good romp this morning. Let's go see!"

Hobo was so excited that he dashed out his second doggie door before Melinda could bundle into her coveralls and snow boots. He barked and yipped, racing figure-eights around the garage and the sleeping garden and burying his nose in the fresh white fluff.

The back steps were easy enough to clear of snow, as was the back sidewalk. She was about to scoop the concrete path all the way around to the front porch, but quickly gave up on that idea. A route to the barn was far more important. In just a few minutes, she was sweating inside her coveralls and puffing for air.

"I don't remember this being so hard," she gasped as she stopped for a breather, momentarily removing her knit cap to cool her scalp. "But then, I haven't shoveled snow since I was a kid." It wasn't very deep, but unlike what she had faced so far this winter, this snow was dense and heavy. Her shoulders slumped as she eyed the distance to the chicken coop.

"I need to pick my battles," she told Hobo when he hustled over, wanting his ears scratched while he took a break from his sprints. "If I can clear a path to the barn and knock down the snow in front of the garage, I should be able to get the car out just fine. I'll just need to hoof it through the snow to reach the chickens."

The low clouds began to break apart, a faint glow of pink in the east announcing the sunrise. Melinda eyed the driveway while she finished the path to the barn.

Should she ask Nathan to plow the driveway and yard? He had a snow blade for his truck, and promised Melinda he would come over and clear the lane just as he always had for Horace and Wilbur. All she had to do was call.

Surely Nathan and Angie were up, but they had chores of their own to do and really, the snow wasn't that deep. With Hobo romping at her side, Melinda started off down the lane, kicking down the few short drifts with her boots and scooping away snow from areas where it seemed the deepest.

She was shuffling back toward the house when there was a rumbling to the south and the metallic flash of fog lights. The county crew's snowplow barreled up the gravel road, clouds of white flying from the front of its blade. She grinned and offered a big wave, and the driver tooted his horn as he churned past the mailbox.

Sunny and Stormy didn't appear on the picnic table as usual, demanding their breakfast. She was worried for a moment but found them in the barn, where it was dry and warm, waiting inside the door. The ewes were antsy, running between their troughs and the locked pasture door and looking restless. Would she let them out for the day?

Annie, who always had at least one eye on Melinda's location, was the first to see her reach for the pasture door's iron latch. With a grunt and a shake of her black ears, Annie turned from her grain and rushed over to push her nose against the door.

"Just a sec," Melinda laughed as more ewes hurried to join Annie. "Girls, come on. Let me get it open, OK?"

Annie paused for only a second when she saw the snow, but then ran out into the pasture, her black legs kicking up puffs of white. The others soon followed. Maybe the sheep would paw down through the snow in search of late-season grass, or maybe they would just run laps and head back into the warmth of the barn.

Either way, they would have their freedom today. It wouldn't be long before the weather would turn colder and the pasture door would stay locked for days on end.

The chickens were only interested in their feed. Pansy gave a squawk of indignation when Melinda slid the hens' small door open to reveal the winter wonderland that now occupied their enclosed run.

"Fine, Pansy," she gave an exasperated sigh. "You don't have to go out in the snow. But you can't say you didn't have the chance."

The kitchen clock showed it was nearly six-thirty by the time she unwound her chore gear. She had to hurry. Hobo was already sprawled out on the living room rug, dozing next to the floor register, when she snatched her purse off the kitchen counter and hurried out to the garage.

"It's a good thing this driveway's pretty flat," Melinda reassured herself as she backed her car around. "I was smart to knock down those little drifts earlier. As long as I give it the gas, it'll be fine."

The tires spun a bit as she pulled out of reverse, but then the car eased down the lane, sliding through the rough spots so easily that she couldn't resist giving a confident thumbs-up to the sheep, who were now clustered along the fence. "Piece of cake," she grinned as the car neared the gravel road.

The car suddenly stopped. It would easily move into reverse, but not forward one more inch. "What's all this?" She got out of the car to get a better look.

"Oh, great!" She rolled her eyes. "The plow guy blocked me in. Why didn't I come down here after he came by?"

Melinda pulled her spare shovel from the car's trunk, adjusted her stocking hat, and got to work. It wasn't as if she had to dress nice for Prosper Hardware, but she still cringed at what a sweaty mess she was by the time the end of the drive was at last cleared of snow. There wasn't time to go back to the house and change, and she didn't want to risk another run up the lane before Nathan could blade it clear.

The gravel road wasn't too bad, thanks to the plow that went by less than an hour ago. The county highway, to Melinda's relief, was even better. She took her time reaching Prosper, and paused for a moment to collect herself before coming in the back door of the store. It wasn't even seven-thirty, but it had already been a long day.

The comforting aroma of hot coffee beckoned as she shuffled up the store's main aisle, her shoulders and knees already stiff and complaining. The men were gathered around the sideboard as usual, their parkas and hats steaming on the coat rack by the Christmas tree.

"We were about to send out the National Guard," Bill said as he got up to refill his cup. "Wondered how it was going out there this morning."

"Well, I got the chores done and some shoveling, too," Melinda gave a casual shrug as she unwound her wraps and sank gratefully into the chair that Auggie kindly set out for her, even though he still wouldn't look her in the eye. "Wasn't too bad, really."

She wasn't about to tell her friends how hectic her morning had already been. If she was going to stay at the farm, she couldn't complain every time it snowed. Especially when spring was months away.

George just nodded and gave her an encouraging smile. Doc buried his face in his coffee cup. Jerry busied himself sawing off another slice from the loaf of pumpkin bread on the sideboard, then started snickering.

"What?" Melinda asked suspiciously. "What are you guys up to now?"

"Oh, us? Nothing," Jerry smothered his amusement with a bite of pumpkin bread.

"It's just, well," Doc said gently, then started laughing. "Melinda, you look like you got dragged backwards over a snow fence by an angry bull. What happened?"

She reached up and felt most of her now-sweaty hair standing on end. Two puddles were forming on the oak floors under her soaked snow boots.

Melinda rolled her eyes and sighed. "OK, OK, so I got stuck at the end of my driveway," she admitted.

The guys burst into such infectious laughter that she had to join in. But then she reached for her phone. "That reminds me, I need to call Nathan and ask him to come down with his truck blade before I get home."

✳ 19 ✳

Ed and Will had already unloaded a partially assembled Christmas tree out of the back of Will's truck by the time Melinda arrived at the Benniger farm.

"It was crazy at the store today. Sorry I'm a little late," she called to Mabel, who was picking her way up the brick sidewalk with a plastic basket of cleaning supplies in her arms. Evan had apparently found a shovel and cleared a path to the stately home's front door, and someone had bladed away most of the recent snow from the long gravel lane. Evan and Chloe, as arranged by Ed, were not at home. A spare key had been left behind the broken lattice under the porch.

"We're just getting started," Mabel called over her shoulder. "This place may be beautiful, but it sure needs a good scrubbing."

"I feel just like Santa," Ed's grin spread ear to ear as he took hold of the top of the fake tree. "Or like those guys on television, giving away that sweepstakes prize money. I tell you, Melinda, we should make this an annual tradition, find some local family that needs help and pitch in like this."

Melinda agreed. She'd volunteered for many years at an animal rescue in the Twin Cities, and served on a committee at WP&S to gather donations of interview-appropriate attire for a women's shelter. But since she'd returned to Prosper, her community involvement hadn't expanded beyond helping with the town's festivals. It was going to be so satisfying to fill Evan and Chloe's living space with not only holiday cheer, but the comforts of a real home. She couldn't wait to get started.

As for her talk with Auggie, Melinda kept the details to herself. She told her neighbors Auggie was reluctant to reach out to Evan, and didn't seem willing to change his mind. "Sounds just like him," Mabel had responded with a shake of her head, and Melinda said no more.

What Auggie had told her was troubling, in more ways than one. Evan and Chloe's situation was apparently far more precarious than Evan had let on. Melinda understood why Evan didn't feel comfortable confiding in strangers, but what was really going on? His hopelessness and weariness were real, she had no doubt about that. But after talking to Auggie, she had to admit that Evan's carefully edited explanation was filled with holes and half-truths.

There was, of course, the possibility that Auggie's view was distorted by a father's anger and anguish over his son's choices. That didn't quite fit, either. Melinda knew Auggie to be forthright and sometimes judgmental, but he always based his pointed comments on the facts.

"I guess the truth is somewhere in the middle," she said to herself as she reached in the trunk of her car for the bags of cat food and litter she purchased for Daisy, along with a small sack of toys and treats. "Maybe Evan really is serious about making a fresh start. Either way, little Chloe is going to have the best Christmas we can give her."

Angie soon arrived, the backseat of her car loaded down with several bags. "I can't believe how many things I found for Chloe," she told Melinda, "pants, sweaters, even a dress with a pair of tights and nicer shoes. If Evan and Chloe go to Auggie's for Christmas, she'll have something nice to wear."

"I don't know if that will happen." Melinda reached for a tote bag that carried a stuffed bear and two dolls. "But I'm not giving up hope yet."

"I decided to wrap a few clothes and toys, I couldn't help it," Angie confessed. "I hope Evan doesn't feel like it's too much. He can hide them for now, then set them under the tree and say they are from Santa."

The Christmas tree was a perfect fit for the sitting room's grand picture window. With a cardboard box at her feet, Helen arranged the stray branches in the tree's center pole.

"Now I know why I could never bring myself to give this tree away," Helen told Melinda and Angie as they came into the room. "Just wait until we get the lights and ornaments on it. Oh, this little girl is going to love it!"

"I'm amazed we were able to gather so many things on such short notice," Melinda said as she surveyed the piles of donated items. Daisy, observing all the commotion from a corner of the faded couch, allowed Melinda to give her a gentle pat on the head.

"And I have some things for you," she told Daisy. "No more dead mice, OK? Stormy and Sunny have no use for toys, apparently, being barn cats. They are happy to share."

"Speaking of mice," Mabel set her hands on her hips, "I've got some traps in the car."

Ed and Will brought in the toddler bed and set it up next to the fireplace while Angie and Melinda started a welcoming blaze in the hearth. Evan, who had kept himself busy breaking up the large twigs that littered the expansive lawn, had told Ed where to find his haphazard wood stack behind the carriage house. Mabel and Helen swept the sitting-room floor and then brought in an area rug woven with shades of red, green and gold that had been tucked away in one of Ed and Mabel's guest room closets. A cozy red throw blanket and colorful pillows were added to the old couch, and the last of the decorations added to the tree's branches.

The sitting room was soon transformed, its worn surfaces softened and the once-lonely space filled with the dreamy glow of the tree. As soon as Angie draped a fluffy white towel over the tree base for a makeshift skirt, Daisy claimed the cozy spot as her own and curled up for a nap.

They tackled the kitchen next. It was shadowy and dull, with only a two-bulb fixture dangling near the high ceiling.

The cabinets may have been white long ago. A tired gray-green linoleum covered the counters as well as the floor.

"Well, we better get at it," Mabel sighed, looking around the shabby space. "They'll be home around seven, I think. Just enough time to scrub this kitchen down and tackle the bathroom off the hall."

It wasn't long before the fresh scent of clean replaced the house's stale air. A few rugs were tossed on the kitchen floor, and extra towels in bright colors stacked on the counter. Helen brought out a cream tablecloth scattered with holly and berries, and centered it on the small round kitchen table.

Will went out to his truck and returned with a spare floor lamp, which chased away the rest of the sitting room's shadows. Ed and Mabel's old television was set up on an end table by the couch. Helen dressed Chloe's new bed with spare sheets and more quilts, and a few extra blankets were folded at the foot of Evan's air mattress.

Ed's phone rang. Evan and Chloe were about to leave Charles City and would be back in twenty minutes. There was just enough time to carry all the cleaning supplies out to the vehicles and make one more pass through the rooms.

"It's so beautiful, I can't believe this is the same place," Angie marveled as they took a moment to survey their efforts and admire the sparkling tree and the popping logs in the fireplace. "It's as if this old house is coming back to life."

"People make a house a home," Mabel squeezed Angie's shoulder. "That, and love. And a little elbow grease, now and then. She's a grand old lady, that's for sure. Oh, look! There's lights at the end of the lane. They're back!"

"Everyone, let's gather around the tree," Helen suggested. "Oh, I can't wait to see their faces!"

As Evan and Chloe came through the vestibule, Melinda could hear the little girl chattering to her father about the deer they spotted along the gravel road. She realized she was holding her breath and her neighbors appeared to be doing the same. What would Chloe's reaction be? Would Evan think they had done too much?

Chloe gasped with delight as they came into the sitting room. She barely noticed her visitors, her wide eyes only seeing the tree.

"It's a Christmas tree, Daddy!" Chloe shouted, jumping up and down. "Such a big tree! Oh, it's beautiful!"

Without removing her coat, Chloe rushed forward and reverently touched one of the tree's evergreen branches. "Daisy, Daisy, look at our tree!" the little girl squealed.

Evan stood just inside the vestibule, unable to move or speak. Then he looked at the floor. For a moment, Melinda thought they had damaged his pride. Then she realized he was trying not to cry.

"We hope we didn't go overboard," Ed said gently.

"Everything's just on loan, Evan," Will added. "Just until you get on your feet. We wanted Christmas to be special for both of you."

"I can't believe this. I can't believe you did all this," Evan finally said, his voice shaking. "It looks great. I didn't want my little girl spending Christmas in a dreary, empty house."

"And now she won't, will she?" Mabel stepped forward and wrapped Evan in one of her trademark hugs.

"Evan, it's been years since I've seen you. But you're home now, if only for a while."

Evan shoulders shook with sobs. "We don't have a home anymore. But now, it's almost like we do."

"Things are going to work out somehow," Mabel comforted him. "I pray that the new year brings you many blessings. As for now, you just need to rest and enjoy time with your little girl."

"And she loves it," Ed broke in, unable to keep from grinning. "Just look at her."

Chloe ran back and forth between the Christmas tree, the now-cozy couch and her new bed. Angie had somehow slowed the little girl long enough to remove her coat.

Chloe shrieked with joy as she touched everything: the bright pillows, the soft blankets, the nubby texture of the floor rug. At last she settled in on the little bed with Daisy in her arms, telling Angie all about her kitty and how much she loved her. "And we have a TV now! I can watch cartoons!"

"Yes, honey, you certainly can," Angie replied as she helped Chloe remove her almost-forgotten snow boots. "I think there's some Christmas shows on tonight. My little girls are going to watch them, too."

Evan at last smiled and wiped at his eyes with his hand. "Chloe's blown away by all this, that's for sure. So am I. I can't thank you all enough. The cookies the other day sure brightened things up around here, and now all this ..."

"I'm Helen, Will's wife," Helen grasped Evan's hand with a warm squeeze. "Over there is Angie; she and her family live in our neighborhood, too. She's got two little girls and found some extra clothes for Chloe."

"Oh, that's wonderful," Evan gasped. "I tried to pack as best I could before I put the rest of our stuff in storage, but I don't think I brought enough."

"And there's more." Melinda reached into her purse and pulled out an envelope. "My aunt and uncle own Prosper Hardware. They sent along a fifty-dollar gift certificate for you to use at the store. We've got a little of everything: clothes, groceries, you name it. Come by anytime. And there's more food and litter for Daisy in the corner of the kitchen."

When Chloe heard there were treats for her kitty, she let out a whoop and ran into the next room to investigate.

Evan only nodded, once more overcome with emotion.

"Angie wrapped a few of the toys and clothes she found for Chloe," Melinda told him in a low voice. "We put them in the cabinets above the kitchen sink. We thought you might want to set them out on Christmas, tell Chloe they were brought by Santa."

"Yes, yes, I will," he nodded gratefully. "I'd saved back a few dollars to get her some new socks and a few storybooks, but that was going to be it. Now, she'll have things to open Christmas morning, and I'm just so ..." He looked around at the group, gratitude showing in his tired brown eyes.

"I don't know what to say," Evan shook his head. "Except

thank you, a million times over. 'Thank you' doesn't begin to cover it. You've given us a Christmas, and I'll never forget your kindness. But you know, it's more than that. You've given me hope."

Ed patted him on the back. "You need anything, you let us know. Hang on to that hope, Evan. It'll see you though."

As Melinda drove down the lane, she glanced in her rearview mirror and admired the beautiful Christmas tree, which glowed in the grand house's picture window like a beacon in the darkness. Auggie might never reconcile with his son; there wasn't anything she could do about that. But she felt an exuberant grin spread across her face as she recalled little Chloe's sheer joy at the sight of the Christmas tree.

Melinda was thrilled with what she and her neighbors accomplished, how easy it had been to reach out and give of their time and possessions to make someone else's holiday brighter. But there was more than that behind the peace she felt, she decided. She understood the despair and defeat Evan tried to hide from them on their first visit. And now, she recognized the glimmer of hope that Evan carried in his heart.

She was soon back in Prosper, driving past the water tower to where Main Street stretched out ahead. A stubborn dusting of snow clung to the lawns and the buildings' roofs, and the snowflake and tree decorations tossed off cheerful beams of light along the tiny business district. She admired the scene's quiet beauty, then started to laugh.

"It's like Bedford Falls! Merry Christmas, vet clinic!" Melinda shouted as she cruised down Main Street. She was laughing like a fool, but she didn't care. "Merry Christmas, Watering Hole! Merry Christmas, Prosper Hardware!"

Once she crossed the state highway, leaving the glow of Prosper's holiday lights behind her, her thoughts turned inward again.

Her past struggles were different than Evan's, but she had once stood at the same crossroads he was at now, afraid and unsure, and had to choose a new path. She'd taken one little step, and then another. It took weeks, then months, and then, somehow, she found herself in a new life. It hadn't happened all at once, and there's wasn't one special day where Melinda woke up and suddenly felt her life was back on track.

But little by little, things fell into place. It would happen for Evan and Chloe, too.

And then, as her car's headlights beamed down the snow-packed gravel road and at last reflected off the mailbox at the end of her lane, tears of gratitude sprang into Melinda's eyes. Her own colorful holiday lights beckoned from her front porch, sending out their cheerful welcome. A soft glow poured out the kitchen windows, the light above the sink visible as she drove into the yard.

She still had to do chores, and find something for supper and wash the dishes that needed her attention. It would be some time yet before she could at last sink into the comfort of her own couch, pull up her own fleece blanket and snuggle with her dear Hobo, who was right now barreling out his doggie door to greet her car by the garage.

"But I'm home," Melinda whispered. "And it's so good to be home."

✻ 20 ✻

A few snowflakes danced past the farmhouse's windows as Melinda sipped her coffee at the kitchen table. She had a few moments before the next batch of sour-cream cookies would come out of the oven, the perfect chance to look over her Christmas to-do list.

"*Clean bathrooms.* Check. *Mop floors.* Check."

She yawned and rubbed her face, enjoying the mini-facial provided by the steam rising from her coffee. And then she sighed. "Oh, yeah, look at all this other stuff on here. *Create reindeer table favors. Dice and blend carrots for root-vegetable soup. Sweep barn aisle. Get holiday collar for Hobo.* Why was I going to do all that again? Because I wanted to make this the perfect Christmas, that's why."

She glanced around the kitchen, shaking her head at the bare-faced cookies waiting to be decorated and the muddy paw prints Hobo had left minutes ago on the just-mopped linoleum floor. Horace's antique-tractor calendar, tacked up next to the wheezing refrigerator, reminded her it was already December 22.

Three days until Christmas. Two days, then, until her out-of-state family arrived. Melinda thought she'd be ready by now, but she was just getting started.

Prosper Hardware had been non-stop crazy Friday and Saturday, packed with harried shoppers from open to close.

Yesterday was a holiday whirlwind as she went to Advent services at her home church in Swanton, enjoyed lunch with cousins passing through on their pre-holiday travels, then attended an afternoon concert and dessert buffet at Swanton's historical society. She came home happy, filled with the Christmas spirit, and nearly sick to her stomach from too many rich treats.

"This list has to go." Melinda ripped the paper in half. "I'm running out of time. I'm tired. I have to work tomorrow. And even through the store closes early on Wednesday, Liz and her family could drive in the yard before I get home."

Hobo had stopped at his water bowl when he came in from outside, melting snowflakes glittering in his brown fur. Seeking a few pats on the head, he turned toward Melinda, his muddy tracks extending even farther across the floor.

"The things on that list? They're not what Christmas is really about, right, Hobo?" She reached for a worn towel kept under the table just for this purpose, and tried to wipe Hobo's white feet. "You don't need a fancy new collar, anyway. Everyone's going to love you just as you are."

The forecast had changed several times in the past few days, but at last, Auggie and the professional weather forecasters agreed: There would be no holiday-week blizzard, and the white Christmas they already had was all they would get. For once, the weather wasn't going to be a factor in Melinda's plans.

"All that matters," she decided, "is that we'll be together."

Not everyone would be so fortunate. Her thoughts turned to Evan and Chloe's troubles and Auggie's continued silence, of the rift keeping their family apart.

She had tried to mend it. All she could do was pray that Auggie would someday set aside his anger and give his son another chance.

And now, after the fuss of the holiday festival, the frenzy of last-minute shoppers at the store and the rush to give Evan and Chloe a special Christmas, Melinda was ready to slow down and really savor the season.

She took a generous gulp of her coffee, kicked her sock-covered feet up on the rungs of the chair across the table, and felt the weight of her unrealistic expectations lift away.

"I'll never get this place spotless in time," she shrugged, "and that's just as well. I don't want to be so exhausted that I can't enjoy having everyone here. If we have clean sheets on the beds, something to eat, and maybe a few presents under the tree, we'll get by just fine."

The timer buzzed on the counter, and she pushed herself out of her chair and over to the oven. She'd frost the cookies, think of something simple she could throw in the slow cooker for Christmas Eve supper, and focus on getting the laundry done and the spare beds ready.

As for Christmas dinner, her parents and Frank and Miriam were pitching in with side dishes, and Melinda's brother-in-law insisted on bringing his new deep fryer and cooking the turkey out in the yard.

She had hesitated at first, due to her hopes to roast the best Christmas turkey ever put on a platter as well as Isaac's questionable culinary skills, but finally agreed to turn the turkey over to him.

"Isaac and his brother did it for Thanksgiving," Liz said the other night on the phone, "and the turkey turned out perfect. Let us do it, Melinda, it will be one less thing for you to deal with."

There were pumpkin pies to bake, but Melinda, in a moment of clarity sometime in the past week, came up with a way to get from-scratch pies and occupy her young nephews at the same time. Christmas Eve afternoon, she'd take Liam and Noah down to the basement and let them make a joyful mess as they scooped out pumpkins Melinda had harvested from her garden and stored in the cellar.

"Horace's garden," she reminded herself as she stirred the frosting for the cookies.

"Next year, the garden will truly be mine. I could expand the strawberry bed, put in an extra row of sweet corn ... but never mind that now. One season at a time."

Melinda turned on the holiday tunes the moment she arrived at Prosper Hardware the next morning. This would be the coffee group's final gathering until after Christmas. Some of the regulars would be out of town tomorrow, and the others would be preparing for their own guests to arrive.

"Whew, it's cold out there," Jerry shivered as he unwound his scarf and shrugged out of his coat, then added them to the pile on the hall tree.

"I'm glad it's not supposed to snow, as we're heading to our son's in Denison tomorrow for Christmas Eve. But a little warm-up would be much appreciated." He gave Auggie a hopeful look.

"Not likely," Auggie shook his head as he offered Jerry a steaming mug of coffee.

Jerry wrapped his chilled fingers around the cup and settled in his usual chair next to the sideboard. "Well then, I'll just be grateful the roads will be good," he said. "This time of year, we're lucky if we catch one break at a time. Melinda, are you ready for all those relatives to show up tomorrow?"

"You know what, Jerry? I think I am," she replied as she polished the oak counter.

"I decided to scale back. The house is sort-of clean, and everyone will have a place to sleep. I'm going to let the rest go. I've been thinking a lot about what the holidays are really about," she continued as she came around the counter and poured a cup of coffee, then helped herself to a slice of the gingerbread George brought in that morning.

"We'll have plenty to eat, and we'll be together. That's all I really want."

Too late, Melinda saw Auggie's shoulders flinch. She quickly steered the conversation away to something else, and the vet clinic was always a safe topic.

"So, Doc, do you have many patients coming in today?"

"Just a few," he stretched out his long legs and took a hearty swig of his coffee. "Had our last surgery for the week yesterday, nothing too serious, thankfully. My family's staying in town this year, and I'm looking forward to it. But Karen's going home, so I'm on call tomorrow night and Christmas Day. In my line of work, you never know when you'll be making a trek to a stable in the middle of the night."

That brought a round of laughter from the group. Even Auggie managed a brief smile.

Melinda finished her coffee, then straightened the display of holiday-themed kitchen towels on the far end of the counter. They were only a few left and, at seventy-five percent off, she expected the last ones to go out the door by noon.

As she turned toward the register, she spotted something that made her heart jump. Or rather, someone. Through the plate-glass windows across the front of the store, she saw Evan Kleinsbach picking his way up the snow-dusted sidewalk. Chloe held his hand, both of them bundled against the cold. The car parked a few spaces down from Prosper Hardware's front door, unfortunately, also looked familiar.

She whirled around to find Auggie busy at the sideboard, his back to the front door, stacking coffee cups on the metal tray as he started his usual clean-up duties.

Maybe Evan and Chloe would walk on by, she hoped, maybe they were heading to the post office. But it wasn't quite eight and, even with extended holiday hours, Glenn didn't open until nine.

And then, Evan was guiding Chloe to Prosper Hardware's entrance. Bill, glancing at the clock, shrugged and hurried over to unlock the door before Melinda could warn him. The bells above it jangled as a cold breeze darted into the store.

"Come on in," Bill said, then grinned. "We're just about to open. Can I help you find anything today? We've got a few specials going on and ..."

Bill paused when he noticed the tension in Evan's posture and on his face. Evan glanced around nervously, then froze when he spotted Auggie across the room. Chloe edged closer to her father.

"Hello, Melinda," Evan said in a shaky voice, not meeting her gaze. Bill at last remembered to close the door, gave Melinda a confused look, and stepped away.

"I'm ... I'm looking for my dad," Evan continued, directing his halting words toward Auggie's back.

There was a moment of charged silence and then a crash, the echo of porcelain mugs shattering on the oak floor. Auggie didn't turn around, but Melinda could see his hands shaking. Everyone looked at each other, and waited.

Bill's eyes grew wide with surprise, but he was the first to recover his composure. He ambled over to Chloe and crouched down to her level.

"Do you know what I do here at the store? I make things for people, just like Santa does. Would you like to see my workshop? It's just in the back there."

Chloe's confusion finally melted into a shy smile.

Evan had gone pale, his mouth set in a firm line. Chloe glanced at her father and then over to Melinda, who gave the little girl an encouraging nod. Chloe let Bill take her hand.

"Wait until you see what I'm making today," he told Chloe, giving Melinda a worried look as he passed by.

Melinda wanted to say something, anything, to diffuse the tension in the room. But what? "Hi, Evan," she offered quietly, then made a futile gesture toward Auggie, who still had his back to his son.

"Dad," Evan tried again, his voice still wavering. "Dad, I need to talk to you. Mom told me you'd be here this morning. I didn't want to show up down at the co-op and ..."

"And what?" Auggie pivoted and glared at him. "Make a scene? What do you call this, Evan?"

Evan only blinked and said nothing.

Auggie looked around at his friends and sighed, as resigned as he was angry. "I think we've had enough scenes over the years. I can't do this anymore. You know that. We've talked about this before."

"But I'm not done talking. And you need to listen." Evan's face began to flush. Melinda could see he was deeply hurt by Auggie's comments. She was thankful Bill had the presence of mind to remove Chloe from the tense situation. "I'm not here to cause trouble."

"That might be," Auggie stayed rooted to his spot by the sideboard, the shards of broken coffee cups forgotten at his feet. "But trouble seems to follow you around."

"If you mean Carrie," Evan said coldly and squared his shoulders, "we're not together anymore. My only focus right now is on Chloe, Dad. I lost my job. I know you know that," he added through gritted teeth. "I know Mom told you."

"You're right about that," Auggie spit out as he marched across the floor to stare down his son.

"She was sobbing. When are you going to grow up, Evan? How many times are you going to disappoint your mother? How many times are you going to let your drinking get you kicked out the door, huh? You've got a little girl to support now, I can't believe ..."

The electronic clang of Doc's phone made everyone jump. He glanced around apologetically and tapped the screen. "Hello? Yeah. Sorry to hear that. I'm on my way." With an air of relief about him, Doc gathered his coat, hat and gloves and rushed for the door.

"We all should leave," Jerry looked warily at Frank. "We don't need to ..."

"No, no, you can stay." Auggie said. "Evan can say what he needs to stay in front of everyone, including those who've worked so hard to give Chloe the Christmas he can't manage on his own." He included Melinda in his gaze.

She wanted to follow Doc out the door. The bitterness between Evan and Auggie was breathtaking. But so was the sadness. She could only go behind the counter and finish her preparations for the store's opening, hope no customers would walk in on this ugly scene.

"I'm not drinking, you know!" Evan shouted. "How dare you throw that in my face! That was years ago. Just so you know, half of my department was eliminated. It wasn't my fault, although I've spent hours trying to figure out what I could have done to save my job. It must be nice to have your own business, Dad," he added sarcastically, "where you can do whatever you want, order everyone around and ..."

"I worked hard for years to put a roof over your head," Auggie's voice was low and cold as he pointed a finger at his son. "You, and your brother and sister. You have no idea ..."

"Yes, I do," Evan snapped. "Because that's exactly what I'm trying to do for Chloe. I'm all she has left. Carrie can't be the mother she should be. Her parents are taking her side. Why do you think we're here? Why would I ever come back here if I had anywhere else to go?"

Melinda cringed as she counted the money in the cash register's drawer. She used to tell herself that, too, sometimes, when things were hard in Minneapolis.

How wrong she had been. Coming home to start over was one of the best decisions she ever made. But what was here for Evan? Maybe not enough.

"I'm doing this for Chloe," Evan said again, his voice softening. "I want her to know you and Mom. She needs you in her life. If you don't want to let the past go, that's fine, I can take it. But I'd like you to make an effort for Chloe's sake."

Auggie's shoulders slumped and he looked at the floor. Evan pressed on. "Mom's invited us to come for dinner tomorrow night." Auggie's head shot up in surprise.

"Just me and Chloe. Just the four of us for Christmas Eve. She said it would be up to *me*," Evan pointed at himself and Auggie flinched, "if we came Christmas Day, when everyone was there. It would be so good to see everybody." He swallowed hard. "But I need to know you're OK with that."

Auggie was still silent. Evan waited, his fists in his coat pockets. Uncle Frank looked as if he was about to say something, then didn't. Melinda wanted to shout at Auggie: *This is your chance!* But she said nothing.

Then Auggie looked up, and there were tears in his eyes. She could see he was tired of fighting and tired of being angry. He hesitated, then turned her way, a mix of disappointment and fear on his face.

She tipped her chin down and gave him a level stare.

You know what to do, she thought. *Let it go. You know it's the right thing to do.*

"All right, then," Auggie gave the barest of nods. "I think we're eating at seven." He put up a cautionary hand.

"We'll see how it goes. And we don't have any presents for Chloe, we weren't expecting ..."

"That's fine, Dad. Not a problem," Evan barely nodded. "She'll be excited enough as it is." He looked as if he wanted to hug his dad, but instead offered his hand. Auggie hesitated for a moment, then reached out and shook it.

"Good," was all Auggie said. "We'll see you tomorrow." He stuffed his hands in his pockets and started for the sideboard. "Well, I've got some dishes to wash, then I better get down to the co-op. Hate to leave Dan alone at the counter, you know."

There was a squeak and the door to the workshop opened. Bill's head popped around it and he raised his eyebrows at Melinda. She gave Bill a nod, and he and Chloe cautiously made their way up the main aisle of the store. The little girl grasped a wooden star in her hands.

"Look, Daddy," Chloe said, her excitement lowering the lingering tension in the room. "Bill cut it out for me. I can hang it on our Christmas tree."

"Maybe someday you can paint it," Bill suggested. "But for now, it will be just fine as it is."

Auggie stood awkwardly to the side, unsure what to say or do. Evan gave Bill a grateful nod and stepped forward.

"Chloe, this is your Grandpa Auggie. We haven't seen him in a long time. You were just a baby then." His face clouded for a moment, then he continued.

"But he and Grandma Jane have asked us to come over for supper on Christmas Eve. Do you know when that is?"

"Tomorrow night!" Chloe exclaimed, not taking her wide eyes off her grandfather.

"That's right, honey," Evan answered.

"Do you like my star?" she shyly asked Auggie. He tried his best to crouch down to his granddaughter's level.

"Why, yes, I do," he said, his voice wavering. "It's so pretty. It is good to meet you, Chloe."

Chloe smiled, then gave her grandpa an unexpected hug.

Auggie couldn't get any words out, but he blinked rapidly and tentatively wrapped his arms around the little girl.

Evan watched his father and daughter embrace with happy tears in his eyes. Then he seemed to think of something, and stepped over to the counter.

"Melinda, thank you again. Mom told me you cornered Dad, I guess he was an emotional wreck when he got home that night. She took the opportunity, then, to pressure him to let the past go."

Evan's brown eyes sparkled now, and he extended his hand. "I'm glad you spoke up, I think it made a difference."

"Oh, I don't know," she shrugged but accepted Evan's handshake. His grip was firm and warm, and the worry and fear that followed him in the door just minutes ago had all but vanished. "Your dad talked some sense into me a few months' back, I was just returning the favor. The important thing is, he's giving you another chance."

Uncle Frank clapped Evan on the shoulder. "Welcome to Prosper Hardware," he said. "I'm Frank Lange, I own this place with my wife, Miriam. Melinda here is our niece. Glad you stopped in."

"Frank," Evan shook his hand. "I really appreciated the gift card. We do need a few things, as long as we're here."

"Well, as Miriam likes to say, we've got 'a little of everything and a lot of nothing,'" Frank said as he handed Evan a plastic shopping basket.

Evan laughed, then reached into a coat pocket for his list. Chloe was telling Auggie all about Daisy, and he was hanging on every word.

"I always say, the first customer sets the tone for the whole day," Frank told Melinda as he leaned over the counter. "I think this will be the best day-before-Christmas Eve Prosper Hardware's ever had."

✳ 21 ✳

Melinda couldn't help it. She kept wandering by the living room's picture window and leaning over the sofa to stare up the gravel road.

"They'll be here any minute," she whispered, glancing around the cozy farmhouse yet again to check that everything was ready. A small fire snapped in the hearth, matching the bright sunshine still streaming through the windows. The oak floors gleamed, as she had found a few minutes that morning to give them a quick sweep. Savory aromas drifted from the kitchen, where sloppy joe filling and macaroni and cheese simmered in two slow cookers, one on loan from Mabel.

The Christmas tree glittered and glowed in its place of honor, but Melinda had to shake her head as she came through from the living room. Hobo had yet again wedged himself under the tree, packages and gift sacks pushed out of the way so he could sprawl out near the floor register. Hobo was snoring, one front paw twitching as he lived out some mysterious escapade in his sleep.

"I never would have guessed a dog your size could fit under my tree," she said softly as she crouched down to give Hobo's brown nose a loving pat. "You're a great deal bigger than Oreo, that's for sure."

How everything had changed since last Christmas. Before Melinda could become too sentimental, however, she heard the muffled rattle of tires on the gravel lane. Hobo's eyes popped open and he jumped to his feet with an excited bark, the Christmas tree rocking dangerously in its stand.

"Hobo, be careful!" she gasped as she reached for two of the tree's branches, its surprising weight tipping her way. "We don't need a disaster before Christmas even gets started!" The slap of the first doggie door told her Hobo was already into the back porch and on his way out to greet his guests.

Melinda steadied the tree, then took a calming breath. Was she really this nervous to see her sister?

She and Liz had been so close growing up, Liz being only two years younger. But when Liz chose to attend college in Chicago and then moved to Milwaukee to start her architectural design career, hundreds of miles and emotional distance caused them to grow apart. Weekly phone calls just weren't the same. Between Liz's hectic schedule with her career and two little boys, and the upheaval of Melinda's year, they hadn't seen each other since last Christmas.

She didn't need Liz to approve of her new life, Melinda reminded herself as she slipped on her shoes and reached for her coat. But oh, wouldn't it be nice if Liz was envious of her lovely acreage, even just a little bit?

"I guess sibling rivalry is alive and well," Melinda muttered as she tugged on a knit cap, then had to smile at the glittering expanse of the snow-covered yard outside the porch windows. "Besides, there's so much here to love."

Before she could get out the back door, little Noah was already barging through, breathless with excitement.

"Aunty Melinda, guess what?" The freckles on Noah's cold-flushed cheeks matched his brown eyes and the crooked knit hat on his head.

He pulled a rumpled fold of paper out of his parka pocket. "I made this snowman for you in school yesterday!"

"Why, Noah, I love it," she took the picture in one hand and wrapped the other arm around her youngest nephew, who at four wasn't in kindergarten yet, but couldn't wait to be. "I'll find a special for it on the refrigerator, OK?"

Noah noticed the layers of winter gear hanging on hooks by the back door. "Can we go see the sheep now? I saw them there by the barn, calling us to come and play with them."

Melinda smothered a laugh as she pulled on her gloves. Noah and his six-year-old brother, Liam, had only ever encountered farm animals at a petting zoo.

The array of critters waiting for them at her farm had been the source of curiosity for several weeks: What did the chickens eat? What did the sheep do all day? Could they take a ride on a sheep, like a pony? She had quickly put an end to that idea.

"I'm sure the sheep will be glad to meet you," she replied, "but we'll need to stay on our side of the fence." Noah's grin began to fade. "But don't worry. We can still reach through and pet their faces. And tonight, you and Liam can help me do chores, OK?"

This promise brought back Noah's smile, and he let out a whoop as he ran down the back steps to where Liz and Isaac were unloading overnight bags and sacks of gifts. Melinda's nerves vanished the minute Liz ran toward her and gave her a long, smothering hug.

"Well, we made it," Liz said as she pushed her sandy blonde hair out of her blue eyes. While Melinda and their brother, Mark, looked like Diane, Liz took after their father. "We didn't get lost! And you should have seen the boys' faces when we turned off on the gravel, you'd think we landed on the moon."

Isaac shifted his armful of luggage enough to pat Melinda on the back. "A few days out here will be good for them." He gazed around the farm yard, his hazel eyes lighting up with awe and approval. "This place is amazing, Melinda. Just look at those fields and trees. And that barn! No wonder you couldn't bear to leave."

"Why honey, I didn't know you longed for the country life," Liz laughed as she relieved Isaac of two of his bags.

"Being an accountant, playing golf is about as close as I get to the great outdoors," he admitted. "You know, I've spent my whole life within ten minutes of a twenty four-hour grocery store. I don't think I'd last very long out here."

Noah ran off to where Liam was petting Hobo under the oak tree. Isaac pointed out a blue tote just inside the SUV's tailgate. "That's where Santa keeps his stash," he whispered to Melinda. "The boys think it's still packed with sports gear. I'll come out tonight after they go to bed and bring the presents in."

Liz's face clouded as they watched the boys play with Hobo. "I wish our schedule wasn't so crazy at home," she sighed. "We'd get a dog in a heartbeat. Liam in particular could use a furry friend. He's in a new class this year for first grade, and it's been a hard transition for him."

Melinda gave her sister's arm a sympathetic squeeze as they turned for the house, memories of her first challenging weeks at the farm flooding back in her mind. "A little time with Hobo will do wonders for Liam," she assured Liz. "Hobo has a special knack for knowing who needs him the most."

Liz's smile returned as she entered the kitchen. "Melinda, your pictures didn't do this place justice. It's so homey and simple, but beautiful. You know, it reminds me of Grandpa and Grandma Foster's farm."

"Me, too," Melinda beamed with pride. "I think that's part of the reason this place called to me so strongly from the beginning. And what's funny is, the built-in bookcases and the oak woodwork are almost identical to what I had in my Minneapolis apartment."

But Liz stopped short when she entered the dining room. Isaac looked over her shoulder, and let out a low whistle when he saw the garish wallpaper. "I'm not sure if those bluebirds are friendly, or if they're going to peck my eyes out."

"That's one of the fun parts about living in an old house," Melinda shrugged. "You've got decades of design decisions to deal with."

"Could you take it down?" Liz suggested. "Or might that offend the Schermanns? Of course, once the farm is yours for good ..." She raised an eyebrow.

Melinda shook her head. "From what I hear, these birds would have flown the coop years ago if anyone could have gotten that wallpaper down. It's all but put on with cement."

Isaac set the boys' duffel bags on Horace's former bed, then Melinda continued the tour upstairs.

"You'll be staying in Wilbur's old room, there at the other end of the hall," she pointed. "I put extra blankets on the bed, and there's more stacked in the closet."

Liz and Melinda checked on the boys from the west window of Melinda's room. They were still playing with Hobo by the picnic table. There was no sign of Sunny and Stormy, but Melinda wasn't surprised. It had taken her months to earn their trust. Christmas visitors would be tolerated but not exactly welcomed.

"What a view," Liz took it all in. "And I can see how it must be in the summer, Melinda. A carpet of green grass, the trees full of leaves, bees buzzing among the flowers. It's beautiful." She turned from the window and gave her sister a knowing grin. "Should we get started on that messy project for the boys? I think they're as eager to try that out as they are to feed the sheep. In their minds, Santa's running about third this Christmas."

Melinda had roasted the pumpkin halves last night and left them in the refrigerator to cool. Isaac and Liz spread newspapers over the canning room's metal-topped table while Melinda showed Liam and Noah how to scoop out the pulp and add it to the crockery bowls she brought down from the kitchen.

"Can we go feed the sheep?" Noah asked as soon as the mess was cleared off the table. "Aunty Melinda, I really want to go see them now!"

Liz ruffled Noah's auburn hair, which was so like his father's. "The sheep and the chickens have a special time they eat supper, just like we do at home. We don't want to mix them up by feeding them too early."

Melinda glanced out the small, dingy window near the ceiling. The sunlight was starting to fade. And she knew it would take extra time to get the boys cleaned up and dressed for church. "Hmmm," she mused as Noah and Liam waited expectantly. "I think it's just about time for chores. Let's go get our coats and ..."

"Yes!" Liam shouted and ran for the stairs.

"I packed the boys' oldest boots," Liz said. "I already told them to be careful where they step in the barn, that you had the house so nice and clean for our visit."

"Don't worry," Melinda laughed. "I track all kinds of stuff into that porch. Wait until you see my new brown coveralls. They're the latest in farmer fashion, purchased at Prosper Hardware, of course."

The boys wanted coveralls too, but were soon distracted by the promise of another project. After they fed the chickens, sheep and cats, they would help Melinda stack bundles of hay in two buckets and set them in front of the barn to gather the special Christmas frost.

"And in the morning, you can help me feed it to the sheep," she promised they boys. "It'll be their special treat."

The chickens were startled by all the strange faces approaching their run, and scuttled into the coop. "It gets a little crowded in there," Melinda gently explained to Noah, who wanted to go inside and pet all the hens. Instead, Liz, Isaac and the boys watched Melinda do the chicken chores through the coop's screen door.

"That one chicken's not a good friend," Liam pointed to Pansy as she pecked one of the other hens out of her way.

"You're right," Melinda tried not to laugh as she latched the coop's outer door tight. Her nephews missed nothing. "I think you'll have more fun in the barn."

The yard light flickered on as they passed the machine shed, the thin layer of snow crunching under their boots. A few stars appeared in the clear, cold sky.

"Looks like a good night for Santa to make his rounds," Isaac told the boys.

"Do you think he'll find us out here?" Noah asked Melinda, doubt in his voice.

"I'm sure he will," she answered confidently. "He keeps a list of all the boys and girls away from home on Christmas, so he knows where to bring their gifts."

Some of the ewes were in the pasture west of the barn, watching their guests approach. Melinda steered the boys to the barn door and ushered them into the main aisle. "OK, say 'here, sheep; here, sheep.' Let's see if they come."

Encouragement to shout didn't come their way often, and the boys made the most of the opportunity. They cheered with excitement as the ewes tumbled in through the pasture door and lined up at the troughs across the aisle fence.

Liam insisted on scooping the grain from the barrel and tossing it into the feed bunks, climbing partway up the fence so he could reach over the partition. Isaac held Noah up so the little boy could drop the fistfuls of hay Liz broke out of the bale at her feet. Melinda let herself inside the sheep's area and, after counting twelve ewes at the feeders, closed and latched their pasture door. Isaac and Liz tossed the rest of the sheep's evening hay while Melinda went into the grain room to feed and comfort Sunny and Stormy.

"Lots going on, huh?" she said to the cats, who rubbed against her coveralls but kept a wary-eyed watch over the commotion out in the aisle.

"Don't worry, I think the boys are too excited about the sheep to want to pet you two. We'll go inside soon, and you can eat in peace."

There was barely time to get everyone dressed and over to the Fosters' home church in Swanton by seven. Then they enjoyed cookies and cocoa at Diane and Roger's house, the boys only willing to leave once Grandma and Grandpa promised they would arrive at the farm in time to open presents Christmas morning.

The farmhouse was quiet at last, the boys sound asleep in Horace's old room while Hobo dozed in his favorite spot at the foot of the bed. Isaac went upstairs, saying he wanted to read for a while, but Melinda suspected he was trying to give Liz some quiet time with her sister.

"Oh, that's just what I needed," Liz sighed gratefully as Melinda brought her a glass of red wine.

"What a day." Melinda stretched out in her reading chair by the fireplace, where she had just started a new blaze, and picked up her own glass. "I think everything is ready, now that the bread's all torn up for the stuffing. I can make the pies in the morning."

Liz pulled one of the cozy fleece throws off the back of the couch and handed the other to Melinda. They sipped in silence for a few minutes as the fire took hold, spreading its warmth into the dimly-lit room.

"I know I've said this already, but I love this house," Liz said in a low voice, determined to not wake the boys in the next room. "And when it's decorated for Christmas, it's even more amazing."

"It's so much more fun to decorate for the holidays than take everything down in January, isn't it?" Melinda mused, admiring the tree around the corner. "A house always looks so bare for a few days, like something's missing."

A gust of wind pushed in from the north, and the clear plastic sealed over the square windows above the bookcases flexed in and out. Melinda shook her head.

"I shrink-wrapped these windows as tight as I could. Extra rows of tape, even. I never got around to doing the window in Wilbur's old room, though. I hope you and Isaac will be warm enough the next two nights."

"Oh, we'll be just fine," Liz waved Melinda's worries away. "There's plenty of blankets. And it's only December. Winter hasn't really kicked in yet. But when it does ..."

Her voice trailed off. She fell silent, then seemed to gather her courage.

"Melinda," Liz set up straighter and set her wine glass on the coffee table. "Do you really mean to stay here? I mean, as in, *forever*?"

Melinda paused for a moment, the weight of that word sinking in. "Well, who knows?" she shrugged at last. "I'm going to buy this place from Horace, once spring comes. I can see myself here, Liz, for years and years to come. But you never know where life will take you, I guess. A year ago, I wouldn't have believed I'd be here in the first place."

She laughed softly, then stopped when she saw the concern on her sister's face. "You think I'm crazy, don't you?"

"No, not crazy," Liz said quietly. "I just ... this is a big commitment, Melinda. Buying a farm? This place is darling but it's, what, a hundred years old? And, I love Frank and Miriam, too, but ... working at the hardware store? You're so creative, you loved Minneapolis so much. I always thought you were happy there."

Melinda swallowed hard, measuring her words carefully.

"I was happy there," she answered sadly. "But then everything changed. Just as I'd finally healed from breaking off my engagement to Craig, things started to go south at WP&S, we were losing clients. Then Oreo died, and ..."

The tears were coming now, and she tried to brush them away with the back of her hand. "Then I lost my job. I didn't know who I was anymore. Nothing made sense."

"And then Mom called to tell you about Uncle Frank," Liz said gently. "And suddenly, you had a purpose again. You were needed. But that's all in the past now, the emergency is over. It's OK for you to move on, to get back to leading your own life."

"This *is* my life," Melinda muttered. How could she make Liz understand? "I may not be married, or have kids, but I ..."

"That's not what I meant. I would never ..." Liz sighed, but didn't say anything more.

Melinda took a sip of her wine, the tension rising in the room. "Maybe things haven't worked out as I suspected they would, OK? I'll be forty in March. Forty! Do you remember when we thought that was ancient?"

"Well, actually, we thought thirty was ancient," Liz said wryly, then became serious. "But that doesn't mean you have to stop trying ..."

"Trying for what? For the white picket fence and all that? For the big corner office?" Melinda tried to keep her voice down. She was suddenly so hurt. Did Liz think that was why she'd stayed on here? Because she'd given up on herself?

"You're right, Liz. I used to have it all," Melinda stared into the fire, remembering. "I had the great job, the closet stuffed with designer clothes, the cute vintage apartment in the 'right' neighborhood. But it wasn't enough. And then, it all went away."

Liz just looked at the floor.

"And then, I went away," Melinda whispered, shaking her head. "And now, I just can't go back, I don't want to. I'm happy here. Why isn't that enough?"

"I wish I could have come," Liz wiped at her cheeks, her voice thick with guilt. "I wish I could have been there when you lost your job. I wanted to just get in the car and drive five hours and be there with you, help you somehow. But I couldn't get away."

"I know, I know," Melinda said gently, trying to get her own sniffles under control.

The door to Horace's room edged open, and a brown nose popped out. Hobo approached Liz for a quick pet, then leaned his head against Melinda's reading chair. She reached down and wrapped her arms around him, and the fuzzy white tip of his tail thumped a comforting rhythm on the floral wool rug.

Liz rose from the sofa and approached Melinda, placing an arm around her sister's shoulders.

"I'm sorry, I shouldn't have questioned your choices. This is a wonderful place, Melinda." Liz reached down and gave Hobo a loving pat on the head. "And any place that comes with a dog as special as Hobo must be the right place for you."

⁂ 22 ⁂

Only the Christmas tree's soft lights greeted Melinda as she tiptoed downstairs the next morning, determined to not wake her guests. Hobo wasn't waiting in the living room, ready to help with chores, but Melinda knew why.

She peeked into Horace's old bedroom and saw Hobo still curled up with Liam and Noah, and all of them sound asleep. *Merry Christmas*, she thought but didn't say, then padded into the dining room to confirm that Santa had indeed arrived after she and Liz, at last finished with their confidences and glasses of wine, called it a night.

Melinda knew Liz meant well, but their situations were so different. She had never considered herself materialistic or shallow but, like so many people, assumed her life would follow a certain path, an expected order. But when things began to unravel, she learned to toss that to-do list aside.

And when she found the courage to let go of her expectations, she discovered a new way forward and realized how blessed she really was.

Sort of like my plans for the perfect Christmas, she thought as she rubbed her eyes and wandered into the kitchen, which was silent except for the refrigerator humming away in the corner. Maybe she didn't need a fancy menu or elaborate place settings to make today special. Even so, she had things to do this morning.

Diane and Roger would be at the farm around nine, and Frank and Miriam said they'd be there by eleven. With such a big meal planned for midday, breakfast would be a simple selection of cereals and some cranberry-bran muffins she pulled from the basement freezer the night before. Isaac, of course, was taking ownership of the turkey. She just had to make the stuffing, and the pies ...

Melinda didn't pause to flip on the kitchen light, but shuffled across the room to turn the preheat knob on the oven. It would be ready by the time she came in from chores. Since she was cheating with store-made pie crust, it would take only a few minutes to blend the pumpkin custard. She could have the pies baking, their wonderful aroma filling the house, by the time everyone came down for breakfast.

The buckets of hay were right where Melinda and the boys left them, the hay's dull green obscured by a thick layer of frost. She was glad no wild animals had knocked the pails over during the night or ran off with mouthfuls of the hay, ruining the boys' fun. So the chickens wouldn't feel left out, she would cut up one of the larger pumpkins in the cellar and let Liam and Noah feed some of the chunks to the hens and give the rest to the sheep.

Melinda had only told Liam and Noah that the frosted hay would be a nice treat for the ewes, and left the rest of the superstition unsaid. The idea that their efforts might protect the sheep in the coming year would go right over the little boys' heads. And worse, she thought with a shudder, if something bad happened to one of her animals, she never wanted her nephews to feel responsible.

Part of her thought the procedure was silly. On the other hand, there was a strange comfort to it, a reassurance she was doing all she could to take care of her animals. Melinda shifted the handle of the cats' food bucket up her arm, and reached down to take the pails of hay inside the barn.

"It's a Christmas tradition at this farm," she told Sunny and Stormy, who greeted her on the other side of the door, their demanding meows drowned out by the calls of the sheep. "And what's wrong with that? We need to pick things up right where Horace left off, don't we?"

Sunny's golden eyes zeroed in on the cats' bucket before he ran ahead to the grain room, but Stormy took a moment to sniff the pails of frosted hay.

"After Christmas dinner, I'll bring you two some gravy and a picked-over buffet of turkey trimmings," she promised the cats as she poured out their breakfast kibble. "Personally, I think you guys are getting the better end of the deal. Your treats will be far tastier than some bunches of hay or chunks of pumpkin."

A smudge of pink was just visible on the eastern horizon as Melinda came out of the barn, the sky fading from a velvet black to a soft gray-blue. There was no wind and, despite the cold, it promised to be a clear, beautiful Christmas Day. She was halfway to the house, mulling over her blessings as she often did on these silent mornings, when her thoughts were interrupted by what sounded like Hobo barking frantically on the back porch.

Then a small figure burst out the door, Liam still in his pajamas and his brown hair a sleepy mess.

"Aunt Melinda!" Liam yelled from the top step, sounding both afraid and excited all at once. "Something's on fire!"

She dropped the cats' food bucket in the snow and sprinted past the garage, rounding the picnic table just as Liz appeared on the back steps.

"Did you turn on the oven before you went out?" she gasped, pulling her fleece robe tighter against the cold.

The unmistakable smell of smoke met Melinda as she rushed past Liz. "Sure, but I didn't put anything in it, just set it to heat for the pies! How can something be burning?"

She kicked off her ice-crusted boots and hurried into the kitchen, where two trays of blackened blobs now huddled on top of the stove, the smoke alarm a shrill screech above Hobo's frenzied barking and everyone talking at once.

Isaac stood on a chair by the sink, reaching for the smoke detector tucked under the high ceiling, and at last the terrible beeping stopped. Liz ripped away the clear plastic sealed over the kitchen windows and opened one of the wooden sashes, allowing a refreshing wave of cold air to rush into the kitchen.

"What happened?" Melinda waved off the smoke and rushed to the crumbled, charred mess scattered on the cookie sheets. "This is ... or it was ... the bread cubes for the stuffing. I left them on the kitchen table to dry, I'm sure of it. I didn't put them in the oven."

She sighed, thinking back. "I was half asleep when I went out to do chores, but I'm sure I only turned the preheat on. Why would I stick the bread in there? I can't imagine ..."

Through the haze of clearing smoke, Melinda caught a glimpse of Liam and Noah huddled in the corner by the refrigerator with Hobo wedged between them. She saw the furtive look that passed between her two young nephews. Liz saw it, too.

"OK, boys," Liz said gently but firmly. "Does anyone have anything to say that could help solve this mystery?"

There was a moment of guilty silence, and Liam busied himself with scratching Hobo's ears.

"Hobo did it!" Noah wailed. "We tried to stop him!"

Melinda blinked. "What do you ..."

"We were trying to help," Noah's voice rose in distress. "We wanted to save the stuffing. We got up to see Santa and the reindeer, and then we heard these noises!"

Isaac covered his face with his hands, but Melinda was sure he was trying to hide a smile. Liz just sighed, being all-too-familiar with trying to get a straight answer from her boys. "OK, you guys. Just tell us what happened."

"Hobo woke up and wouldn't go back to sleep," Liam took a tentative step toward his mom. "We got up and he took us to the front window, where we saw these deer out front. The one was really big, with the big antlers."

Liam raised his hands above his head and Noah nodded vigorously in agreement.

"We watched the reindeer," Noah added, his eyes growing wide at the memory, "hoping to see Santa when he came back around the house. There was all this rattling out in the kitchen. I thought Santa had come in the back door."

Liam shook his head, still disappointed by what they found. "We ran in here, but it wasn't Santa. Hobo was up on a chair and eating the bread off the table, Aunt Melinda."

"When was all this?" Isaac was nearly choking on suppressed laughter. "Why didn't you come get us?"

"Everyone was asleep," Liam said matter-of-factly. "We told Hobo to get off the chair because we wanted to have stuffing for Christmas. We tried to hide the bread. But the refrigerator was full. So we set it in the oven. We were going to get it out this morning and put it back on the table before everyone got up. But Aunt Melinda, you get up so early!"

"We didn't want Hobo to get in trouble," Noah whimpered, patting Hobo on the head. Hobo turned and licked the little boy's hand. "Hobo is a very nice dog and he just wanted some of the bread. It was really good."

Melinda suspected Hobo wasn't her only taste-tester. She imagined Hobo and the boys padding around the kitchen in the dark, sampling the bread cubes and then trying to find a place to hide the rest.

"I got the broom and swept the floor," Liam said proudly, gesturing to the covered trash can by the back door. "I cleaned everything up."

The boys watched Melinda with cautious eyes and Hobo, sensing his crime had been discovered, lowered his head and leaned closer to Noah. She didn't know whether to laugh or cry. She'd been planning this meal for weeks, purchasing a package of raisins to put in the special stuffing her Grandma Foster always made, the one with the apples and the spices.

Even when she ran short on time and energy, Melinda had refused to give up the idea of serving this family dish at her first Christmas at the farm. But the charred blobs still smoking on the scorched cookie sheets told her there would be no homemade stuffing this year.

In the awkward silence, she realized everyone was waiting for her to say something. This was her house, after all. Her home. She could voice her disappointment, put a damper on everyone's Christmas cheer, or just roll with things and get on with the holiday.

"It's OK," she said at last, hurrying over to her nephews, who burst into happy grins as she hugged them close.

"You wanted to do the right thing. And I shouldn't have turned the oven on and then went outside like that, even if I thought it was empty. I was trying to save time."

"We'll get breakfast on the table," Liz gestured to the upper cabinets and Melinda pointed to where the cereal bowls were kept. "You go get changed. And if you show me where to find the recipe for the pumpkin pies, I'll get those going after we eat."

"There's one in the recipe box up on the top shelf by the stove," Melinda answered as she gave Hobo a reassuring hug. "Horace insisted we use it for the pies, he said it was his mom's and she made the best pumpkin pies ever."

"What's the secret ingredient?" Isaac asked as he set the milk and butter on the table.

"None that I can see," she shrugged. "I called Ada about it, and she laughed and said it's just the recipe off the cans of pumpkin you get at the store."

Liam and Noah, their transgressions now behind them, poured out their cereal. Liam began to speculate about what was in the mysterious packages under the tree, and exactly how Santa knew to drop their presents at Aunt Melinda's farm. Noah, however, was still so quiet.

"What is it, buddy?" Isaac ruffled his youngest son's hair. "Aunt Melinda's not mad."

"I wanted stuffing for Christmas." Noah whispered as he wiped his face with the flannel sleeve of his pajama top. "Now we don't have any."

Liz and Melinda looked at each other, nearly as disappointed as Noah. Their grandmother's stuffing was a tradition they both treasured. Melinda could only shake her head. "Sorry, Noah. But there's lots of potatoes in the cellar. We'll just have more of those with lots of yummy gravy."

"Too bad the one grocery store in Swanton is closed today," Liz said, "or Mom and Dad could stop on their way out of town."

"Wait a minute. Why didn't I think of this sooner?" Melinda reached for her phone.

"Uncle Frank? Hey, it's Melinda. Merry Christmas! We've had a, well, a change in plans with our menu. Could you and Aunt Miriam stop by the store and check on something before you leave town?"

The boys regained their good cheer as they handed out the treats to the chickens and the sheep. The hens clucked over their pumpkin pieces, pecking at them greedily, and the ewes eagerly accepted the extra handfuls of hay the boys tossed over the fence. Noah and Liam both cheered when Melinda went into the sheep's area and opened the pasture door. "They're excited about Christmas, too!" Noah shouted as the sheep rushed out to enjoy the calm, sunny day

Isaac was setting up the turkey fryer by the picnic table when Melinda and the boys returned from the barn. Liam pointed out Roger and Diane's car, which was coming down the gravel road and soon turned up the drive, a small wreath anchored to its front grill.

"We're loaded down with gifts," Diane told Melinda, giving her oldest daughter a warm hug. "Merry Christmas, honey. It's too bad your brother couldn't make it home, but I've got everyone else under one roof today. I consider myself very blessed."

Once everyone was settled in the living room, with coffee for the adults and mugs of hot chocolate for the boys, Isaac handed out the presents.

Liam and Noah were thrilled with their toys, ticking off their wish lists and shouting over how, yet again, Santa had come through. As Melinda suspected they would, everyone received a hand-knitted scarf from Diane. Hers was a herringbone pattern in two soft shades of lavender.

"Mom, this is so beautiful," she said as she examined the intricate design. "You could sell these, I know you could."

"Oh, it's just a hobby," Diane waved away the suggestion, but Melinda could see her mom was pleased. "I got a bit carried away, I was even going to knit a sweater for Hobo. But your father wisely talked me out of it. I think Hobo's just as happy with the treats and toys we brought him." She reached over and scratched Hobo's chin.

"Melinda, you've got another present there," Roger pointed. He was so excited about whatever was in the last box, which was heavy for its size. She gave him a questioning look and ripped off the holly-themed paper.

"A drill?" She turned the box over. "Two drills?"

"It's a cordless drill-and-driver set," Roger could barely contain his enthusiasm. "There's two bases. One to use, and one to charge. Lots of power there. If you're taking over this farm, you're going to need better tools. I've seen Horace's stash. Some of his stuff looks to be as old as I am."

"Oh, Dad!" Melinda got up and gave Roger a hug. Then she laughed. "Even a year ago, I would have thought you were crazy to give me this. But it's perfect! This is just what I need."

"Only one thing," Roger raised an eyebrow. "Promise me that if you're going to use that for any extended period of time, that you let me come over and help."

He lowered his voice and looked longingly out the picture window. "I really miss my parents' farm. I never realized how much, until you moved back and landed here, Melinda. I'm offering free labor whenever you need it."

"I'll take you up on that," she replied. "You might be sorry you offered, though."

After the presents were opened, Isaac bundled up and went outside to watch over the turkey fryer, Hobo tagging along. Sunny and Stormy soon appeared, drawn by the savory aroma, and stretched out on the picnic table, angling themselves to catch the feeble sun's rays.

"I swear your kitties are expecting more company," Liz said as she pulled the pumpkin pies from the oven. "The fluffy orange one appears to be asleep, but I think he's really watching the driveway."

Frank and Miriam soon arrived. Uncle Frank had a casserole dish of green beans tucked in his arms, and Aunt Miriam carried a canvas tote bag.

"So ... did we get lucky?" Melinda almost hated to ask.

"Two boxes of stuffing!" Miriam cheered and plopped them on the kitchen counter with a flourish. "One still on the shelf, and one up in storage. The very last we've got."

Miriam took off her coat and then pulled a package of rolls from the bag. "You know, those apples and raisins and spices will taste almost as good in this boxed mix. Get me a cutting board, and I'll get this ready and in the oven."

Melinda had discovered an embroidered white tablecloth in the dining room's built-in buffet, and carefully hand-washed and ironed it for the occasion. She now spread it over the ornately carved table, then let Liam and Noah set out her white, everyday dishes and plain glassware.

A group of cut-glass dessert bowls in the buffet had also caught her eye, but she hesitated to use them. Ada, however, insisted otherwise.

"You get them out," Ada had told her last week. "They probably haven't been used since our mother died. Horace and Wilbur weren't exactly hosting fancy dinners out there. Mother would love for someone to enjoy them again."

Melinda had carefully washed seven of the dessert dishes, deciding to scoop Liam and Noah's gelatin into paper cups instead. There were only nine bowls, meaning at least one broke years ago, and she didn't want to add to that tally.

Just before noon, everyone gathered around a beautiful table loaded down with steaming platters and bowls. All except Hobo, who took up his new favorite place under the Christmas tree, where there was at last plenty of room to stretch out. Besides, Hobo had already enjoyed his holiday dinner. Isaac had shared several choice bits of turkey while carving the bird in the kitchen.

The turkey's appearance in the dining room earned a round of applause. It turned out just as Isaac promised it would, tender and juicy but with a crisp skin.

Melinda was proud to add a jar of her plum jam to the table, to pair with Aunt Miriam's from-scratch rolls. And there was a ripple of laughter when she returned from the kitchen with a small cut-glass serving bowl heaped with the pungent, colorful corn relish.

"It's a holiday tradition in this house," she told her family. "So we've got it on the table. That doesn't mean we have to eat it. But if you're feeling brave, by all means help yourself."

Melinda asked her dad to lead grace. But before Roger could begin, Uncle Frank raised his hand. "I've got something I'd like to say first, Roger, if you don't mind."

"The floor's all yours, Frank."

Uncle Frank looked around the table, took a moment to give each member of the family a grateful glance. "I'm lucky to be here, as you all know. That day back in June, when I had that heart attack and collapsed right there on the floor of Prosper Hardware, I thought I was done for." Aunt Miriam reached over and grasped Frank's hand. "But what I thought was the end turned out to be a new beginning."

"That's a great line, Uncle Frank," Liz suddenly spoke up. "I think it belongs in a song." Everyone laughed.

Frank beamed but shook his head. "Just so you know, I didn't just pull that one out of my hat. Took me awhile this morning to think about what I wanted to share with all of you today." The room fell silent again.

"I got another chance," Frank continued. "Maybe I can't work at the store the way I used to, but I can still live my life with thankfulness and gratitude. And out of all that fear and pain, another great thing happened."

Frank turned to Melinda, who sat at the head of the table. "Melinda came home. And then? She decided to stay. I can't thank you enough, Melinda, for what you've done for us."

"Neither can I," Miriam chimed in. "Honey, it's wonderful to have you back."

"I couldn't agree more," Diane said with happy tears in her eyes as she gazed around the table. "There's nowhere I'd rather be on Christmas Day than right here, with all of you."

Melinda took in everything around her, the happy faces of her family members, the glowing Christmas tree, Hobo dozing underneath its branches. A cheerful blaze sizzled in the fireplace.

If she turned her head just so, she could see out the dining room's south windows to where the sheep frolicked in the snowy pasture, dashing about in the bright sunshine.

"I know it's Christmas, and not Thanksgiving," Melinda began, "but I think every day is a good day to count your blessings. So, I'm thankful for all of you, for this wonderful house, this farm, and every crazy thing that comes with it. For better or worse."

Liz caught Melinda's gaze and gave her a knowing wink.

"I got a Christmas card from Horace the other day," Melinda continued. "He asked me to wish you all a Merry Christmas, and to thank you for helping this old house come alive again at the holidays."

"It's wonderful how strangers can become friends, and friends can turn into family," Roger said, then raised his wine glass. "To family, of all kinds. And here's to a bright future, for all of us."

Melinda ended her Christmas Day where she started it, out in the barn. The sun had already set by the time Frank and Miriam left for home. It was completely dark when she zipped up her coveralls and started her evening rounds, Diane and Liz taking charge of the homemade pizzas that would serve as their supper.

She was solo for chores again, but she didn't mind. Hobo would get back to his rounds tomorrow, when Liz and her family left for Milwaukee and Melinda returned to Prosper Hardware and her regular routine. She paused on the back steps to switch on the headlamp settled over her knit cap, then set off across the yard to the chicken house, mushing through the snow with the toes of her insulated boots.

She gazed up at the full moon, which gave the snow-frosted yard a pearly glow. What had Auggie told her about this moon?

Oh yes, it was known as the cold moon, signaling winter's arrival. But he'd reminded her of something else the other day: The winter solstice had come and gone. So although the sun set early this time of year, they were now at last moving, slowly but surely, toward spring.

She pondered this as she fed the chickens and changed their water. There was something about the sun gaining strength, a little more every day ... Melinda decided she liked that idea. She was getting stronger, too. The worst weather of the season was sure to come. It would get colder before it got warmer, and there was likely to be heavy snow, even ice. But Melinda was ready, and she would persevere.

After she settled Stormy and Sunny in the grain room with more turkey scraps and their usual kibble and water, she turned her attention to the sheep waiting expectantly on the other side of the aisle fence.

"Yes, ladies, yes, I know," she cooed to them as she scooped out their grain. "Did you think I'd forgotten? I'd never do that to you." She reached for slabs of hay torn from the bales parked in the aisle, and made a mental note to bring more down from the haymow tomorrow.

Christmas had been special, but such a whirlwind of activity. She put her arms on the aisle fence, taking a moment to enjoy the peace she always felt out here, in the barn with her animals, and patted a few sheep on their wooly heads.

"You all are such good girls, you rarely give me any trouble. Except you, Annie," Melinda turned to address the ewe at the far end of the line.

"But that's just because you're so independent. And spoiled. I can thank Horace and Wilbur for that."

She evaluated her little flock, admiring their healthy appearance. The sheep's cream wool was thick and curly, and every one of them had a hearty appetite. But even so, a few of the girls looked a little, well ... wider.

Melinda had been so busy the past few weeks, and it had turned so cold for both the morning and evening rounds of chores, that she hadn't stopped to examine the sheep closely.

But now, she leaned over the wooden fence as far as her bulky layers would allow and studied them, one by one.

Karen had said any lambs on the way would arrive in the middle of February. She and Doc cautioned Melinda that it could be a few weeks into the new year before it would be clear which ewes were pregnant.

"We're less than two months out now," she reminded the ewes as they munched their hay and grain. "Who has a secret to share, huh?"

Annie appeared to be the same old Annie, and Melinda was relieved that her feisty girl didn't seem to have motherhood in her future. Lambing would be hard enough, she suspected, without having to deal with Annie's moods.

But what about No. 18? She peered closer. Maybe. And No. 7 also seemed to be carrying a few extra pounds.

No. 33 looked to be all but a lock, if Melinda correctly remembered how she used to look. She decided No. 21 also could be in the family way.

"So, there's maybe three or four," she mused as she checked that the lids on the metal feed barrels were tight and secure. "Out of a dozen sheep. Are those good odds?"

She reached over and petted No. 33 on the nose. "If we average two lambs apiece, that's six or eight babies that could be coming."

Melinda eyed the feed bunks in the vacant area on the other side of the aisle. Whatever would she do with more sheep? Could they all eat together, or would she need to get another trough in the barn? Would it be better to keep the new lambs once they were weaned, or sell some, or all? Could she get a good price for the adults' wool when they were sheared in the summer?

Her mind ran in circles. There was so much she didn't know, so many decisions that would have to be made. But she didn't need the answers tonight.

Stormy, finished with his supper, jumped up on the fence and demanded Melinda turn her attention to him. "It's been a wonderful Christmas, hasn't it?" she whispered to Stormy, then cuddled him against her coveralls. "As for what the new year will bring, we'll just have to wait and see."

She set Stormy down on the concrete floor and he padded toward the back of the barn, eager to curl up in the cats' heated hideaway under the stairs. She opened the barn door, then reached back to flip off the lights.

As Melinda turned around again, she saw the farmhouse glowing with warmth, pools of welcoming light pouring out its windows. There was Liz in the kitchen, taking the pizzas out of the oven. Roger was setting a stack of paper plates on the dining room table, the Christmas tree glittering in the corner behind him.

Melinda was tired, but she was content. There would be plenty of time to enjoy the memories from this wonderful Christmas after everyone went home. But for now, she was determined to embrace every busy, crazy minute.

It was only right that this farmhouse was once again filled with people and love on this special day. If not for the modern vehicles lined up by the garage, she decided, this cozy scene could be from any Christmas years ago.

Time stood still, if only for a moment, as she paused there in the barn's sheltering doorway. Her thoughts turned to two elderly brothers, dozing in their easy chairs after a full day of celebrating with Ada and Kevin, of a miniature Christmas tree glowing in a basket on a nearby table. She would be sure to call them tomorrow.

"*Merry Christmas, Horace. Merry Christmas, Wilbur,*" Melinda whispered. She gathered up her buckets, heard the satisfying click of the sturdy barn door as it latched tight against the cold, and stepped out into the night.

WHAT'S NEXT

"Waiting Season" sneak peek: Read on for a special excerpt from the fourth title in the series, which follows Melinda through the next few months. She's got some big challenges ahead of her, including a rough Iowa winter and those pregnant sheep out in the barn. "Waiting Season" arrives in December. And, additional titles are planned for this series. Look for Book 5 sometime in 2019.

Recipes and more: Part of the fun is discovering what Melinda cooks up in her farmhouse kitchen. Head over to fremontcreekpress.com to find recipes inspired by the novels!

About the books: Details on all the novels follow the excerpt from "Waiting Season." Then discover "A Tin Train Christmas," a short story set on the Schermann farm during the Great Depression!

Stay in touch: Sign up for the email newsletter when you visit fremontcreekpress.com. You won't hear from me too often, but when you do, it'll be something worthwhile ... like release dates for future books in the series.

So, what did you think? If you've got something to say about "The Peaceful Season," please hop on to Amazon.com and leave a review. Or, share your thoughts with your friends on Goodreads.

Thanks for reading!
Melanie

FOURTH IN A SERIES

Waiting Season

* *a novel* *

BY MELANIE LAGESCHULTE

Coming December 2018

SNEAK PEEK
AT 'WAITING SEASON'

January: Prosper Hardware

It was already after seven, and still no sign of Auggie. Melinda thought it strange, and began to set out the folding chairs and make the coffee. Jerry soon wandered in, then George.

"I can't believe I'm saying this," George sighed as he pulled off his coat. "But it's too warm and humid out there, for this this time of year, anyway. Rain in January? Feels like this storm could be a big one, too, given how my knees ache this morning."

They had just settled in with their coffee when there was an urgent pounding on the store's front door. The huddled-over man on the other side offered a friendly wave and pointed at the handle. Melinda glanced at the round clock above the sideboard. Prosper Hardware didn't open for twenty minutes, but she felt bad leaving the guy standing out there like that. It was raining hard now, the gloomy skies a heavy shade of slate, and the store's dark-green canvas awning offered little protection from the bracing wind.

She hesitated for only a moment, then slipped the deadbolt to the side. A rush of damp air, noticeably colder than even an hour ago, blasted her face as she opened the door. "Can I help you?"

"I need ice melt and batteries," the man gasped, pushing back the hood of his parka and wiping the cold rain out of his eyes. "Thanks for opening early. I live twelve miles out, and I want to get back home as soon as I can."

Melinda's confusion must have been obvious, as the customer gave her a surprised look.

"Haven't you heard?" He shook off his heavy gloves, which were soaked through. Water dripped down his lined face and out of his trimmed gray beard.

"Weather service just updated their forecast. A winter storm warning, starting at noon. Eight inches on the way."

"Oh, sorry, I didn't know," Melinda replied. She was about to add that Auggie, unlike the professional forecasters, had predicted that outcome the day before. But the urgency on the man's face told her he didn't have time to chat.

"We've got some ice melt right up front here," she said instead, "and batteries are in the second aisle. Anything else?"

The man paused for a moment and looked around the store. "I better get some milk and eggs."

George, trying to fight down his laughter, gestured at the refrigerator case and then the grocery aisle. "French toast tastes good in this kind of weather. Bread's over there in row three, while you're here."

Before Melinda could ring up the man's purchases and lock the door behind him, three new people rushed in. Then two more customers, then five. The stack of plastic hand baskets was nearly empty, and oversized snowflakes suddenly appeared outside Prosper Hardware's plate-glass windows. She had never been so glad to see Bill hurrying up from the back, still wearing his parka.

"Where did they all come from?" he shook out his soaked cap and surveyed the crowd. "The back lot is full already."

"One guy wanted in, so I opened the door," Melinda said in a low voice so she could be heard over the rising din in the store. "Then, like, a dozen more just came out of nowhere. Word now is eight inches of snow, just like Auggie predicted. I guess we're open early today."

Then the phone rang. It was a woman wondering if Prosper Hardware had flashlights in stock. When Melinda said there were a few left, the woman begged her to save one back and said she was on her way to the store.

Before Melinda could ask Bill to grab a flashlight, two men started to argue over the last bag of ice melt by the front counter. Bill quickly stepped between them.

"We've got more, don't worry. Pull around back after you pay. It's on a pallet right inside the door."

Melinda could barely keep up with the line at the register, and the store buzzed with a mix of anxiety and excitement.

Jerry folded the chairs back against the wall and elbowed through the crowd to reach the counter. "I guess no coffee club this morning, huh? I encouraged George to head home. Doc just called me, said he's working a round of farm calls before things get worse. What can I do to help?"

"Check that grocery aisle for me, will you? Bill's parceling out ice melt and shovels. There's more bread and such in the storeroom, if you can bring some down. I'm afraid the milk and eggs in the cooler is all we've got, though."

Jerry ferried supplies for nearly an hour before a phone call sent him across the street to City Hall. Then Uncle Frank arrived. Melinda was surprised but relieved, as Bill was still busy in the back.

"I couldn't stay away," Frank said defensively, his tone telling Melinda he'd already been chastised by Aunt Miriam, who was down with the flu. "I knew it would be crazy in here, and it's only three blocks, you know. They're dismissing school at ten, so this rush isn't going to let up anytime soon."

"Well, if you're going to stay, we could use the help," Melinda said. "Let Bill handle the heavy stuff, OK? No lifting. Here, you take the register and I'll check the shelves."

The eggs were nearly gone, and only two cartons of milk remained. A few random boxes of cereal were still on the grocery shelf. She counted four loaves of bread. The soup had been raided as well. There were more non-perishable groceries in the upstairs storeroom, but when they ran out, that was it. The truck wouldn't come again for two days.

Melinda was bringing down packages of toilet paper when the weather radio screeched on the counter. The storm alert had been upgraded to a blizzard warning, with gusts over 45 mph, whiteout conditions and up to a foot of snow. The flakes were now falling thick and fast, City Hall and the library erased into mere shadows as the wind whipped down Main Street. She hurried behind the counter to sack purchases while Uncle Frank continued to ring up orders.

Bill came in from the back, clutching his phone. "Tony just texted everyone, said the roads are getting worse and we need to be ready." Bill, like Doc, was a volunteer with Prosper's emergency department. "There's already a pileup on the state highway north of here. If any more accident calls come in, Prosper needs to take the lead."

"There goes our last gallon of milk," Uncle Frank sighed as one woman, bundled in warm layers but with a triumphant smile on her face, hurried for the door.

Melinda was trying to mop up puddles of slush from inside the front door when Esther's car pulled up.

"Melinda, you are to get out of here, right now," Esther rubbed at her frozen cheeks. "Miriam just called me. She'd come herself if she wasn't so sick."

"Oh, Esther, thank you so much for coming!" Melinda hugged her friend, then grabbed her coat, hat and gloves.

The driving snow stung her face as she staggered out Prosper Hardware's back door. Even here, in the relative shelter behind the two-story brick building, the wind was relentless. Her car was already covered in slushy snow with an underbelly of ice, and she rushed to clear the windows and get behind the wheel. She flipped on the lights and wiper blades, but left the radio off. All of her attention had to stay on the six long miles that stood between her and home.

As Prosper's buildings and trees fell away, the view out the windshield faded to white. It was as if all the color had been erased from the sky and fields, and the blacktop became only two gray tire tracks on the snow-covered road.

Melinda crawled along, trying to get her bearings in the changed landscape, straining to spot the junction with the state highway that was somewhere up ahead.

"I'll get home just fine. I just need to go slow, that's all," she told herself, leaning over the steering wheel as she drove straight into the furious storm. "Oh, but this is bad."

"Waiting Season" arrives in December 2018.
Look for it in Kindle, paperback and hardcover editions.

ABOUT THE BOOKS

*Don't miss any of the titles
in this heartwarming rural fiction series*

Growing Season (Book 1)

Melinda Foster is already at a crossroads when the "for rent" sign beckons her down a dusty gravel lane. Downsized from her job at a Twin Cities ad agency, she is struggling to find her way forward when a phone call brings her home to rural Iowa. It's not long before she is living in a faded farmhouse, caring for a barn full of animals, and working at her family's hardware store. And just like the vast garden she tends under the summer sun, Melinda soon begins to thrive.

Harvest Season (Book 2)

Two months into an unexpected sabbatical from her bustling life in Minneapolis, Melinda's efforts at her rented farmhouse are starting to pay off. But even in Prosper, nothing stays the same. One member of the hardware store's coffee group shares a startling announcement, and a trip back to the city makes Melinda realize how deep her roots now run in rural Iowa. As the seasons change, she must choose between the security of her old life or an uncertain future.

Waiting Season (Book 4)

Melinda finds herself struggling to keep the worst of winter's threats from her door. She pushes on because Horace's offer still stands: If she wants to stay, he'll sell her the farm in the spring. But as winter tightens its grip on rural Iowa, Melinda's biggest challenges are still to come. A series of events threatens to break her heart and shatter her hopes, and it will take all of her faith and the support of her family and friends to see the season through.

Coming December 2018

A TIN TRAIN CHRISTMAS

Travel back in time to Horace's childhood for this special holiday short story inspired by the "Growing Season" fiction series

From the author of the heartwarming "Growing Season" series comes this old-fashioned story of family and faith to brighten your holidays!

The toy train in the catalog was everything two young boys could ask for: colorful, shiny, and the perfect vehicle for their wild imaginations. But was it meant to be theirs? As the Great Depression's shadows deepen over the Midwest, Horace and Wilbur start to worry that Santa might not stop at their farm. But with a little faith and their parents' love, the boys just might discover the true spirit of Christmas. (Approx. 12,000 words)

And there's more: At the end of the story, you'll discover three holiday recipes handed down in the author's family!

"A Tin Train Christmas" is available in Kindle format as well as a paperback version that's perfect for holiday gift giving!

CPSIA information can be obtained
at www.ICGtesting.com
Printed in the USA
LVHW091507141118
597114LV00007B/27/P

9 780998 863894